Our People

Woody Guthrie strummed his guitar. From his home in Oklahoma, he traveled across the whole United States. In New York City, he wrote a song about the nation he had crossed. He called his song "This Land Is Your Land." Other Oklahomans have done great things too. They are all part of Oklahoma's story.

What part do you play in Oklahoma's story?

Woody Guthrie wrote more than 1,000 folksongs. His songs tell about happy times and sad times.

★ HISTORY ★

J.C. Watts served in the United States House of Representatives from 1995 to 2002. Before that he was the quarterback for the Oklahoma Sooners.

Shannon Lucid traveled 75 million miles in 188 days. That was the last of five space flights she took as an astronaut. Outer space is a long way from Bethany, Oklahoma, where Lucid grew up.

Our Land

Oklahoma's "land is made for you and me." It has steep mountains, rolling hills, rivers and lakes, too. Some people farm Oklahoma's land. Others dig for minerals. Still others enjoy Oklahoma's cities.

What is special about where you live?

▲ Black Mesa
Highest Point
in Oklahoma
4,973 ft.

．Guymon

Gloss Mountain State Park

Cimarron River

Did you know?

★ Dinosaurs lived in Oklahoma. You can walk in their footprints at Black Mesa State Park.

★ There is a chocolate festival in Norman every February.

WICHITA MOUNTAINS

Lawton

Red River

OK4

★ GEOGRAPHY ★

The Gloss Mountains are also called the Glass Mountains. They got their name because of the sparkly mineral on their surface. The mineral makes the mountains look like they are covered in glass.

Oklahoma City, the capital of the state, has more people living in it than any other city in Oklahoma.

Sooners Are Good Citizens

There are many ways for you to be a good citizen. You may help at a recycling center. You can show how you care about your community by throwing litter in trashcans. Good citizens are responsible for the way they act in public places.

What do you do as a good citizen?

The state capitol in Oklahoma City was built in 1915, right on top of an oil well. Government leaders work here to create laws for Oklahoma citizens.

★ CITIZENSHIP ★

The state flag flies with the United States flag. Citizens of Oklahoma are also citizens of the United States.

Working together is one way to show good citizenship. These children help to plant a tree in their schoolyard.

Your Social Studies Book

What do you know about Oklahoma, your state? Where is Oklahoma in the United States? Where do you live? Which cities are near where you live? What do people do there for work? This year you will learn the answers to these questions and more.

★ Your book has stories and maps.

★ There are holidays, too.

★ You can work on activities and projects with classmates.

Oklahoma has learning goals called PASS. The goals will help you learn skills and remember ideas about what you have read. It's going to be a good year. Let's learn together.

Get ready for an Oklahoma Adventure!

HOUGHTON MIFFLIN
SOCIAL STUDIES

NEIGHBORHOODS

Visit **Education Place®**
www.eduplace.com/kids

HOUGHTON MIFFLIN BOSTON

OKLAHOMA

LIBERTY EDITION

AUTHORS

Senior Author
Dr. Herman J. Viola
Curator Emeritus
Smithsonian Institution

Dr. Cheryl Jennings
Project Director
Florida Institute of
 Education
University of North
 Florida

Dr. Sarah Witham Bednarz
Associate Professor,
 Geography
Texas A&M University

Dr. Mark C. Schug
Professor and Director
Center for Economic
 Education
University of Wisconsin,
 Milwaukee

Dr. Carlos E. Cortés
Professor Emeritus, History
University of California,
 Riverside

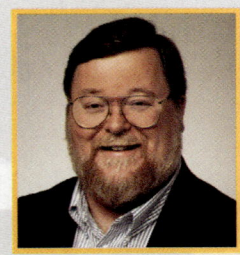

Dr. Charles S. White
Associate Professor
School of Education
Boston University

Consulting Authors

Dr. Dolores Beltran
Assistant Professor
Curriculum Instruction
California State University, Los Angeles
(Support for English Language Learners)

Dr. MaryEllen Vogt
Co-Director
California State University Center
for the Advancement of Reading
(Reading in the Content Area)

HOUGHTON MIFFLIN

SOCIAL STUDIES

★ NEIGHBORHOODS ★

HOUGHTON MIFFLIN   BOSTON

OKLAHOMA

LIBERTY EDITION

Consultants

Philip J. Deloria
Associate Professor
Department of History
and Program in
American Studies
University of Michigan

Lucien Ellington
UC Professor of Education
and Asia Program
Co-Director
University of Tennessee,
Chattanooga

Thelma Wills Foote
Associate Professor
University of California,
Irvine

Stephen J. Fugita
Distinguished Professor
Psychology and Ethnic
Studies
Santa Clara University

Charles C. Haynes
Senior Scholar
First Amendment Center

Ted Hemmingway
Professor of History
The Florida Agricultural &
Mechanical University

Douglas Monroy
Professor of History
The Colorado College

Lynette K. Oshima
Assistant Professor
Department of Language,
Literacy and Sociocultural
Studies and Social Studies
Program Coordinator
University of New Mexico

Jeffrey Strickland
Assistant Professor, History
University of Texas Pan
American

Clifford E. Trafzer
Professor of History and
American Indian Studies
University of California,
Riverside

Teacher Reviewers

Sharon Blount
Meadowbrook
North Kansas City, MO

Jane Cregg
Mendell Elementary
Roxbury, MA

Bonnie Ewing
Ideal Elementary
Countryside, IL

Lori Martinez
Woodland Charter
Elementary
Atlanta, GA

Kathleen Mastaby
Mendell Elementary
Roxbury, MA

Shari Moleterno
Jefferson School
Berwyn, IL

Fred Richardson
West Zephyrhills
Elementary
Zephyrhills, FL

Phyllis Yamaguchi
Alvarado Elementary
Signal Hill, CA

Donna Zaccaria
William Cramp Elementary
Philadelphia, PA

All maps created by Maps.com

Photography Credits
OK1 Jorge Delucca/Acclaim Images. OK2 (cr) Getty Images. (bkgd) James Steinberg/Photo Researchers, Inc. OK3 (bl) Downing Larry/CORBIS. (tr) AP/Wide World. OK5 (tr) Kim Baker/Oklahoma Travel and Nature Photography. (br) J&J Photo James Heathcock/Painet Stock Photos. OK6 Ken Sharpe Photography. OK7 (b) Michael Newman/PhotoEdit. (t) Denny Eilers/Grant Heilman Photography, Inc.

© 2008 Houghton Mifflin Company. All rights reserved.

No part of this work may be reproduced or transmitted in any form or by any means, electronic or mechanical, including photocopying and recording, or by any information storage or retrieval system, without the prior written permission of Houghton Mifflin unless such copying is expressly permitted by federal copyright law. Address requests for permission to reproduce Houghton Mifflin material to School Permissions, Houghton Mifflin Company, 222 Berkeley St., Boston, MA 02116.

Printed in the U.S.A.

ISBN-10: 0-618-81341-1
ISBN-13: 978-0-618-81341-4

123456789-VH-15 14 13 12 11 10 09 08 07 06

Contents

Introduction

- **About Your Textbook** 14
- **Reading Social Studies** 18
- **Constitution Day** 20

Bringing the world to your classroom!

UNIT 1 — People and Places ... 22

Vocabulary Preview
Reading Strategies: Summarize, Predict/Infer ... 24

Lesson 1
- Core — All Kinds of Groups ... 26
- Extend — *Literature* — "Recess Rules" ... 30
  - **Map and Globe Skill** Review Maps, Globes, Symbols, Directions ... 32

Lesson 2
- Core — Living Together ... 36
- Extend — *Biography* — Maggie Cervantes ... 40
  - **Map and Globe Skill** Use a Grid ... 42

Lesson 3
- Core — Cities and Suburbs ... 44
- Extend — *History* — A City Grows Taller ... 48
  - **Graph and Chart Skill** Read a Calendar ... 50

Lesson 4
- Core — Rural Communities ... 52
- Extend — *Economics* — Markets ... 56

Unit 1 Review **WR** Current Events Project ... 58

UNIT 2 Places Near and Far 62

Vocabulary Preview
Reading Strategies: Question, Monitor/Clarify 64

Lesson 1	Core	Your Address	66
	Extend	*Biography* — Sally Ride	70
		Map and Globe Skill Parts of a Globe	72
Lesson 2	Core	Land and Water	74
	Extend	*Literature* — **The Great Smokies**	80
		Map and Globe Skill Use Intermediate Directions	82
Lesson 3	Core	Weather and Climate	84
	Extend	*Readers' Theater* — Big Storm Coming	88
Lesson 4	Core	Regions	92
	Extend	*Geography* — Hurricane Regions	96
		Reading/Thinking Skill Identify Main Idea and Details	98
Lesson 5	Core	Resources	100
	Extend	*Literature* — "Maple Talk"	106

Unit 2 Review **Current Events Project** 108

UNIT 3 Ways of Living 112

Vocabulary Preview
Reading Strategies: Summarize, Predict/Infer 114

| Lesson 1 | Core | Families from Many Places .... 116 |
| | Extend | Primary Source — Immigrants at Ellis Island . 122 |

Graph and Chart Skill Read a Timeline 124

| Lesson 2 | Core | Sharing Cultures .... 126 |
| | Extend | Citizenship — Yo-Yo Ma .... 132 |

Study Skill Conduct an Interview 134

| Lesson 3 | Core | America's Symbols .... 136 |
| | Extend | Literature — "The Star-Spangled Banner" ... 142 |

| Lesson 4 | Core | We Celebrate Holidays .... 144 |
| | Extend | Biography — Cesar Chavez .... 148 |

Citizenship Skill Make a Decision 150

Unit 3 Review Current Events Project 152

UNIT 4 People at Work 156

Vocabulary Preview
Reading Strategies: Question, Summarize 158

Lesson 1 | Core — Needs, Wants, and Choices 160
Extend — Literature — The Milkmaid 162

Reading/Thinking Skill Compare Fact and Fiction ... 164

Lesson 2 | Core — Work 166
Extend — History — First Farmers 170

Lesson 3 | Core — Goods and Services 172
Extend — Biography — Scientists Serving Others 174

Graph and Chart Skill Read a Bar Graph 178

Lesson 4 | Core — People Save Money 180
Extend — Economics — Spend Your Dollar 184

Study Skill Use Reference Books 186

Lesson 5 | Core — From Field to Market 188
Extend — History — Keeping Food Cold 194

Lesson 6 | Core — People and Nations Trade 196
Extend — Geography — Money Around the World 200

Map and Globe Skill Use a Map Scale 202

Unit 4 Review (WR) Current Events Project 204

7

UNIT 5 — America's Past 208

Vocabulary Preview
Reading Strategies: Predict/Infer, Monitor/Clarify 210

Lesson 1
- Core — First Americans 212
- Extend — Literature — The Young Woman and the Thunder Beings 218

Lesson 2
- Core — Explorers Travel the World 222
- Extend — History — The Magnetic Compass 226

Lesson 3
- Core — Jamestown and Plymouth 228
- Extend — Readers' Theater — The Mayflower Crossing 234

Reading/Thinking Skill Identify Cause and Effect 238

Lesson 4
- Core — A New Country 240
- Extend — Biography — Two Patriots 246

Reading/Thinking Skill Compare Fact and Opinion ... 250

Lesson 5
- Core — Past Heroes 252
- Extend — Primary Source — Learn from a Letter 258

Lesson 6
- Core — Communities Change 260
- Extend — Biography — Inventors in Transportation 264

Citizenship Skill Understand Point of View 266

Lesson 7
- Core — Communication Changes 268
- Extend — History — Runners with a Message 272

Unit 5 Review WR Current Events Project 274

8

UNIT 6 America's Government ... 278

Vocabulary Preview
Reading Strategies: Summarize, Question 280

Lesson 1	Core	Government and People	282
	Extend	Literature — The Fire Station	288
Lesson 2	Core	Citizens Make a Difference	292
	Extend	Reader's Theater — Solving Problems	296
Lesson 3	Core	Laws	300
	Extend	Biography — Rosa Parks	304

Graph and Chart Skill Read a Pictograph 306

Lesson 4	Core	Leaders	308
	Extend	Citizenship — Voting with Ballots	312

Citizenship Skill Resolve a Conflict 314

Lesson 5	Core	National Government	316
	Extend	Citizenship — Democracy	320
Lesson 6	Core	Our Nation and the World	322
	Extend	Geography — Flags of Different Nations	326

Unit 6 Review (WR) **Current Events Project** 328

Holidays

Veterans Day 332
Thanksgiving 333
Martin Luther King, Jr. Day 334
Presidents' Day 335
Memorial Day 336
Flag Day 337
Independence Day 338

9

References

Citizenship Handbook R1

Our Flag R2

Songs of Our Nation R4

Character Traits R8

Resources

Geographic Terms R10

Atlas R12

Picture Glossary R20

Index R36

Credits/Acknowledgments R43

Extend Lessons

Connect the core lesson to an important concept and dig into it. Extend your social studies knowledge!

Literature

"Recess Rules"	30
The Great Smokies	80
"Maple Talk"	106
"The Star-Spangled Banner"	142
The Milkmaid	162
The Young Woman and the Thunder Beings	218
The Fire Station (excerpt)	288

Readers' Theater

Big Storm Coming	88
The Mayflower Crossing	234
Solving Problems	296

Economics

Markets	56
Spend Your Dollar	184

Citizenship

Yo-Yo Ma	132
Voting with Ballots	312
Democracy	320

Primary Sources

Immigrants at Ellis Island	122
Learn from a Letter	258

More primary sources at www.eduplace.com/kids/hmss05/

Geography

Hurricane Regions	96
Money Around the World	200
Flags of Different Nations	326

Biography

Maggie Cervantes	40
Sally Ride	70
Cesar Chavez	148
Scientists Serving Others: Marie Curie, Louis Pasteur, George Washington Carver, Eloy Rodrigues	174
Two Patriots Abigail Adams and Paul Revere	246
Inventors in Transportation: Granville T. Woods and Taylor G. Wang	264
Rosa Parks	304

More biographies at www.eduplace.com/kids/hmss05/

History

A City Grows Taller	48
First Farmers	170
Keeping Food Cold	194
The Magnetic Compass	226
Runners with a Message	272

Skill Lessons

Take a step-by-step approach to learning and practicing key social studies skills.

Map and Globe Skills

Review Maps, Globes, Symbols, Directions	32
Use a Grid	42
Parts of a Globe	72
Use Intermediate Directions	82
Use a Map Scale	202

11

Graph and Chart Skills

Read a Calendar	50
Read a Timeline	124
Read a Bar Graph	178
Read a Pictograph	306

Study Skills

Conduct an Interview	134
Use Reference Books	186

Citizenship Skills

Make a Decision	150
Understand Point of View	266
Resolve a Conflict	314

Reading and Thinking Skills

Identify Main Idea and Details	98
Compare Fact and Fiction	164
Identify Cause and Effect	238
Compare Fact and Opinion	250

Reading Skills/Graphic Organizer

Compare and Contrast 26, 52, 74, 222, 228
Main Idea and Details 36, 84, 92, 126, 268, 300
Cause and Effect 44, 196
Classify 66, 136, 144, 172, 212, 252, 292, 316
Sequence 100, 188, 240, 260, 308
Draw Conclusions 116, 166, 282
Predict Outcomes 160, 180
Problem and Solution 322

Visual Learning

Maps, graphs, and charts help you learn.

Maps

North Pole, South Pole	32
World Map	33
Smithfield	35
Three Tampa Neighborhoods	38
Use a Grid	43
San Diego and Spring Valley	47
Brown Elementary School	60
The United States of America	67
World Continents	68
North America	69
Northern, Southern, Western, and Eastern Hemispheres	73
Sierra Nevada	74
San Juan Mountains	75
Florida	76
Nebraska	77
Massachusetts	78
Cincinnati	79
United States	83
Two Cities	86
Landform Regions of the United States	93
Plant Regions of the United States	94
Rainfall in the United States	99
Some Land and Water in North America	108
Parts of a Globe	110
Southwestern States	110
San Francisco, Havre, New York City	118
Where Our Ancestors Came From	120
Landmarks in the United States	138
Mesopotamia	170
Trading Bananas and Wheat	198
Money Around the World	201
Eastern United States	203
Route to Airport	206

12

Four First American Groups	213
Route from Europe to Asia	223
Christopher Columbus's First Journey, 1492	224
Routes to North America	229
Routes of the Pilgrims, 1620	239
The Thirteen Colonies	241
Lakota Homelands	253
Israel	254
Plainfield, Illinois, in 1873	261
Plainfield, Illinois, Today	261
Inca Lands	272
The United States of America	284–285
World Leaders Meet	324
Mexico, Japan, Ghana	326
The World: Political	R12–R13
The World: Physical	R14–R15
Canada, United States, Mexico	R16–R17
The United States	R18–R19

Charts and Graphs

Calendar	51
Where People Live	58
Calendar	60
Weather Chart	84
Your Culture Comes From	152
Sally's Choices	161
Milk Produced Each Year	179
Money in Gina's Savings Account	183
Resources	191
Producers and Consumers	204
Number of Workers in Our School	206
Compare Groups	214–215
Services	286
How to Solve a Problem	295
Number of Cans Collected	307
Government Leaders	309
A Citizen's Government	328
Votes for Our Field Trip	330

Diagrams

From Tree to Barrel	54
Changing the Environment	103
Jamestown	230–231
Plymouth	232–233
Citizens' Responsibilities	294
Geographic Terms	R10–R11

Timelines

Andrea's Family History	124–125
Dan's Life History	154
Keeping Food Cold	194–195
Road to Independence	242–243
Abigail Adams	246
Paul Revere	248
Transportation Changes Plainfield	262–263
Timeline in American History	274

Fine Art

The Boy, Thomas Hart Benton	129
Totem Pole	129
Mount Rushmore	138
Marco Polo portrait	222
Marco Polo at the Court of Kublai Khan	223
Christopher Columbus portrait	225
Battle of Lexington	242
Washington Crossing the Delaware	244
Benjamin Franklin portrait	245
Samuel Adams portrait	245
Abigail Adams portrait	246
Abigail Adams statue	247
Paul Revere portrait	248
Paul Revere statue	249
Sitting Bull portrait	253
Inca Runners	273
The Constitutional Convention	317

About Your Textbook

1 How It's Organized

Units The major sections of your book are units. Each starts with a big idea.

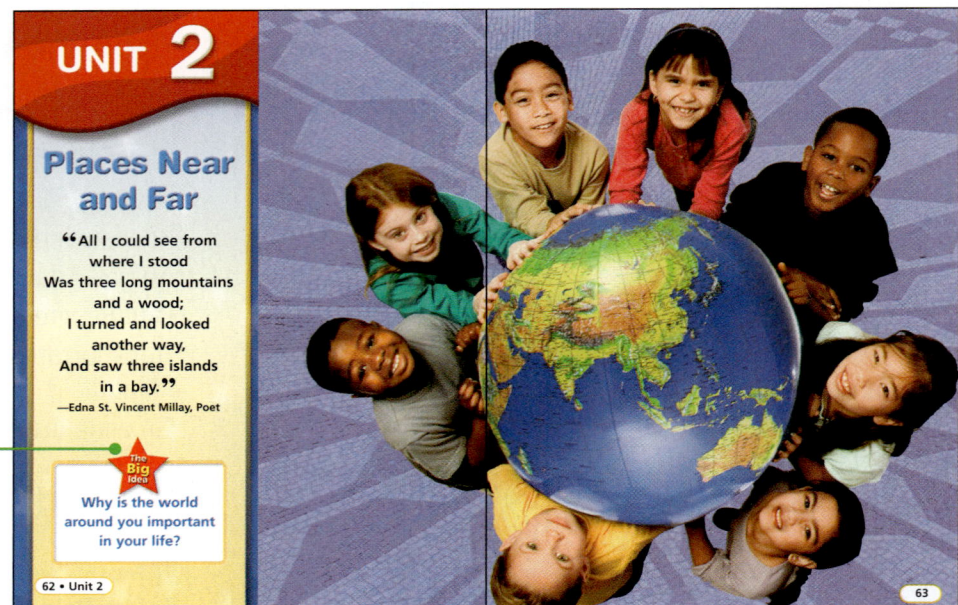

Explore big ideas in geography, history, economics, government, and culture.

Get ready for reading.

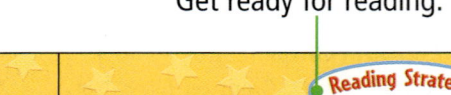

Each unit opens with a vocabulary preview.

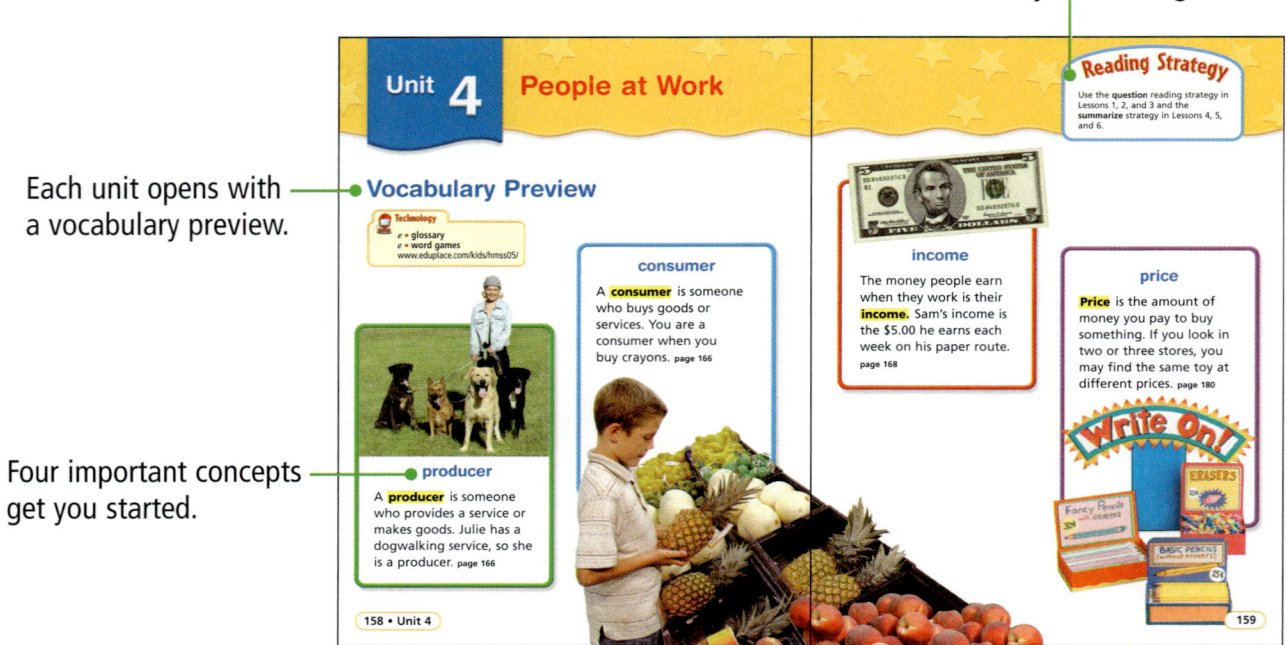

Four important concepts get you started.

14

2 Core and Extend

Lessons The lessons in your book have two parts: core and extend.

Core Lessons
Lessons bring social studies to life and help you meet your state's standards.

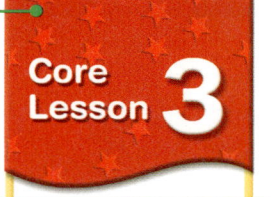

Extend Lessons
Go deeper into an important topic.

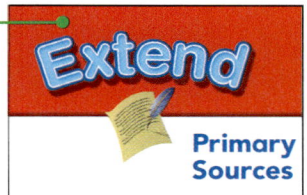

Core Lesson

Vocabulary lists give you the words you need to know.

Reading skills support your understanding of the text.

Core Lesson 1: Your Address

Vocabulary
country
state
continent
nation

Reading Skill
Classify

Build on What You Know
What do you call the community where you live? Do you know the rest of your address?

States in a Country
Carlos is going to mail a letter to his cousin Len. Len lives on Green Street in the city of Columbus. Look at the envelope to see the rest of the address. What is Ohio? What does U.S.A. mean?

Before you read, use your prior knowledge.

Main ideas are underlined to show you what is important.

The United States is on the continent of North America. The United States shares North America with two other large countries. They are Canada and Mexico. Seven small nations and many island countries are part of North America too. **Nation** is another word for country.

Which oceans touch North America?

Review What is one way that Mexico and the United States are alike?

As you read, check your understanding.

After you read, check what you have learned.

Lesson Review

1. **Vocabulary** Write a sentence that tells where you live. Use the words **country**, **state**, and **continent** in the sentence.
2. **Main Idea** What are the earth's seven continents?
   Activity Draw an envelope for a letter to a friend. Write your address and your friend's address on it.

15

About Your Textbook

Extend Lesson — Learn more about an important topic from each core lesson.

Dig in and extend your knowledge.

Write, talk, draw, and role-play!

Look for literature, readers' theater, geography, economics—and more.

16

3 Skills

Skill Building Learn map, graph, and study skills, as well as citizenship skills for life.

Practice and apply each social studies skill.

Skill lessons step it out.

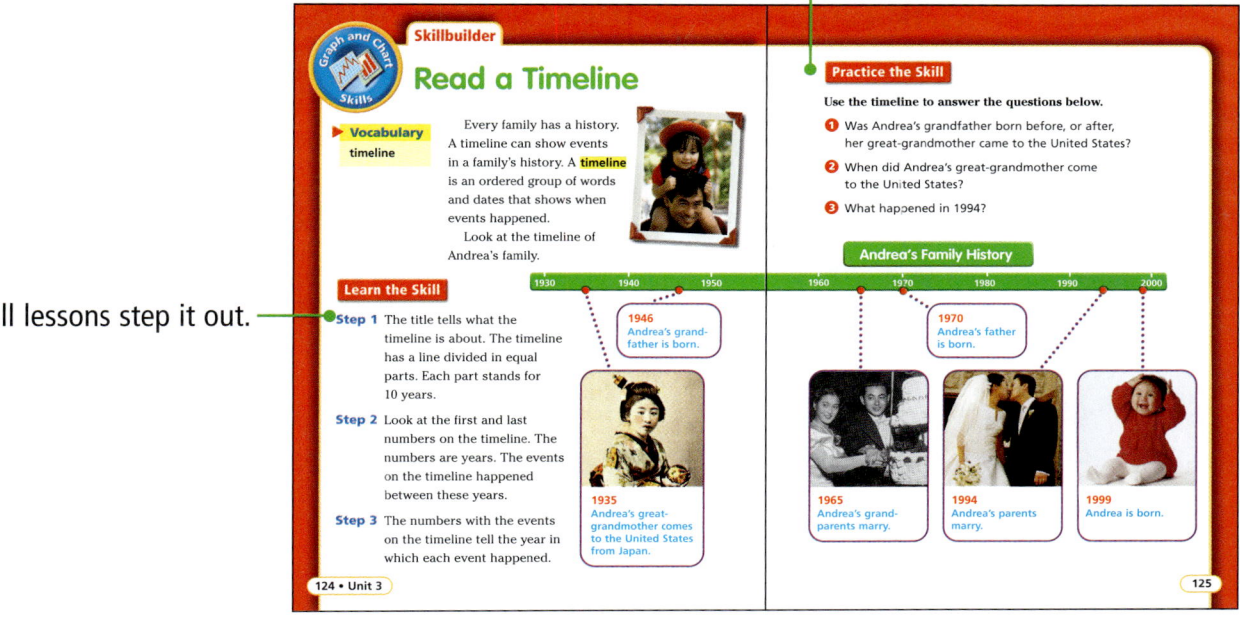

4 References

Citizenship Handbook

The back of your book includes sections you'll refer to again and again.

Resources

Look for atlas maps, a glossary of social studies terms, and an index.

17

Reading Social Studies

Your book can help you be a successful reader. Here's what you will find:

VOCABULARY SUPPORT

Preview Learn four important words from the unit.

Lesson Vocabulary Learn the meanings of lesson vocabulary.

Vocabulary Practice Reuse words in the reviews, skills, and extends. Show that you know your vocabulary.

READING STRATEGIES

Look through your book and find the reading strategies at the beginning of each unit.

Predict and Infer

Monitor and Clarify

Question

Summarize

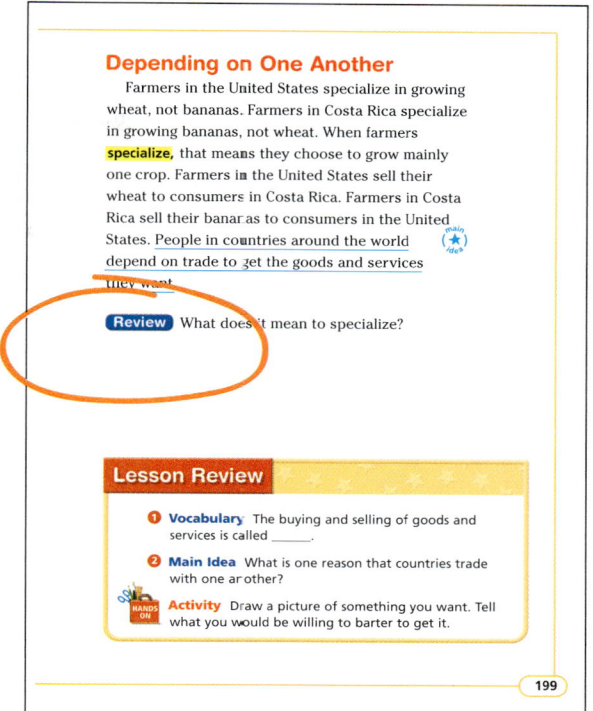

READING SKILLS

As you read, use the reading skills to organize the information.

Sequence

Cause and Effect

Compare and Contrast

Problem and Solution

Draw Conclusions

Predict Outcomes

Classify

Main Idea and Details

COMPREHENSION SUPPORT

Build on What You Know
Ask yourself what you know about the lesson topic. You may already know a lot!

Review Questions
Answer questions as you read. Did you understand what you read?

19

Constitution Day

Our country is a special place. One reason is because of the freedoms people have here. Citizens of the United States are free to say and print what they think, as long as the words do not hurt others. People are free to join groups. These freedoms are described in a paper called the United States Constitution.

The Constitution is a written plan that says what the nation's government can and cannot do. It was written more than 200 years ago by a group of leaders. They signed the Constitution on September 17, 1787. Today we celebrate Constitution Day and Citizenship Day during the week of September 17.

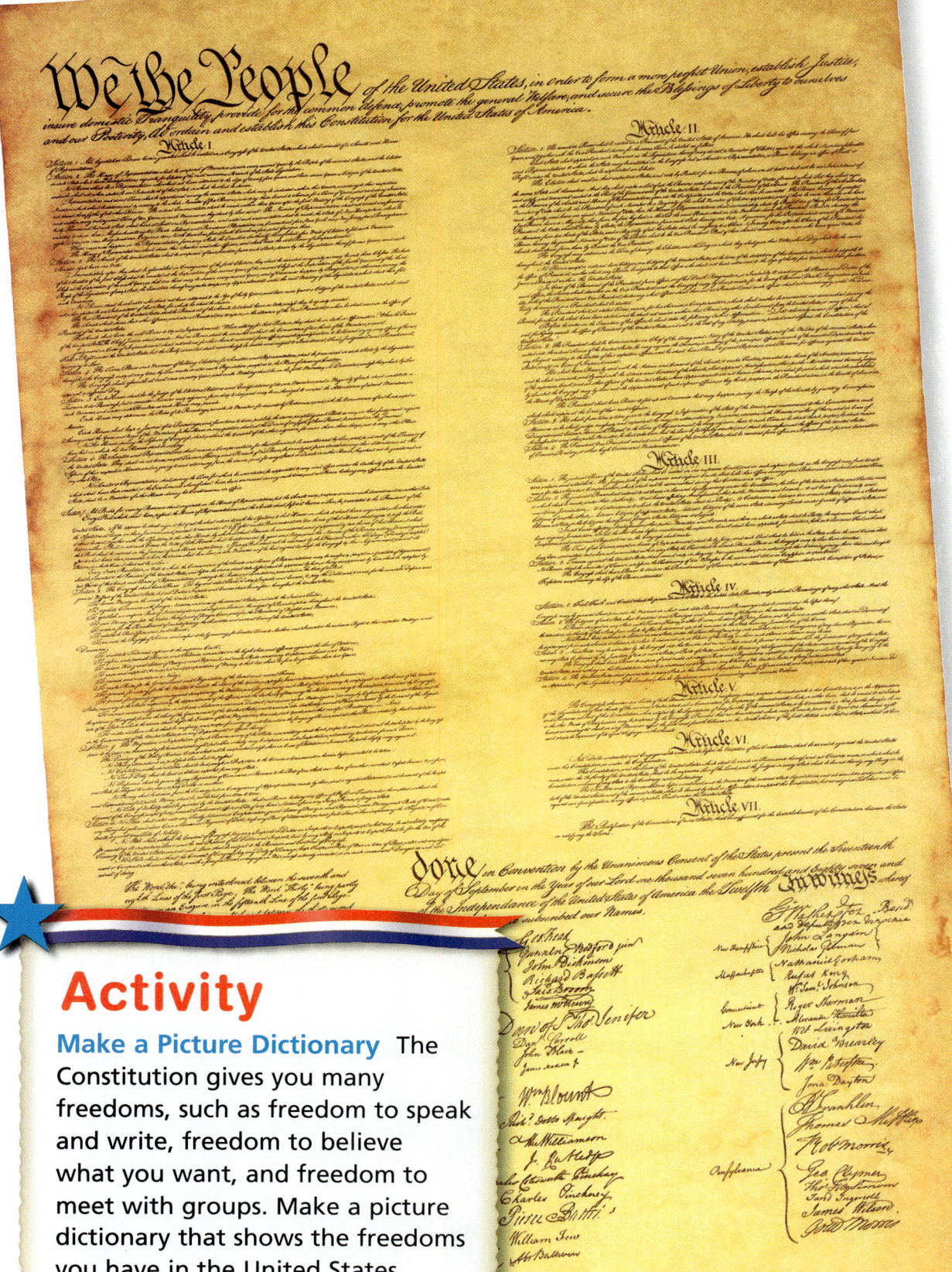

Activity

Make a Picture Dictionary The Constitution gives you many freedoms, such as freedom to speak and write, freedom to believe what you want, and freedom to meet with groups. Make a picture dictionary that shows the freedoms you have in the United States.

UNIT 1

People and Places

"I live in a city, yes I do
I live in a city, yes I do
I live in a city, yes I do
Made by human hands"

—Malvina Reynolds, Poet

The Big Idea

How do land and people make up a community?

Unit 1 People and Places

Vocabulary Preview

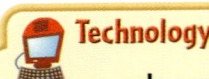

Technology
e • glossary
e • word games
www.eduplace.com/kids/hmss05/

rule

A **rule** tells you what you should and should not do. Some rules are written. page 29

urban area

An **urban area** is a place where many people live and work close together.
page 44

Reading Strategy

Use the **summarize** reading strategy in Lessons 1 and 2 and the **predict and infer** strategy in Lessons 3 and 4.

suburb

Some people live in suburbs. A **suburb** is a community near a city.

page 46

rural area

A **rural area** has more open space and fewer people than a suburb or urban area. page 53

25

Core Lesson 1

All Kinds of Groups

Vocabulary
group
leader
rule

Reading Skill
Compare and Contrast

Build on What You Know
Do you take a class after school? Are you on a team?

Groups
A **group** is a number of people who live together, work together, or spend time together. Your family is a group. Your school class is a group. A church choir is a group too. Families, classes, teams, and choirs are alike because they are groups.

Charan belongs to these three groups. What other group or groups do you think he might be in?

Review What groups do you belong to?

Family

Class

Afterschool art

27

Leaders

A **leader** is someone who leads others. The leader of a band helps everyone in the band play music together. Teachers are leaders of their classes. In some classrooms, children take turns being leaders of activities or games. Most groups have leaders.

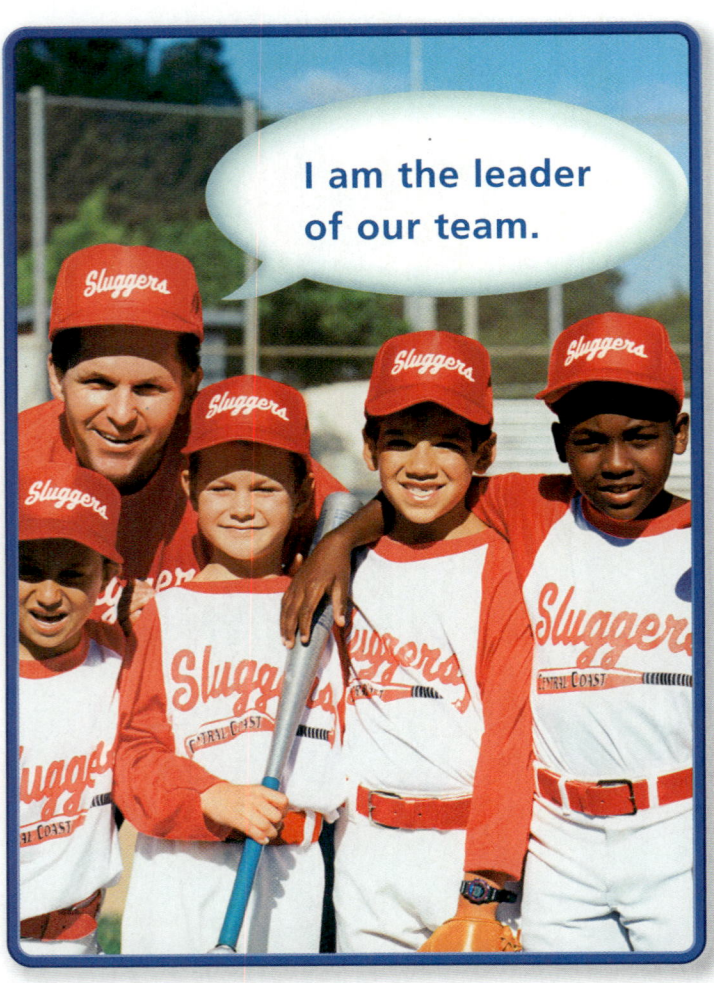

I am the leader of our team.

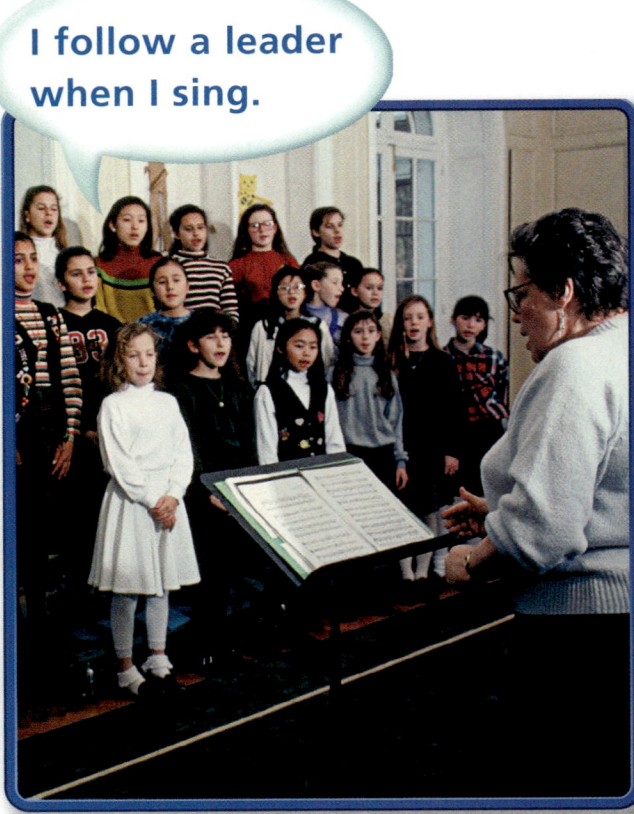

I follow a leader when I sing.

Rules

A **rule** helps people know what they should and should not do. Most groups have rules. Rules are meant to help people get along. They help people work or play together in the group. Following rules can help the people in a group be safe. In some groups, people talk about their rules. They may make or change their rules together.

Review Why are rules important in a group?

Some groups have a list of printed rules.

Lesson Review

1. **Vocabulary** Give an example of a **rule** for a **group.**

2. **Main Idea** Give an example of a group that has a leader. Tell what the leader does.

3. **Activity** Think about a group leader that you know. Write or tell what the leader does for the group.

29

Extend Lesson 1
Literature

Rules

From the book **Lunch Money and Other Poems About School** by Carol Diggory Shields

Recess Rules

No sliding down the handrails.
No climbing up the slide.
No bouncing on the seesaw.
No throwing sand outside.
No twisting on the swings.
No climbing up the trees.
No jumping from the fences.
No hanging by your knees.

Max slides down the handrails.
He climbs right up the slide.
Max bounces on the seesaw.
He throws the sand outside.
Max twirls the swings up double.
He calls me from a tree.
I climb up. Who gets in trouble?
Max sure doesn't.
Only me.

Activities

1. **Talk About It** Does your school have any recess rules that are not in the poem?

2. **Write About It** Look at the drawing on this page. Write or tell why you think Max does not get in trouble.

Skillbuilder

Review: Maps and Globes

> **Vocabulary**
>
> globe
> world map

A **globe** is a model of the earth. It shows that the earth is round like a ball. Maps are drawings of places as seen from above. A **world map** is a flat picture of the earth. You can use a globe and a world map to find continents, oceans, and other places.

Learn the Skill

Step 1 Look at the globe. Oceans are usually colored blue on globes and maps.

Step 2 Find the Atlantic Ocean on the globe and on the world map. In what way is the ocean the same on the map and the globe?

Step 3 Continents are the big bodies of land you see on a globe and a world map. Find North America on the globe and the world map. Globes and maps show countries too. Find Canada on the globe and map.

North Pole

South Pole

32 • Unit 1

Practice the Skill

Look at the globe and the map. Then follow the directions.

❶ Compare the globe and the world map. Tell how they are alike and different.

❷ Look at the globe and find the continent and country where you live. Then find them on the map. Write their names on a sheet of paper.

Skillbuilder

Review: Symbols and Directions

> **Vocabulary**
>
> compass rose
> symbol

Directions help people find places on globes and maps. A **compass rose** shows directions.

Symbols are pictures that stand for real things. Most maps use symbols. A map key explains what the symbols stand for.

Learn the Skill

Step 1 The North Pole is at the top of the globe. North is the direction going toward the North Pole. The South Pole is at the bottom of the globe. South is the direction toward the South Pole. When you are facing north, places to the right are east. Places to the left are west.

Step 2 Look at the map. Find the compass rose. The letters N, E, S, and W stand for the direction words north, east, south, and west.

Step 3 Look at the map key. The symbol for forest is a tree. Find the symbol for forest on the map.

North Pole

South Pole

34 • Unit 1

Practice the Skill

Look at the map. Then follow the directions.

❶ Look at the map key. Describe the symbol for road.

❷ Find the roads on the map.

❸ Look at the river symbol on the map key. Find the river on the map. What is a symbol that touches the river?

❹ Use the compass rose and map key to answer the question: What is west of the farm?

35

Core Lesson 2

Vocabulary
neighborhood
community

Reading Skill
Main Idea and Details

Living Together

Build on What You Know

Who are some people who live near you? They are your neighbors.

Neighborhoods

You and your neighbors live in a neighborhood. A **neighborhood** is a part of a city or town. Most neighborhoods have homes. Many neighborhoods also have stores, parks, and schools.

36 • Unit 1

Neighborhood Activities

People in a neighborhood do many things together. Children in a neighborhood may play together. They may go to the same school. The grownups may work together to make their neighborhood look better. People may also work together to make their neighborhood safer.

Review What activities take place in your neighborhood?

What are some places on this map that are in your neighborhood?

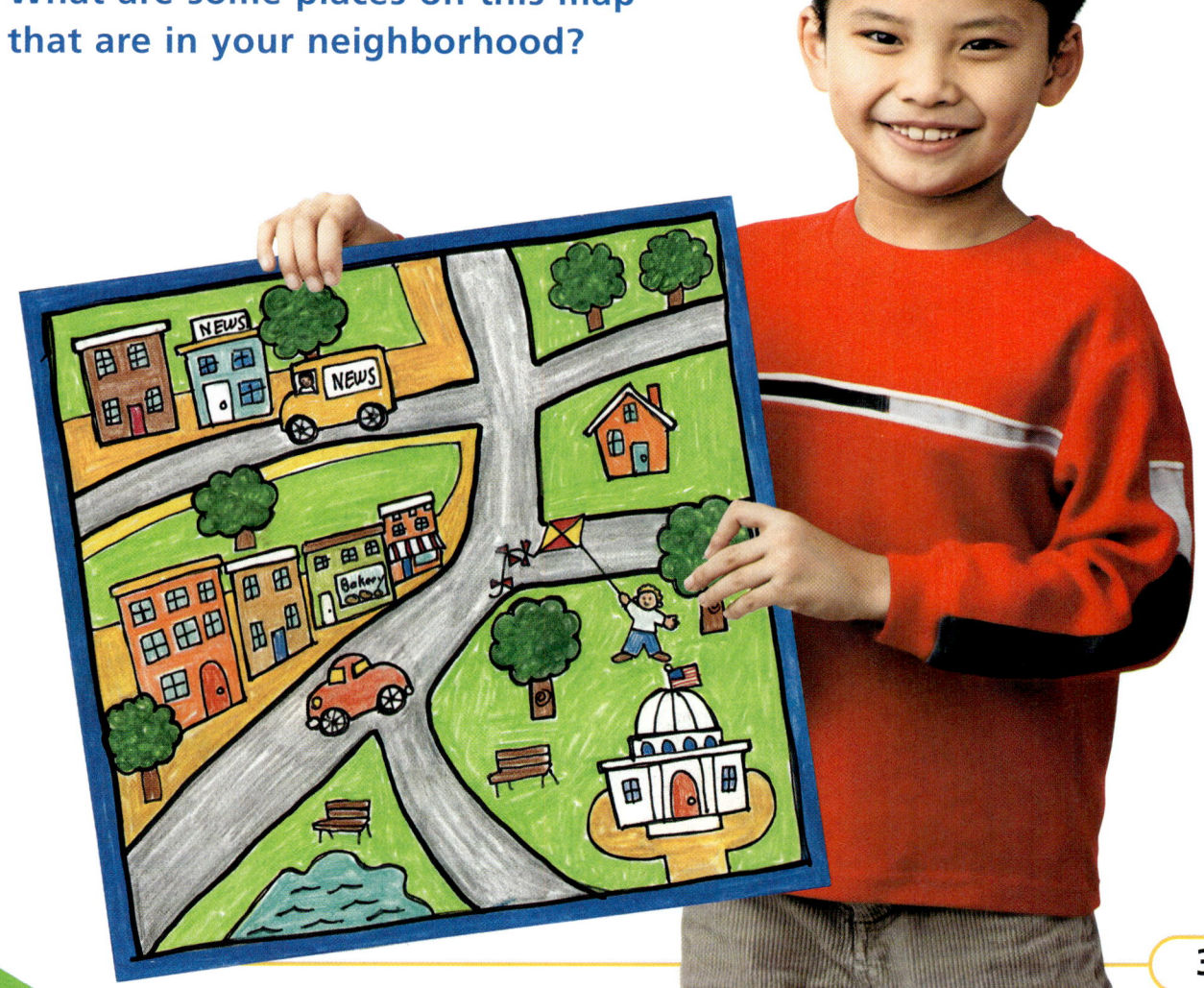

Communities

A **community** is a place where groups of people live. Cities and towns are communities. A community may have a few or many different neighborhoods.

Three Tampa Neighborhoods

- Northeast Macfarlane
- Macfarlane Park
- Oakford Park

Map Key
- Northeast Macfarlane
- Macfarlane Park
- Oakford Park
- Park
- School
- Library
- Boys and Girls Club

Skill **Reading Maps** Name the neighborhoods on this map.

38 • Unit 1

People in a Community

People in a community get together for many reasons. Perhaps the community has a fair every year. Often people from different neighborhoods work together to get ready for the event. Others help out on the special day. On Paint Day in Tampa, people work together to help others paint their homes.

Review What are some reasons people get together in communities?

Lesson Review

1 Vocabulary Explain what a **community** is.

2 Main Idea What are some ways people work together in neighborhoods and communities?

Activity Think about the places you go in your neighborhood. Then draw a picture map that shows those places.

Extend Lesson 2

Biography

Maggie Cervantes

Maggie Cervantes (suhr VAHN tays) is a community leader in the city of Los Angeles, California. She makes sure that neighbors of all ages meet and help each other. As a child, Cervantes saw that many of her neighbors needed jobs. Some needed better places to live. Cervantes promised herself that some day she would help her community.

Maggie Cervantes as a baby

Maggie Cervantes kept her promise. Today she leads a group that helps people in Los Angeles. Her group helped build safe housing for women and their children. In the buildings are child care centers and places where women learn job skills.

CHARACTER TRAIT: Civic Virtue

BIOGRAPHY

Cervantes says that most of all she loves "bringing people together to get a project done."

Activities

1. **Talk About It** Why did Maggie Cervantes want to help the people in her community?

2. **Write About It** Write or tell two questions you would ask Maggie Cervantes if she visited your class.

Technology Visit Education Place for more biographies. www.eduplace.com/kids/hmss05/

41

Skillbuilder

Use a Grid

Vocabulary
grid
location

Grids can help you find places and things on many kinds of maps. A **grid** is a pattern of lines. The lines make columns and rows. Each column has a letter, and each row has a number. The letters and the numbers name each square.

Learn the Skill

Step 1 Look at this grid. Put your finger on the star. Move it straight up to the top of the column. What is the letter?

Step 2 Put your finger on the star again. Move it sideways to the beginning of the row. What is the number?

Step 3 Together, the letter and number name the square. The name of the square with the star is B3. That is the place, or **location,** where the star can be found.

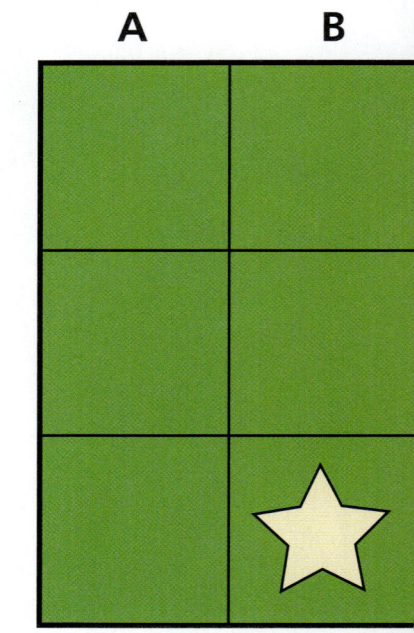

42 • Unit 1

Practice the Skill

Look at the map. Then answer the questions.

1. Where is the library located? Name the square.

2. Where is the post office located? Name the square.

3. What is located in square D4?

43

Core Lesson 3

Cities and Suburbs

Vocabulary
urban area
suburb

Reading Skill
Cause and Effect

Minneapolis, Minnesota

Build on What You Know

Maybe you live in a community that has houses with big yards. Or do you live where buildings are close together?

Cities

A city is a place where many people live and work. Cars, trucks, and buses fill the streets. In some urban areas, tall buildings rise into the sky. **Urban area** is another name for city. Buildings are close together in cities. There may be little space for grassy yards. Children play in city parks.

44 • Unit 1

Skill **Reading Visuals** Compare business centers in two urban areas.

Cities Are Different

Not all cities are alike. Not even all parts of one city are alike. Often one part of a city has many office buildings close together. Another part of the city may have a zoo, a river, a park, or smaller buildings that are farther apart.

Review What things can you see in urban areas?

Suburbs

Some people live in suburbs. A **suburb** is a community near a city. Spring Valley is a suburb of San Diego.

Spring Valley has many homes like this one.

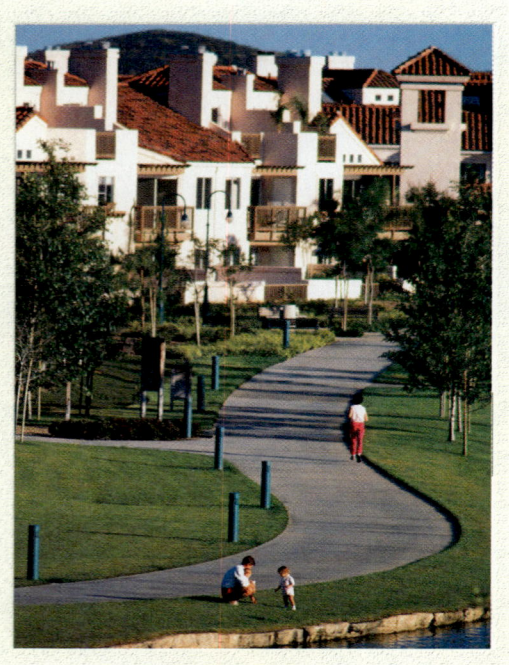

Spring Valley also has apartments and homes like these.

Spring Valley is a big suburb. It has a large amount of land and a large number of people too. In some ways, Spring Valley is like a city. With so many people, Spring Valley needs 18 schools. It has many grocery stores, pizza shops, and other businesses.

46 • Unit 1

Suburbs Depend on Cities

Usually a city has more places to work and shop than any of its suburbs has. Many people who live in suburbs depend on the nearby city for jobs. Also, people come to have fun in a city. People from suburbs all around San Diego can visit the famous San Diego Zoo. Visitors also like Old Town. It shows the way San Diego looked long ago.

Skill Reading Maps Find Spring Valley and San Diego. What other suburbs do you see?

Review Compare your community to Spring Valley or San Diego.

Lesson Review

1. **Vocabulary** Write a sentence that tells two ways that an **urban area** is different from a **suburb**.

2. **Main Idea** What is one way that a suburb depends on a city?

Activity Draw a picture map that shows your community and the nearest city or suburb.

47

Extend Lesson 3

History

A City Grows Taller

Long ago, New York City was not a city at all. It was a small town. Not far from the center of town, people farmed the land. They grew vegetables and raised animals.

New York once looked like this.

48 • Unit 1

Over the years, more and more people moved to New York. It became a city. In time, the city had a problem. It started to run out of open space.

To solve their problem, New Yorkers began to build skyscrapers. These tall buildings could hold many people and businesses. They used little land space. Today New York City has more than eight million people and many skyscrapers.

Activities

1. **Talk About It** Why did New York City grow taller?

2. **Write About It** Use the words **sky** and **high** to write a poem about a city.

Skillbuilder
Read a Calendar

Cities and suburbs have community events. A calendar can help citizens keep track of the events. A **calendar** is a way of showing time. A calendar shows months, weeks, and days.

Vocabulary
calendar

Learn the Skill

Step 1 Name the months of the year in order. Start with January. Then look at the calendar page at right. What month does it show?

Step 2 Each row on the calendar shows one week. Name the seven days of the week. Start with Sunday.

Step 3 Every day of the month has a number, or date. Find the square with the number 6. The date of that day is November 6.

Step 4 Find the community event on the first Saturday of the month. What is it?

50 • Unit 1

Practice the Skill

Look at this community calendar page. Then answer the questions.

1. What holiday is on November 11?
2. What day of the week is Thanksgiving?

Core Lesson 4

Rural Communities

Vocabulary

rural area
market

Reading Skill

Compare and Contrast

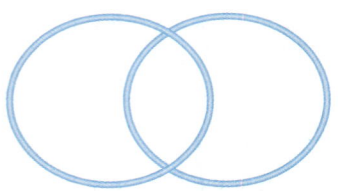

Build on What You Know

Do you live on a farm or in a small town? In some ways, your community is different from a city or a suburb.

Small Towns

Outside of cities and suburbs are rural areas. People in rural areas may live in small towns. Small towns have fewer stores, schools, and homes than cities or suburbs have.

52 • Unit 1

Farms

Rural areas are places with more open space than cities and suburbs. That is why most farms are in rural areas. Farmers need a lot of space to raise animals or crops, such as corn and beans.

The corn that you eat may come from farm fields like this one.

Review Why don't you find farms in cities?

Forests

The wood people use for buildings, chairs, and other things comes from trees. Trees grow in forests. <u>Most forests are found in rural areas because trees need space to grow.</u> (main idea)

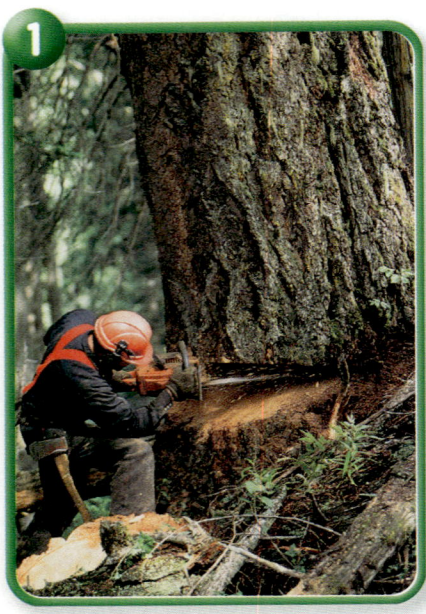

❶ **Lumber companies have workers that cut down trees and saw them into logs.**

❷ **Logs go to a sawmill to be cut into boards.**

❸ **Barrels are an example of something that might be made from wood.**

Review What are some ways that land is used in rural areas?

54 • Unit 1

Markets

Forest workers and farmers sell their wood and the things they grow. They send those things to markets. A **market** can be anywhere people buy and sell things. People in rural areas may send things they make or grow to markets in cities and suburbs.

Food grown in rural areas is sold in city markets.

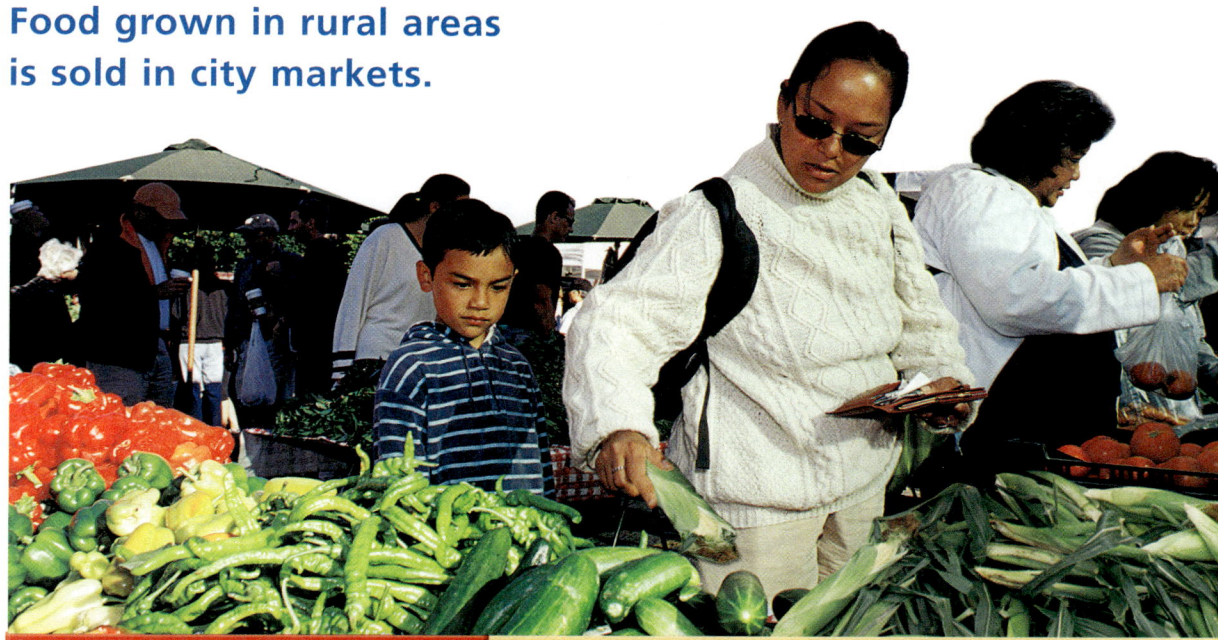

Lesson Review

1. **Vocabulary** Describe a **rural area** in one or two sentences.

2. **Main Idea** What are two ways that rural areas are different from urban areas?

   Activity Look around your classroom or your home. Make a list of all the things that you see that are made of wood.

Extend Lesson 4

Economics

Markets

Are you buying? Are you selling? You are in a **market**. In smaller markets, people buy the things they want for their own use. In large markets, businesses buy materials they need to make things. For example, you might have a business that makes chairs. You would go to a big market where many kinds of wood are sold.

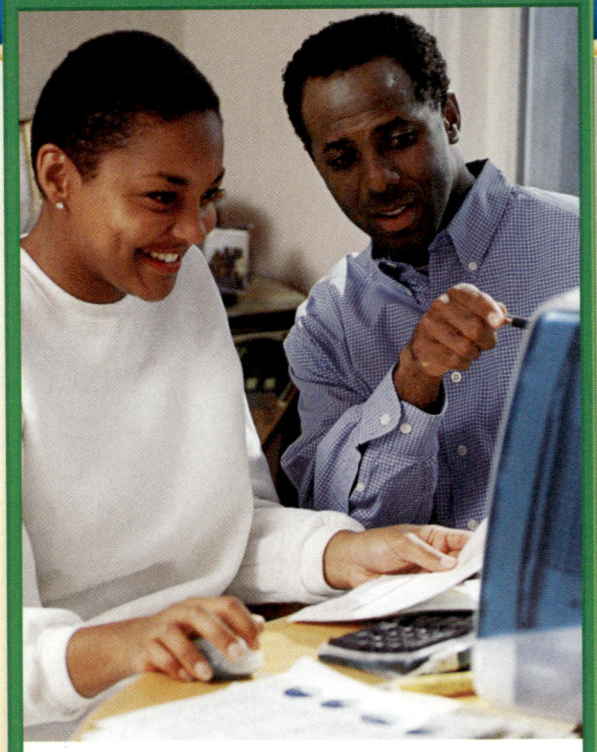

People can buy many different things on an Internet marketplace.

This man sells spices in an open market in Marrakesh, Morocco.

56 • Unit 1

Market

ECONOMICS

A supermarket is filled with many kinds of foods and other things.

Fishers send their catch to markets like this one in Japan. Here business owners buy large amounts of fish.

Activities

1. **Make It** Make a poster showing the names and prices of some things you would find in a market.

2. **Write About It** Write or tell the kinds of things you would sell if you owned a market.

57

Unit 1 Review and Test Prep

Big Ideas

Where People Live

Rural Area

Suburb

Urban Area

Choose the missing words that help describe the chart.

An **1.** _____ has the most buildings and people.
A **2.** _____ is close to a city. A **3.** _____ has the fewest buildings and people.

Facts and Main Ideas

4. What can leaders do to help a group? (page 28)

5. Why are rules important to a group? (page 29)

6. Why are markets important to people in rural and urban areas? (page 55)

7. What is one way that people can help a community? (pages 37, 39)

Vocabulary

Choose the letter of the correct word.

8. A person who leads others

9. Anywhere people buy and sell things

10. Something that tells what people should or should not do

11. A number of people who work, live, or spend time together

12. A place where a group of people live, work, and follow the same rules and laws

A. **market** (page 55)
B. **rule** (page 29)
C. **community** (page 38)
D. **group** (page 26)
E. **leader** (page 28)

 Test Practice

13. What does the word **neighborhood** mean?

    A. a person who leads others
    B. a part of a city or town
    C. anywhere that people buy and sell things
    D. something that tells people what to do

Critical Thinking

Compare and Contrast

14. What are some ways that a suburb is the same as a rural area?

59

Review and Test Prep

Skillbuilders — Use a Grid

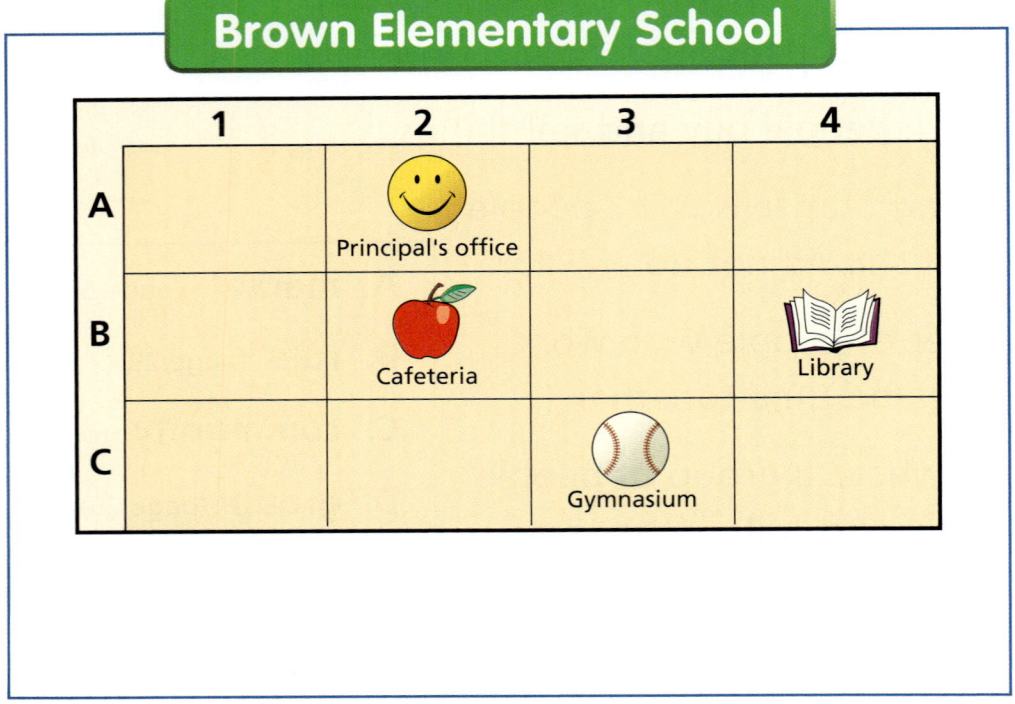

15. Where is the cafeteria? Use the grid to name the square.

16. What is in square 4B?

Read a Calendar

17. Which holiday is on October 23?

18. What is the date of Columbus Day?

Unit Activity

The Big Idea

Give a Short Report

Choose one of the lessons you have read. Get ready to give a short report about it. Make note cards to help you tell about the lesson.

❶ On one card, write something you learned in the lesson.

❷ On another card, write or draw something you liked about the lesson.

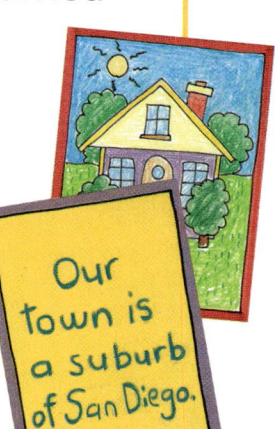

CURRENT EVENTS WEEKLY WR READER

Current Events Project

Find out about what leaders in your community are doing. Make a **Leaders in the News Chart.**

LEADER'S NAME	JOB	PLACE

 Technology

Read articles about current events at **www.eduplace.com/kids/hmss/**

In Your Classroom

Look for these Social Studies Independent Books in your classroom.

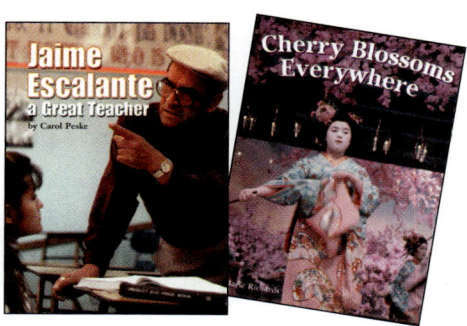

At the Library

You may find these books at your school or public library.

On the Town: A Community Adventure

by Judith Caseley

School Rules

by Larry Dane Brimner

61

UNIT 2

Places Near and Far

"All I could see from where I stood
Was three long mountains and a wood;
I turned and looked another way,
And saw three islands in a bay."

—Edna St. Vincent Millay, Poet

The Big Idea

Why is the world around you important in your life?

Unit 2 Places Near and Far

Vocabulary Preview

- e • glossary
- e • word games
www.eduplace.com/kids/hmss05/

continent

The United States is on the continent of North America. A **continent** is a large body of land. page 68

landform

A **landform** is one of the shapes of land found on the earth. One kind of landform is a plain. page 74

64 • Unit 2

Reading Strategy

Use the **question** reading strategy in Lessons 1, 2, and 3 and the **monitor and clarify** strategy in Lessons 4 and 5.

climate

Climate is the usual weather of a place over a long time. People in a cold climate need warm homes to live in. page 85

natural resource

Water is an important natural resource. A **natural resource** is something in nature that people use. page 100

65

Core Lesson 1

Your Address

Vocabulary
country
state
continent
nation

Reading Skill
Classify

Build on What You Know
What do you call the community where you live? Do you know the rest of your address?

States in a Country
Carlos is going to mail a letter to his cousin Len. Len lives on Green Street in the city of Columbus. Look at the envelope to see the rest of the address. What is Ohio? What does U.S.A. mean?

Carlos

return address
stamp
address

The United States of America

The city of Columbus is in the state of Ohio.

The letters U.S.A. on the envelope stand for the country called the United States of America. A **country** is a land where people have the same laws and leaders. Ohio is a state in the United States. A **state** is a part of a country. The United States is a country made up of 50 states.

Len

Review Which state do you live in?

67

Continents

If you were an astronaut looking at the earth from a space station, you would see mostly oceans. You would also see some very large bodies of land. Most of those large bodies of land are **continents**.

World Continents

Skill **Reading Maps** Find and name the seven continents on the map. Find and name the four oceans.

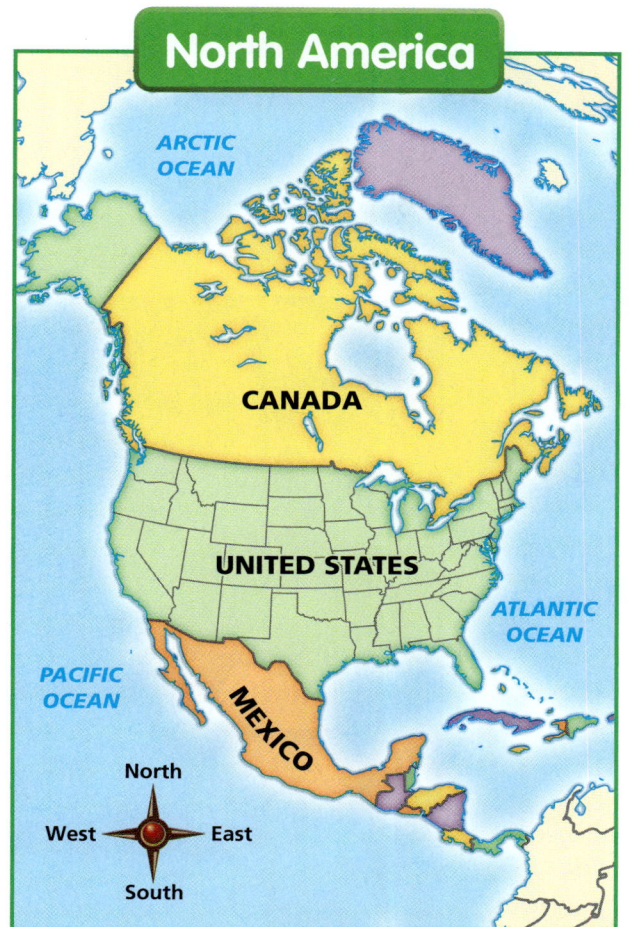

The United States is on the continent of North America. The United States shares North America with two other large countries. They are Canada and Mexico. Seven small nations and many island countries are part of North America too. **Nation** is another word for country.

Which oceans touch North America?

Review What is one way that Mexico and the United States are alike?

Lesson Review

❶ **Vocabulary** Write a sentence that tells where you live. Use the words **country**, **state**, and **continent** in the sentence.

❷ **Main Idea** What are the earth's seven continents?

Activity Draw an envelope for a letter to a friend. Write your address and your friend's address on it.

69

Extend Lesson 1

Biography

Sally Ride

Imagine being able to look down at the continents on Earth from far, far above. If you become an astronaut like Sally Ride, you will be able to do that.

When Sally Ride was a young girl, she liked to read science books. She dreamed of flying in space. After years of hard work in school, she was chosen to train to be an astronaut. On June 18, 1983, she became the first American woman to fly into space.

In her free time, Sally Ride liked to look out the space shuttle window. She was too far away to see people and houses. She could see the Mississippi River and the shapes of farm fields along it.

CHARACTER TRAIT: Responsibility

BIOGRAPHY

Sally Ride liked to "gaze down at the sparkling blue oceans . . . and rugged mountaintops of the Earth below."

Activities

1. **Talk About It** What are some ways that Sally Ride has shown responsibility?

2. **Write About It** Write two questions about space travel that you would like to ask Sally Ride.

Technology Visit Education Place for more biographies.
www.eduplace.com/kids/hmss05/

Map and Globe Skills

Skillbuilder

Parts of a Globe

To show locations on a globe, we use the **poles,** the **equator,** and **hemispheres.**

> **▶ Vocabulary**
>
> pole
> equator
> hemisphere

Learn the Skill

The North and South poles are imaginary. You cannot see them on the earth, only on a globe.

North Pole

South Pole

Step 1 The equator is an imaginary line around the middle of the earth. It is halfway between the North Pole and the South Pole.

Step 2 The equator divides the earth into the Northern Hemisphere and the Southern Hemisphere.

Step 3 The maps on page 73 show that the earth may also be divided into Eastern and Western hemispheres.

Practice the Skill

Look at the maps. Then follow the directions.

1. Find the continent where you live. Tell which hemispheres you live in.
2. Which continent has land in all four hemispheres?
3. Name two continents in the Southern Hemisphere.

Northern Hemisphere

Southern Hemisphere

Western Hemisphere

Eastern Hemisphere

73

Core Lesson 2

Land and Water

Vocabulary

landform
valley
island
peninsula
lake

Reading Skill

Compare and Contrast

Build on What You Know

Think about your community. Is it flat? Is it hilly? Is there a body of water nearby?

Landforms

The land on the earth is shaped in many different ways. Each different shape, such as a hill or mountain, is a **landform.** The pictures on pages 74 to 77 show some different landforms.

Sierra Nevada in California

mountains

74 • Unit 2

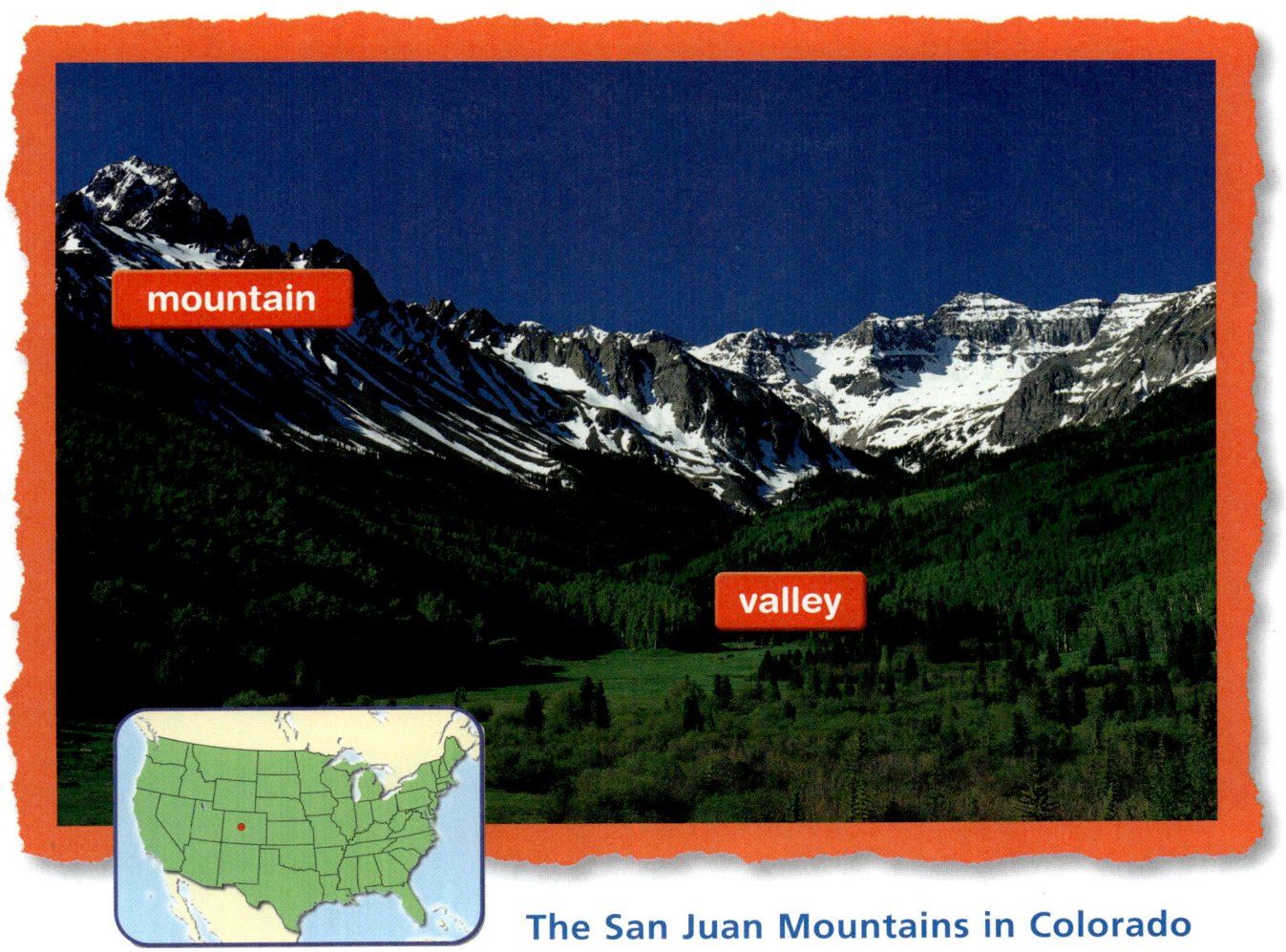

The San Juan Mountains in Colorado

A **valley** is low land between mountains or hills. Often a valley has been carved out by a river running through it. More people choose to farm in valleys than on the steep sides of mountains.

Review Why do you think people are more likely to farm in valleys than in mountains?

A peninsula and an island in Rhode Island

Islands and peninsulas are a little alike. An **island** is land with water all around it. A **peninsula** is land that has water on three sides. Most of the state of Florida is a peninsula. The Delmarva Peninsula has all of Delaware and parts of Maryland and Virginia.

A plain in Nebraska

A plain is mostly flat land. Most of the middle of the United States is covered by plains. Other plains are found on the land along the Atlantic Ocean and the Gulf of Mexico.

Review What is one landform in your state?

77

Water

Water comes in many shapes and forms too. You have read that most of the earth is covered with ocean water. Ocean water is salty. Most bodies of water found on land have fresh water.

A lake in Massachusetts

A **lake** is a body of water with land all around it. Most lakes have fresh water. Lakes come in many sizes. Some are small mountain lakes. Others, like Lake Superior, are huge. Find Lake Superior and the other four Great Lakes on a map of the United States.

78 • Unit 2

The Ohio River flows next to the city of Cincinnati, Ohio.

A river is a long, moving body of fresh water. Rivers flow downhill into oceans, or lakes, or other rivers.

Review What is a difference between an ocean and most lakes?

Lesson Review

❶ **Vocabulary** Write one or two sentences that tell what you know about **landforms**.

❷ **Main Idea** What are some kinds of land and water on the earth?

Activity Draw a picture of how people use land and water in your community.

79

Extend Lesson 2

Literature

The Great Smokies

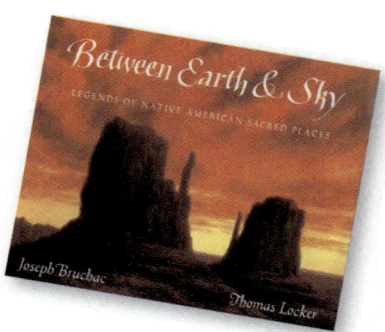

A legend is a story that is told and retold over many, many years. Joseph Bruchac retold this Cherokee legend about **landforms.**

If we should travel
far to the South,
there in the land
of mountains and mist,
we might hear the story
of how Earth was first shaped.

Water Beetle came out
to see if it was ready,
but the ground was
still as wet as a swamp,
too soft for anyone to stand.

Great Buzzard said, "I will help dry the land." He began to fly close above the new Earth. Where his wings came down, valleys were formed, and where his wings lifted, hills rose up through the mist.

So the many rolling valleys and hills of that place called the Great Smokies came into being there.

Activities

1. **Talk About It** How does the Cherokee legend say that valleys were formed?

2. **Write About It** Make up a story about how another landform came to be.

Skillbuilder

Use Intermediate Directions

> **Vocabulary**
> northeast
> southeast
> southwest
> northwest

When people travel from one city to another they often use maps to find their way. A compass rose shows them the directions.

Learn the Skill

Look at the compass rose below.

Step 1 Point to the directions north, south, east, and west. The letters N, S, E, and W stand for each direction word.

Step 2 Find the line halfway between north and east. This line points in the direction called **northeast.**

Step 3 Now find the line halfway between south and west. This line points in the direction called **southwest.**

Step 4 Find the letters NE, SE, SW, and NW. These letters stand for the direction words **northeast, southeast, southwest,** and **northwest.**

82 • Unit 2

Practice the Skill

Look at the map. Then follow the directions.

❶ Find Gettysburg, Pennsylvania. In what direction do you go to get to Selma, Alabama?

❷ Find Columbus, Ohio. What direction do you go to get to St. Paul, Minnesota?

❸ Leave Reno, Nevada, and travel northeast. Which city on this map do you reach first?

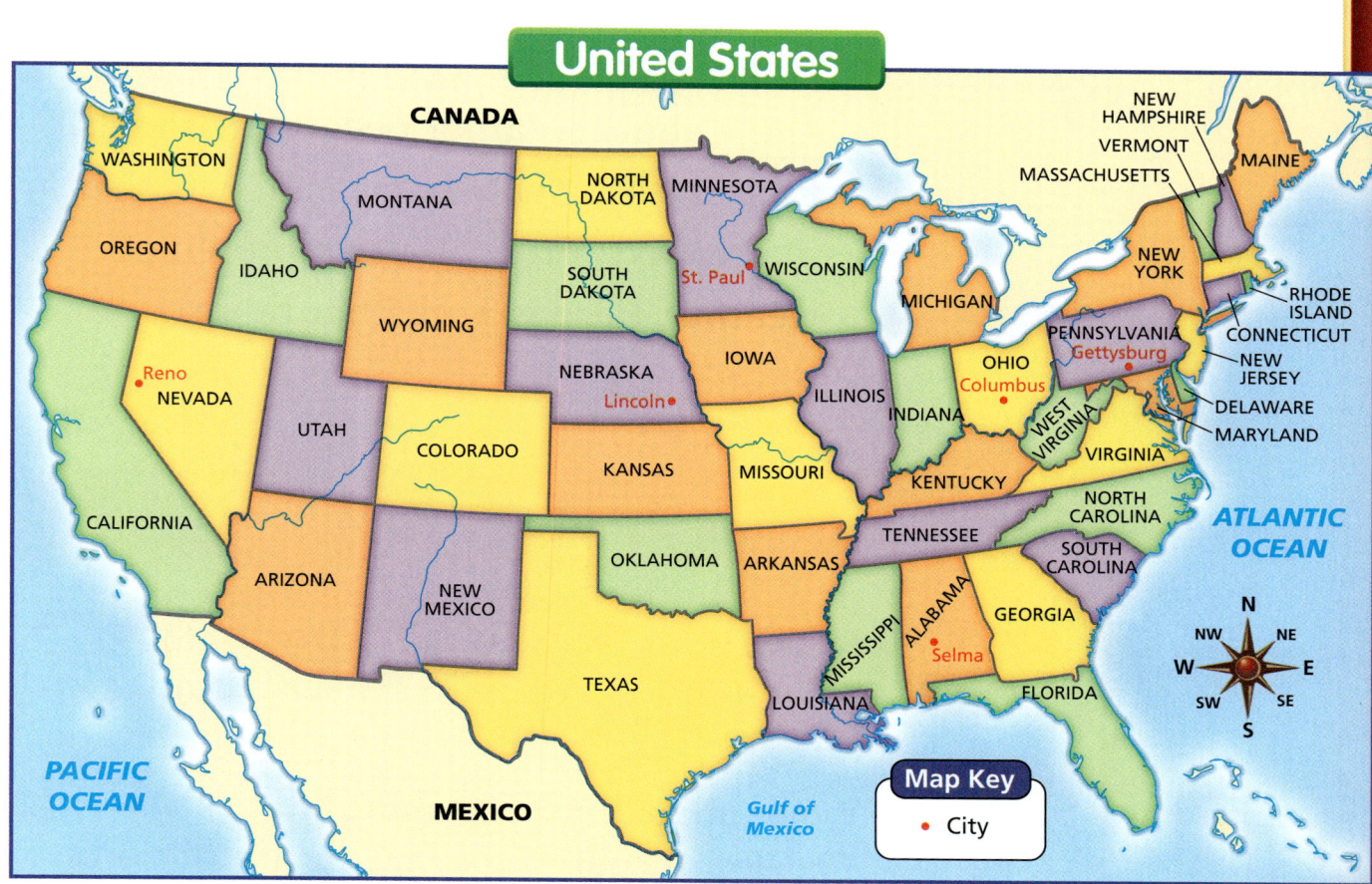

83

Core Lesson 3

Weather and Climate

Vocabulary
weather
climate

Reading Skill
Main Idea and Details

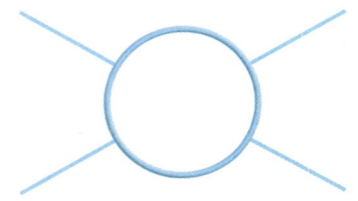

Build on What You Know

Is it raining, snowing, or sunny today? What it is like outside makes a difference in the activities you do each day.

Weather

Weather is what the air is like outside at any given time. People often want to know about weather because it affects their lives. Scientists measure weather in many ways. They also try to predict weather. Here is a weather report.

Today	Tomorrow
Sunny, warm 65° – 70°F	Cloudy 60° – 62°F
Winds up to 10 miles an hour	Chance of rain

Skill Chart Reading What do the words, numbers, and pictures tell about weather?

Climate

Climate is the usual weather of a place over a long time. A climate can have different kinds of weather. Jim and Jenna tell about the climate where they live.

July can be very hot in Milwaukee, Wisconsin.
Jim

January can be really cold.
Jim

Mobile, Alabama, has warm weather most of the year.
Jenna

Rain storms are part of our climate too.
Jenna

Review What are two kinds of weather that could be in one climate?

85

Living in Different Climates

Climates make a difference in the way people live. In what ways are these two climates different?

main idea

Two Cities

Palm Springs, California
has a climate that is hot and dry in daytime.

People need:
- cool air in buildings and cars year round
- light clothes to wear

Fargo, North Dakota
has a climate that is very cold in winter.

People need:
- warm air in buildings and cars in winter
- clothes to keep out snow and cold

Cold Climate Job
How do you know that this picture was not taken in Palm Springs?

Farmers raise plants and animals that do well in their climate. Builders think of climate when they plan homes and other buildings. Also, some jobs fit one climate and not another. Driving a snowplow is one example. Mostly, though, people have found ways to live in almost all climates.

Review What is one way that climate makes a difference in what people do?

Lesson Review

1. **Vocabulary** Write sentences to explain the difference between **weather** and **climate.**

2. **Main Idea** Explain how weather and climate are related.

Activity Draw a picture that shows how climate affects people where you live. Explain your drawing.

87

Extend Lesson 3

Readers' Theater
Big Storm Coming

The Gale family lives in a cold climate. See how a weather prediction helps them.

CAST
Grandmom
Mom
Dad
Annie: age 7
Dean: age 10
Carol Reed: weather forecaster
Narrator
Chorus: blizzard sounds

Scene 1

Narrator: It's a cold Monday night in February. The Gale family is at home watching Carol Reed's weather report on TV.

Carol Reed: We've got a big blizzard headed our way tonight, folks. Strong winds will bring us more than twenty inches of snow. Get ready!

Annie: How can we get ready for the blizzard?

Dad: I'll get out the snow shovels. Then I'm going to the store to get batteries, candles, milk, and bread.

Grandmom: Let's cook now in case we lose electricity.

Mom: I'll fill up some water bottles and start a fire in the fireplace.

Dean: I'll charge the phone and check the radio batteries.

Annie: I'll bring in more logs, too.

Narrator: Four hours later, the family watches the latest weather report.

Carol Reed: Blizzard winds are up to 50 miles per hour. Driving is very dangerous. The airport is closed.

Chorus: (howling wind sounds)

89

Scene 2

Narrator: The family is watching the weather report on Wednesday afternoon.

Carol Reed: We now have 33 inches of snow. This is the worst blizzard in ten years!

Dad: I'm glad we got our supplies ready.

Grandmom: Yes! The electricity was out for nine hours.

Annie: Toasting marshmallows in the fireplace was fun!

Grandmom: Once when I was a girl, I was stuck at school overnight. A big storm surprised us, and no one could travel. People couldn't predict the weather very well then.

Dad: Predictions are much better today.

Mom: Carol Reed predicted this one right.

Dean: I predict we'll dig lots of snow tomorrow.

Annie: Let's make a whole bunch of snow people, too! I wonder if school's going to be closed again?

Carol Reed: The snow should stop late tonight, but most schools will be closed tomorrow. Check the list on your screen.

Annie: Look! Our school's on the list!

Carol Reed: See you tonight at six!

Chorus: (howling wind sounds)

READERS' THEATER

Activities

1. **Talk About It** Tell ways that weather prediction helps people.

2. **Write About It** Write or tell about a storm that you know about. Tell what people did to stay safe.

91

Core Lesson 4

Regions

Build on What You Know

Think about your neighborhood. What makes it different from a nearby neighborhood?

Vocabulary
region

Reading Skill
Main Idea and Details

Regions

A **region** is an area that has some shared natural or human feature. People use regions as a way of describing places. Some regions are natural regions such as climate, landform, or plant regions. Other regions are human regions. They are described by human features. The languages that people speak and the work they do are two human features.

Mountains

Highlands

Landform Regions

Areas with shared landforms are landform regions. The United States has many landform regions. The map shows the main ones.

Review What is one landform region that your state has?

Skill Reading Maps Which part of the United States has more mountains, eastern or western?

Landform Regions of the United States

Map Key
- Plains
- Great Plains
- Highlands
- Mountains
- River
- Water

Plains

Water

93

Plant Regions of the United States

[Map showing Plant Regions of the United States with Map Key: Forest, Grassland, Desert Plants, Cold-Climate Plants, Other Plants]

Which states have desert plants?

Plant Regions

Places may be regions because they have the same kinds of plants growing naturally. The United States has large forest regions and grassland regions. It also has places where few kinds of plants grow. Some places are too dry for most plants. Other places are too cold and windy.

Prickly pear cactus, a desert plant

94 • Unit 2

Hawaii

New England

The United States has many kinds of forests. The forest on the left has the kinds of trees that grow in the hot climate of Hawaii. The forest on the right has the kinds of trees that grow in New England's cool climate.

Review What are two kinds of plant regions?

Lesson Review

❶ **Vocabulary** Describe one kind of landform **region.**

❷ **Main Idea** What region do you live in?

HANDS ON **Activity** Use the map on page 94. Draw a picture of the kinds of plants that grow naturally in your region.

Extend Lesson 4

Geography

Hurricane Regions

A hurricane is a giant storm with high winds and heavy rain. Hurricanes happen in different parts of the world. In the United States, the area along the Gulf of Mexico is one place where hurricanes hit. It is known as a hurricane region.

In 2005, Hurricanes Katrina and Rita hit this region. The hurricanes changed many people's lives. Thousands lost their homes to floods. People around the world came together to help.

Communities work together to rebuild after every hurricane. This family builds a home in New Orleans, Louisiana.

96 • Unit 2

GEOGRAPHY

New Orleans

Florida

Gulf of Mexico

Activities

1. **Describe It** Tell what you see in this photo of Hurricane Katrina taken from space. How could studying this photo help people prepare for a hurricane?

2. **Create It** Make a fact card listing at least two things you have learned about hurricanes.

97

Skillbuilder

Identify Main Idea and Details

Vocabulary

main idea
detail

Knowing about main ideas and details can help you understand what you read.

Learn the Skill

Look for the **main idea** and **details** in this paragraph.

> Different kinds of trees grow in different regions of the United States. Honey mesquite (meh SKEET) trees grow where it is hot and dry. White spruce trees grow where it is cold in winter. Live oak trees grow in warm, wet regions.

main idea

Step 1 The main idea tells what the whole paragraph is about. In this paragraph, the first sentence tells the main idea. But the main idea can be any sentence that tells what the whole paragraph is about.

Step 2 The other sentences in this paragraph give the details. Each detail tells more about the main idea.

Live oak leaves and acorns

98 • Unit 2

Practice the Skill

Read the paragraph below and look at the map.

❶ Tell the main idea of this paragraph.

❷ Give one detail from the paragraph and one detail from the map that tell more about the main idea.

Some regions of the United States get more rain than others. It rains the most on the northwest coast of the United States. The southeast region gets a lot of rain, too. The region that gets the least rain is the southwest.

Rainfall in the United States

Map Key
Inches of Rain Each Year
- Under 10
- 10–30
- 30–50
- Over 50

99

Core Lesson 5

Resources

Vocabulary
natural resource
environment

Reading Skill
Sequence

Build on What You Know

Do you have plants in your classroom? What do plants need to grow? Most plants need air, soil, water, and sunlight. These things are all found in nature. People did not make them.

Different Kinds of Resources

People use different kinds of resources. Like plants, people use things from nature. Something in nature that people use is called a natural resource. Air, soil, and water are natural resources. So are trees, rocks, oil, and some kinds of rubber.

100 • Unit 2

A woman cuts grooves in the bark of rubber trees to get the liquid from which natural rubber is made.

Two Kinds of Rubber

At one time, people had only natural rubber. They made it from a liquid found in some trees. Then scientists found a way to make rubber in their labs. This kind of rubber is called synthetic (sihn THET ihk) rubber. It is an example of another kind of resource. It is a synthetic resource. A synthetic resource is not found in nature. It is made by people.

Review Resources may be found in nature. What is another way people get resources?

101

Can People Get More of It?

Some natural resources can be replaced. Others cannot be replaced. If you cut down a tree, you can plant another one. But if you keep pumping oil out of a well, someday it will run dry. You cannot get more oil from the same place. You might look for oil somewhere else.

Resources that can be replaced

Trees

Resources that cannot be replaced

Oil

Review What is another resource that can be replaced?

Changing the Environment

The natural world around you is called the environment. Land, water, plants, animals, and people are all part of the environment. People change their environment. To build many homes, roads, and businesses, they cut down trees or smooth away hills. People drill wells for water, build dams across rivers, and drain swamps.

Consequences

Everything people do to the land and resources has a consequence. For example, one important resource in our environment is plants. The roots of trees and other plants help hold the soil down. If you cut down trees, the soil may blow away in the wind. Rain may wash away soil. Losing soil is a consequence of people's actions.

People have planted trees to replace some of the ones they cut down.

104 • Unit 2

People recycle paper, plastic, and metals to save resources.

In the past, people did many things to hurt the environment. Some countries made laws to protect the environment. People had to start to clean up the land and water. They had to find ways to keep the air and water clean. Because of the laws and people's actions, some parts of our environment are cleaner than they used to be.

Lesson Review

❶ Vocabulary Write a sentence explaining how you use a **natural resource**.

❷ Main Idea How are synthetic and natural resources different?

Activity Write or tell about something that you can do to help take care of the environment.

105

Extend Lesson 5

Literature

Maple Talk

Think of ways that trees are natural resources. Read about natural resources in the poem "Maple Talk" from **Poems Have Roots** by Lilian Moore.

Plant us.
Let our roots go
deeply down.
We'll hold the soil
when rain tugs
at the earth.

Plant us.
You will better know
how seasons come
and go.

Watch for
   our leaves unfurling
   in spring green,
   our leafy roofs of summer
   over pools of shade
   our sunset red and gold
   igniting autumn's blaze.

When cold winds
leave us bare
we'll show you treetop nests
where songbirds hid
their young.

And when
in early spring
the sweet sap flows again,
have syrup for your pancakes!

Plant us.

Activities

1. **Talk About It** What are two ways that the maple tree is useful to people?

2. **Make a List** Find as many natural resources in the poem as you can.

Unit 2 Review and Test Prep

Big Ideas

Some Land and Water in North America

Map Key:
- Mountains
- Plains
- River
- Water

What are the missing words?

1. The map shows part of the _____ of North America. 2. A body of water on this map is _____. 3. A landform shown is _____.

Facts and Main Ideas

4. Which kind of landform has water all around it? (page 76)

5. How are weather and climate related? (pages 84, 85)

6. Describe two types of regions. (page 92)

7. Name a natural resource that can be replaced. (page 102)

108 • Unit 2

Vocabulary

Choose the missing word in each sentence.

8. A _____ is low land between hills or mountains.

9. A nation may also be called a _____.

10. The _____ is the natural world around us.

11. A landform that has water on three sides is a _____.

A. **country** (page 67)
B. **region** (page 92)
C. **valley** (page 75)
D. **peninsula** (page 76)
E. **environment** (page 103)

Test Practice

12. What do the words **natural resource** mean?

    A. something that people make
    B. something in nature that people use
    C. a place where people cannot live
    D. something that can never be replaced

Critical Thinking

Compare and Contrast

13. Describe a way that people have harmed the environment.

14. Describe a way that people have cared for the environment.

109

Review and Test Prep

Skillbuilders — Parts of a Globe

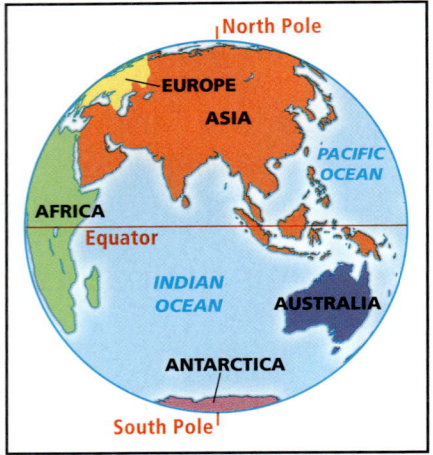

15. What are two bodies of water on the globe?

16. Which two continents are completely in the Southern Hemisphere?

17. On a globe, the equator passes through three continents. Which three are they?

Use Intermediate Directions

18. In which direction do you go to get from Phoenix, Arizona, to Carson City, Nevada?

19. If you go southeast from Salt Lake City, which city do you reach first?

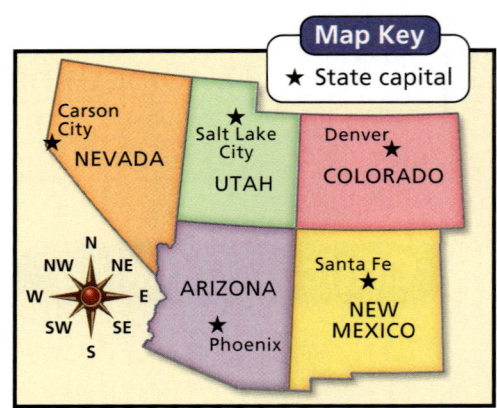

110 • Unit 2

Unit Activity

Keep a Weather Log

Keep track of the weather for a week. Use that information to make a weather log.

❶ Record the temperature each day.

❷ Note whether it is cloudy, sunny, raining, or snowing.

❸ Make a weather map for one day to go with your log.

CURRENT EVENTS WEEKLY WR READER

Current Events Project

Find information about places in your region. Make a **3-D Landform Map**.

Technology

Read articles about current events at www.eduplace.com/kids/hmss/

In Your Classroom

Look for these Social Studies Independent Books in your classroom.

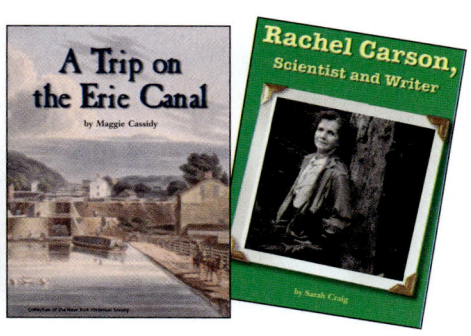

At the Library

You may find these books at your school or public library.

Mountains
By Claire Llewellyn

Hottest, Coldest, Highest, Deepest
By Steve Jenkins

111

UNIT 3

Ways of Living

"The world's a lovely
Place to be
Because we are
A family."
—Mary Ann Hoberman, Poet

The Big Idea

What are some of the cultures that make up your community, state, and nation?

Unit 3
Ways of Living

Vocabulary Preview

Technology
e • glossary
e • word games
www.eduplace.com/kids/hmss05/

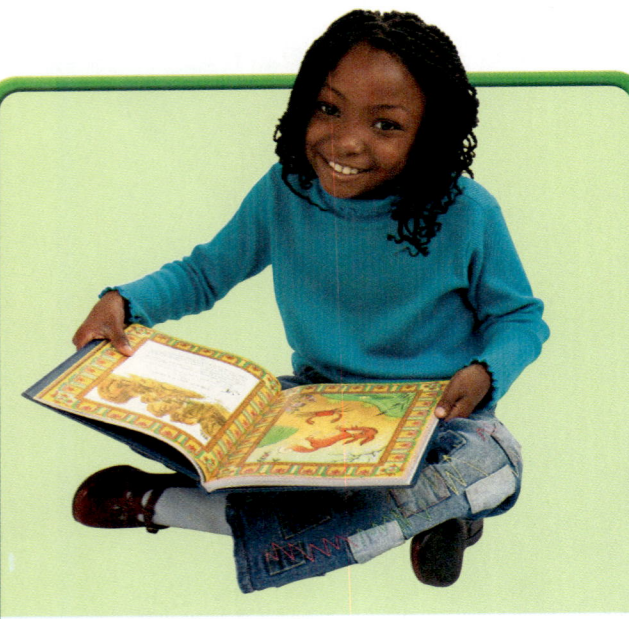

culture
Culture is the way of life of a group of people. Stories are a part of culture. page 117

tradition
A **tradition,** such as Thanksgiving, is something that people do the same way year after year. page 126

114 • Unit 3

Reading Strategy

Use the **summarize** reading strategy in Lessons 1 and 2 and the **predict and infer** strategy in Lessons 3 and 4.

landmark

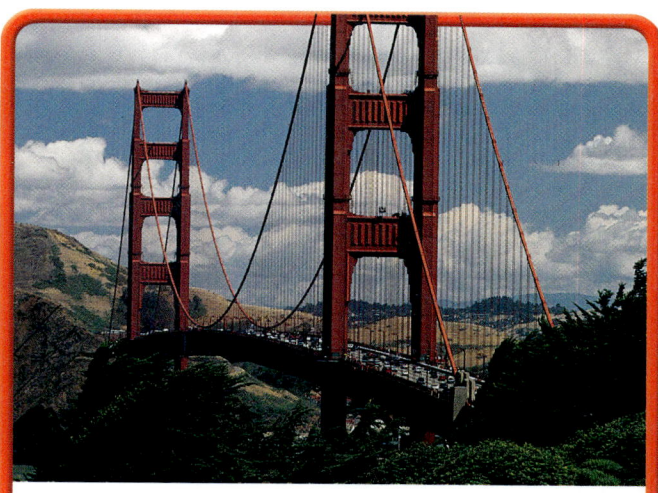

The Golden Gate Bridge is a San Francisco landmark. A **landmark** is something that helps people know a place. page 138

memorial

A **memorial** honors a hero or an event. The Crazy Horse Memorial honors a chief of the Lakota people. page 140

115

Core Lesson 1

Families from Many Places

Vocabulary
custom
culture
immigrant
ancestor

Reading Skill
Draw Conclusions

Build on What You Know
What are some special times when your family meets with other families or with relatives?

Family Customs
A **custom** is something that people usually do at a certain time. Most families have customs. Look at examples on these pages.

main idea

Mary's family sings in church on Sundays.

116 • Unit 3

Families and Cultures

Culture is the way of life of a group of people. The clothes you wear and the foods you eat are part of your culture. Music and language are part of culture. Your religion and your customs are part of your culture too. You learn about your culture from your family, by doing things and by talking together.

Carla's grandma always makes a piñata for her birthday.

Review What is a custom that is part of a culture you know?

Many Cultures in One Country

The United States has many different cultures. Some cultures come from American Indian groups. Some cultures come from immigrant groups. **Immigrants** are people who move from one country to live in another. Many immigrants have come to the United States for freedom. Immigrants from many countries have brought their ways of living to the United States.

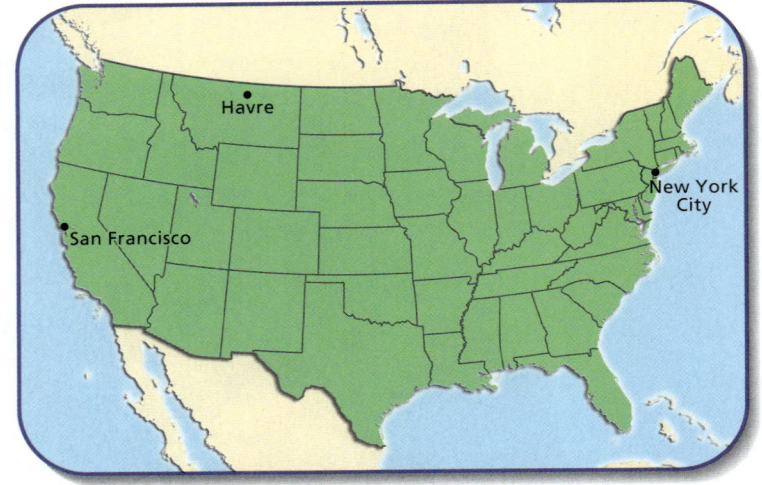

A Chinese New Year's Day parade in San Francisco.

Many American Indian groups celebrate their cultures in powwows like this one in Havre, Montana.

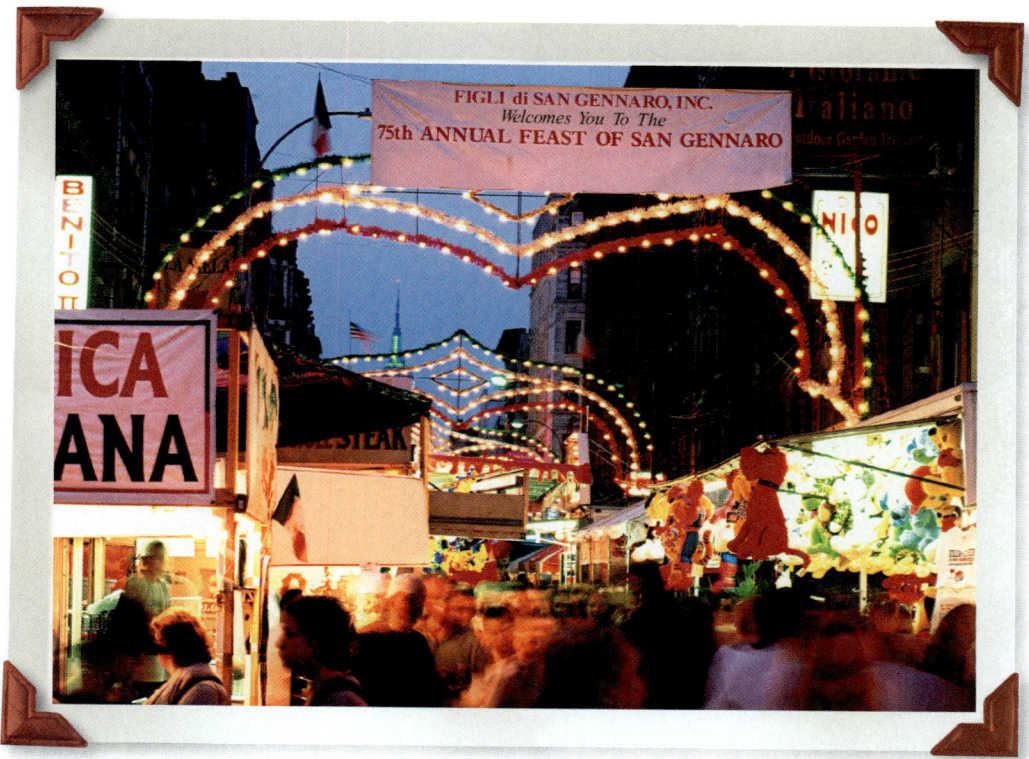

Immigrants from Italy brought customs such as this street fair in New York City.

Review What are two celebrations that came from immigrant groups?

119

Cultures from Ancestors

An **ancestor** is someone in your family who lived before you were born. You can learn about your culture by learning about your ancestors. You can learn from old pictures of them. You can also look at things that once belonged to them. Even your name can tell about your ancestors and their cultures. One family can have more than one culture.

My first name, Kumar, comes from India, where my mother was born. My last name, Bloomstein, comes from Russia, where my father's grandparents were born.

120 • Unit 3

My first name is Isabel, from my mama's Latina family from Ecuador. My middle name is Taysin, from my mama's Chinese culture. My last name is Carter, from my father's ancestors in England.

Review What is one way that children can learn about their ancestors?

Lesson Review

1. **Vocabulary** Tell something about the United States using the words **immigrant** and **ancestor.**

2. **Main Idea** Does the United States have only one culture? Tell why you answered yes or no.

Activity Write or tell about a custom in your family. Tell when, where, and why your family does it.

121

Extend Lesson 1
Primary Sources

Immigrants at Ellis Island

A boy named Yehuda (yeh HOO duh) came to America from Russia in 1922. Visit Ellis Island with him.

Yehuda saw a man approaching with a big bucket filled with milk and a basket of long yellow fruit. He was stopping at every child, giving each one a cup of milk and one of the strange pieces of fruit. Yehuda watched as one boy bit right into the yellow skin, made a face, and spit it out. Then he saw someone pull the skin down in strips and eat the soft, white fruit inside. Yehuda smiled to himself—every day in America he was learning something new!

Women and children at Ellis Island getting snacks

Activities

1. Act It Out Role-play the story about getting fruit and milk.

2. Write About It Describe the face, hair, and clothes of a person in the picture.

PRIMARY SOURCES

123

Skillbuilder

Read a Timeline

Vocabulary
timeline

Every family has a history. A timeline can show events in a family's history. A **timeline** is an ordered group of words and dates that shows when events happened.

Look at the timeline of Andrea's family.

Learn the Skill

Step 1 The title tells what the timeline is about. The timeline has a line divided in equal parts. Each part stands for 10 years.

Step 2 Look at the first and last numbers on the timeline. The numbers are years. The events on the timeline happened between these years.

Step 3 The numbers with the events on the timeline tell the year in which each event happened.

1930 1940 1950

1946
Andrea's grandfather is born.

1935
Andrea's great-grandmother comes to the United States from Japan.

124 • Unit 3

Practice the Skill

Use the timeline to answer the questions below.

1 Was Andrea's grandfather born before, or after, her great-grandmother came to the United States?

2 When did Andrea's great-grandmother come to the United States?

3 What happened in 1994?

Andrea's Family History

1960 — 1970 — 1980 — 1990 — 2000

1970
Andrea's father is born.

1965
Andrea's grandparents marry.

1994
Andrea's parents marry.

1999
Andrea is born.

125

Core Lesson 2

Sharing Cultures

Vocabulary
tradition
legend

Reading Skill
Main Idea and Details

Build on What You Know

Have you sung songs with words in another language? When people share songs of different languages, they share cultures.

Traditions from Cultures

A **tradition** is something that people do the same way year after year. It might be a special holiday meal or clothes for an event. Often families keep a tradition that comes from the culture of their ancestors. Families share their cultures by sharing their traditions with others.

126 • Unit 3

Sharing Traditions

Izumi's (ih ZOO mihz) grandmother learned origami, a paper-folding tradition, from her parents in Japan. She taught it to Izumi. Together they taught origami to other children in Izumi's class.

Review What traditions do you follow in your family?

127

Sharing Stories and Art

Every culture has stories. People share their cultures by sharing stories called legends. A **legend** is a story that people have passed along for years and years. Many legends come from a time when people told stories but did not write them. Later, people wrote them in books.

"The Fox and the Crab" is a legend from China. It is in a book of legends from many different countries.

128 • Unit 3

Art is another way of sharing cultures. People can see art in many different places.

Review What are two ways of sharing culture?

Thomas Hart Benton was famous for painting scenes from the Midwest, such as this painting called "The Boy."

Indians of the Pacific coast carved beautiful totem poles like this.

Artists Who Teach

Some artists share their culture by teaching. Alan Hezekiah (hehz ih KEYE uh) is a musician who teaches drumming to children and adults. Alicia Adame-Molinar (ah LEE see uh ad DAHM ay MOH lee nahr) teaches Mexican dances.

"Drums are in every culture, all around the world. I always wanted to be a drummer. I chose to play drums from Africa because I am an African American. When I play my drum I feel that I am connecting across the oceans, across the years!"

130 • Unit 3

"I was born in Mexico, where music and dancing are very important. I learned many dances when I was growing up. Now I want to share my culture with people in this country. They can learn so much about Mexico when they learn the music and dances!"

Review What is one way that the drummer and dancer on these pages are alike?

Lesson Review

1. **Vocabulary** Write or tell an example of a **legend** and an example of a **tradition**.

2. **Main Idea** How can one family learn about another family's culture?

Activity Draw a picture of someone who has shared his or her culture with you. Tell about your picture.

131

Extend Lesson 2

Citizenship

Yo-Yo Ma

Yo-Yo Ma was only four years old when he learned to play a cello (CHEHL OH). While still a boy, Yo-Yo Ma moved with his family from France to the United States. He kept studying the cello. His music amazed people.

Yo-Yo Ma plays with musicians from other cultures. He believes that music helps people from all cultures understand one another.

Sharing Musical Traditions

As a grownup, Yo-Yo Ma has become a famous musician. He has played concerts around the world. He is excited about music from many cultures. In 1998, he started bringing together musicians from many cultures. They share their musical traditions. They learn from one another and make new music too.

Today Yo-Yo Ma is a U.S. citizen.

Activities

1. **Discuss It** Why does Yo-Yo Ma want musicians to share traditions?

2. **Write About It** Write or tell two things you learned about Yo-Yo Ma.

Technology More biographies at www.eduplace.com/kids/hmss05/

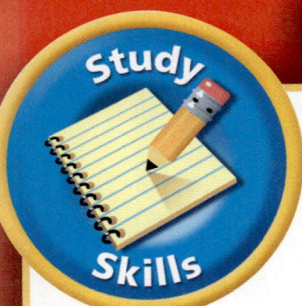

Skillbuilder

Conduct an Interview

Vocabulary
interview

In an **interview,** a reporter asks a person questions about a topic.

Learn the Skill

Think of someone you know in your community. What would you like to know about that person's past or traditions?

Step 1 Prepare your interview questions. Write four or five questions you can ask. Good questions start with words like **who, what, where, when, how, why,** and **what kind of.** . . .

Step 2 Practice asking your interview questions. Ask one question at a time.

Step 3 You may want to rewrite some of your questions.

Practice the Skill

Set up a time to do your interview. Then follow the directions.

❶ Think about what you want to know. Write your questions. Decide the order in which you wish to ask them.

❷ Bring a notebook and pencil so that you can take notes. If possible, bring a tape recorder.

❸ Be polite. Listen carefully to each answer. Thank the person when you are finished.

Hints for Tape Recording

Make sure your tape recorder is working and has a tape. Ask whether you can tape record the conversation.

Where and when were you born?

What did you like to do when you were young?

How did your family celebrate traditional ways?

What kind of stories did your family tell?

Core Lesson 3

America's Symbols

Vocabulary
symbol
landmark
President
monument
memorial

Reading Skill
Classify

Build on What You Know What would you put in a picture to stand for the United States? Pictures, buildings, and statues can stand for a country.

Culture and Symbols

In the United States, people have traditions that have come from many cultures. They also share traditions that began in this country. The United States has a culture from those traditions.

What are some symbols in the seal of the President of the United States?

136 • Unit 3

A **symbol** is a picture, place, or thing that stands for something else. For example, a picture of a bicycle may be a symbol for a bike path.

Symbols for the United States remind people that they are part of one country. The American flag is the symbol people use most often for the United States.

Review Why are symbols for the United States important to people who live here?

Uncle Sam

American Landmarks

A **landmark** is something that helps people know a place. A sign or statue may be a landmark. Many landmarks are symbols for America. Look at some on these pages. The map shows where they are.

main idea

Mount Rushmore
Black Hills, South Dakota

The leader of the United States of America is called the **President.** An artist and many helpers carved the faces of four important Presidents in the stone of this mountain. The faces are 60 feet high!

George Washington

Thomas Jefferson

Theodore Roosevelt

Abraham Lincoln

138 • Unit 3

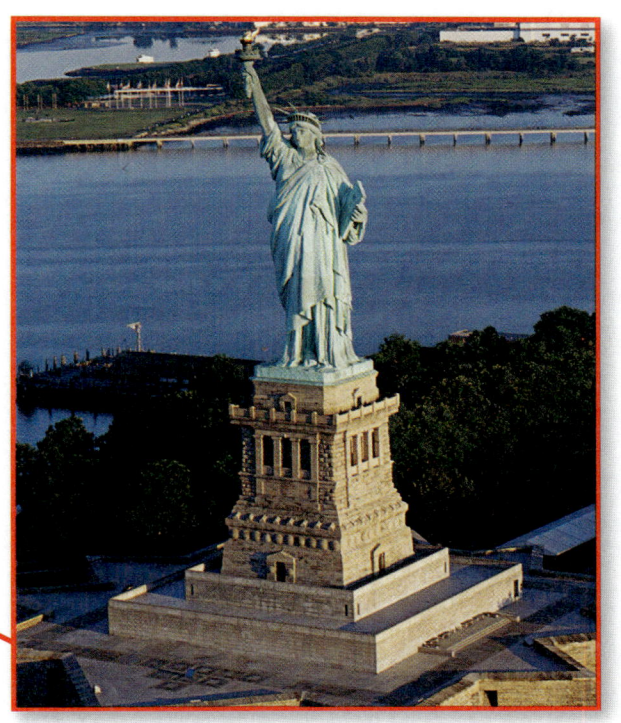

Statue of Liberty
New York Bay, New York

This statue is the size of a tall building. A French artist sent the great statue as a gift from his country more than a hundred years ago. The statue still welcomes immigrants and visitors to America.

Liberty Bell
Philadelphia, Pennsylvania

Americans rang this bell at the start of their new country in 1776. You can still visit it in Philadelphia. Pictures of the Liberty Bell are symbols for freedom in America.

Review Why is the Statue of Liberty an important landmark?

139

Monuments and Memorials

Many buildings and statues honor heroes or events. Some are called **monuments.** Others are called **memorials.** Both can be landmarks. Monuments and memorials help people remember. These monuments and memorials are in Washington, D.C.

Lincoln Memorial

Abraham Lincoln was the President of the United States during the Civil War. Two of his best known speeches are printed on the walls of the memorial.

Washington Monument

The Washington Monument honors George Washington. He was the first President of the United States. He was known for being brave, strong, and honest.

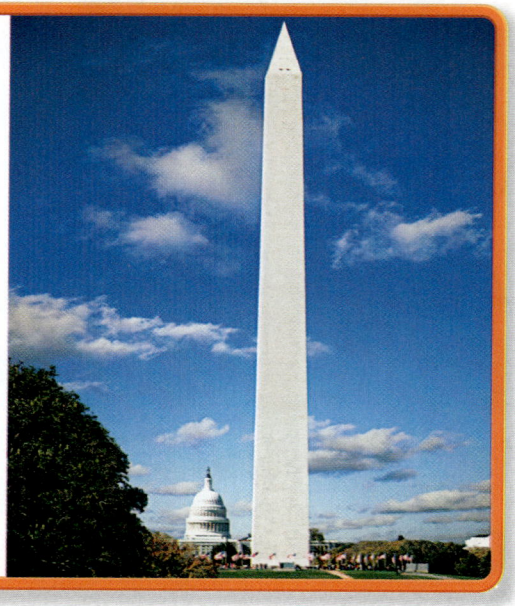

Thomas Jefferson Memorial

Thomas Jefferson was the third President. He wrote the Declaration of Independence. That was the paper that said that the United States should have freedom from Great Britain. Some of his words are printed on the walls of the memorial.

Review Why do people build monuments and memorials to Presidents?

Lesson Review

❶ **Vocabulary** Tell what is the same about **monuments** and **memorials.**

❷ **Main Idea** What are some symbols that remind us that we are all members of one country?

Activity Draw one of the symbols of the United States. Tell what you think and feel about the symbol.

141

Extend Lesson 3
Literature

The Star-Spangled Banner

The year was 1814. The United States was at war. All night Francis Scott Key watched the British fire cannons at an American fort. Its flag stayed up during the battle. This proved to Key that the United States was strong. He was so proud, he wrote a poem.

The poem that Key wrote was set to music. It became the anthem of the United States. An anthem is a song that is a <mark>symbol</mark> of a place.

Fort McHenry in Baltimore, Maryland

142 • Unit 3

The Star-Spangled Banner

Oh, say can you see, by the dawn's early light,

What so proudly we hailed at the twilight's last gleaming?

Whose broad stripes and bright stars, through the perilous fight,

O'er the ramparts we watched, were so gallantly streaming?

And the rockets' red glare, the bombs bursting in air,

Gave proof through the night that our flag was still there.

O say, does that star-spangled banner yet wave

O'er the land of the free and the home of the brave?

Activities

1. **Talk About It** Explain how a song can be a symbol of a country.

2. **Write About It** Choose a line of words in the song and tell what you think the words mean.

Core Lesson 4

We Celebrate Holidays

Vocabulary
national holiday
religious holiday

Reading Skill
Classify

Build on What You Know Name some holidays you celebrate. Find out how holidays are alike and different.

National Holidays

A holiday is a day that honors a person or an event. A **national holiday** honors someone or something that is important to the country. The date for a national holiday is the same everywhere in the country. Schools and many workplaces are closed so that families and friends can celebrate together.

Presidents' Day is a national holiday that honors two American Presidents, George Washington and Abraham Lincoln.

144 • Unit 3

State Holidays

Some holidays are state holidays. A state holiday usually honors an event or a person who is important to that state. Schools and workplaces may be closed, but only in the state where people celebrate that holiday. In California, for example, people celebrate Cesar Chavez Day of Service and Learning.

Review What is a way that state holidays are different from national holidays?

Massachusetts and Maine celebrate Patriots' Day. It honors events that took place in those states during the American Revolution.

145

Religious Holidays

People who belong to a religion share a set of beliefs about God. They may have times each year to honor events that go with the beliefs of their religion. These times are called **religious holidays.**

Ramadan
For the month of Ramadan, Muslims do not eat or drink during the day. They say prayers at certain times. After sunset, people eat and visit with one another.

Easter
For Easter, Christians say special prayers in church. Some Christians give up certain foods for a time before Easter. Eggs and flowers are symbols of the holiday.

Passover
For Passover, Jews have a meal called a seder, with prayers, songs, and symbols. For about a week, Jews do not eat most kinds of bread, cakes, or cookies.

Review What are some things people do on religious holidays?

Other Holidays

Some holidays are not religious, state, or national holidays. Some holidays honor traditions of a culture.

A Saint Patrick's Day parade

Lesson Review

1 **Vocabulary** Write a sentence about a **religious holiday** and a sentence about a **national holiday.**

2 **Main Idea** Explain how a national holiday is different from a religious holiday.

Activity Draw a picture of people celebrating a holiday you like. Tell if it is a national, state, or religious holiday.

147

Extend Lesson 4

Biography

Cesar Chavez

When Cesar Chavez was ten, his life changed for the worse. His family lost their home and became farm workers. Both grownups and children worked very hard in fields for very low pay. Often they were treated unfairly.

Cesar Chavez wanted to change how farm workers were treated. As a grownup in California, he led farm workers in their struggle for better pay and safety. Chavez was a strong, caring leader. He often said, "¡Si se puede!" (see say PWAY day). It means "Yes we can!" People believed in him. In California many schools do service projects on the state holiday that honors him.

CHARACTER TRAIT: Fairness

BIOGRAPHY

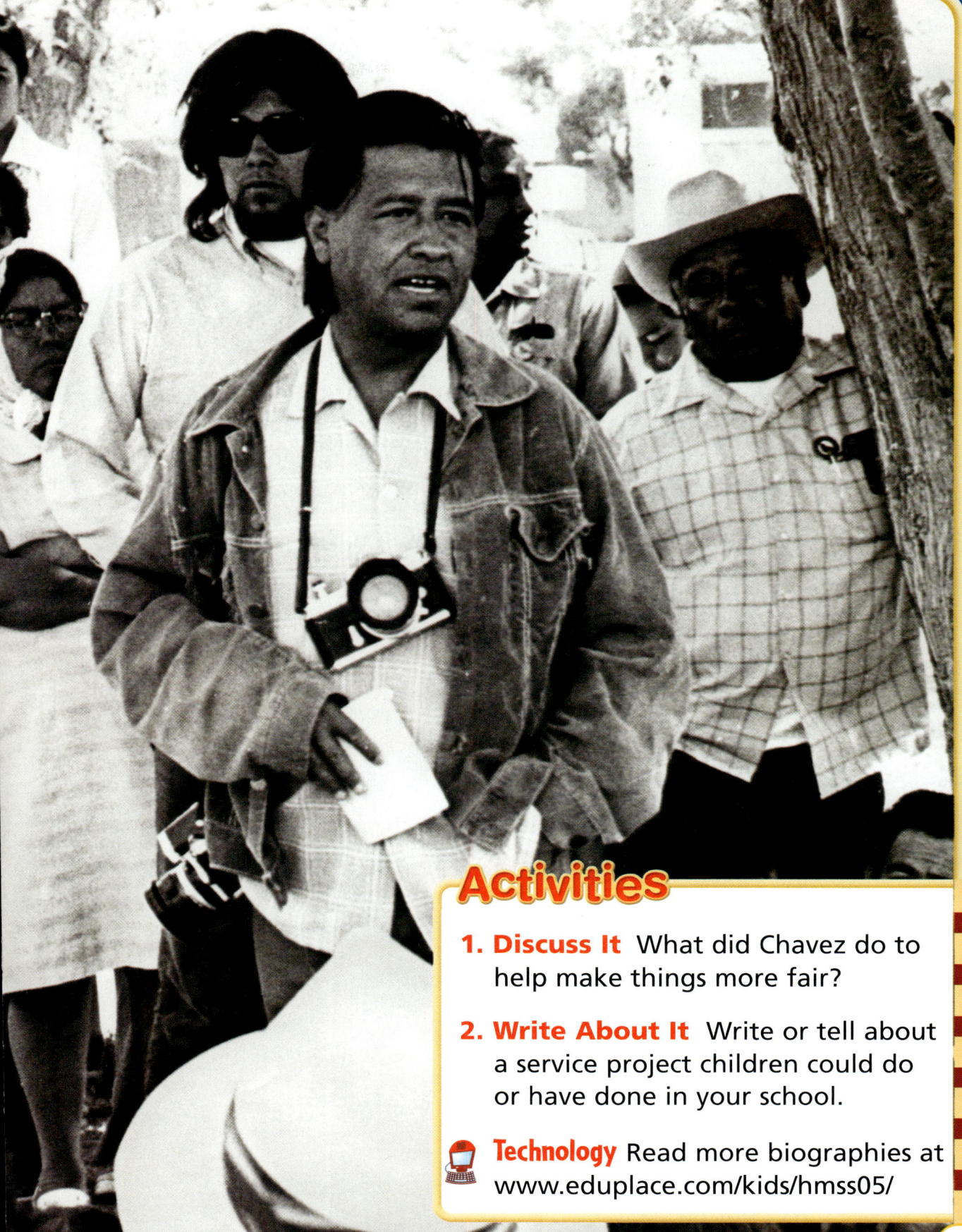

Activities

1. **Discuss It** What did Chavez do to help make things more fair?

2. **Write About It** Write or tell about a service project children could do or have done in your school.

Technology Read more biographies at www.eduplace.com/kids/hmss05/

Skillbuilder

Make a Decision

Vocabulary
decision

Good citizens think before they make decisions. To make a **decision**, you make up your mind. It may help to compare choices in a chart.

Learn the Skill

Suppose that your class wants to do a project that helps the school. Many children like two different ideas. How do you make a decision?

Step 1 Put the ideas in a chart that shows what is good and not good about each choice. Use plus (+) for good and minus (-) for not good. Look at the example on this page.

Step 2 Think and talk about what is good and not good about each choice. Write your thoughts in the chart.

Step 3 Compare choices in the chart. You might ask: Which choice will help more people in the school? Decide which choice is better.

150 • Unit 3

Apply Critical Thinking

Practice the Skill

Follow the directions to help Nino make a decision.

❶ Look at the pictures and read the words. Tell what Nino's choices are.

❷ Make a chart to show what is good about each choice and what is not good about each choice.

❸ Think of a question Nino might ask to help him decide. Use the question and the chart to make a choice.

Will you come play soccer?

Will you help me in the yard?

I can't decide!

151

Unit 3 Review and Test Prep

Big Ideas

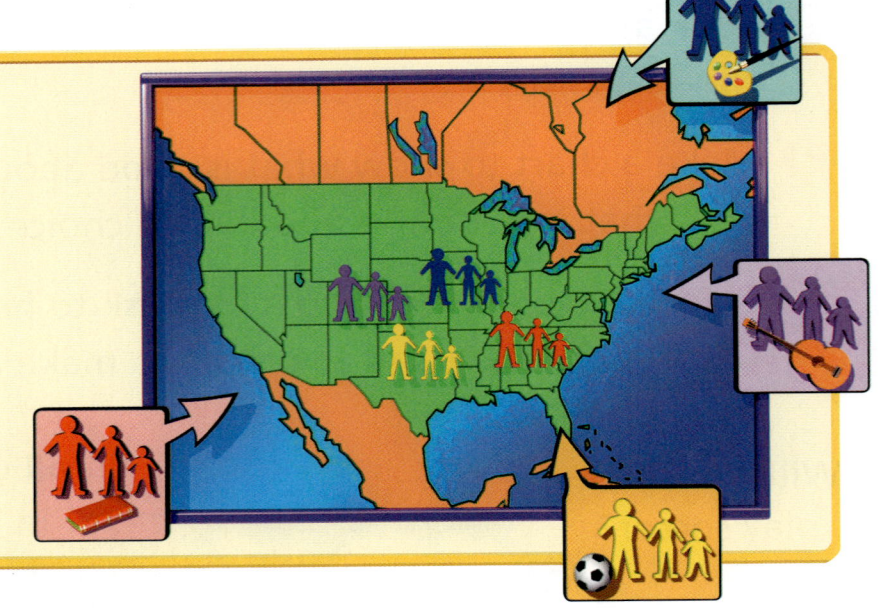

American Culture
- Your Family
- Your Country
- The World

Choose words that help describe the picture.

Your culture comes from your **1.** _____ and your **2.** _____. Languages and traditions are part of **3.** _____ .

Facts and Main Ideas

4. In what way do immigrants change American culture? (pages 118, 119)

5. What are two languages that people might speak in the United States? (pages 118–121)

6. Who has been honored by an American monument or memorial? (pages 138, 140–141)

7. What are two symbols of the United States? (page 139)

8. What is one tradition that is part of a religious holiday? (page 146)

Vocabulary

Choose the letter of the word to match the correct sentence.

9. A story that has been passed along for a long time

10. Something that people keep doing in the same way

11. A person who lived before us

12. A building or monument that helps people know a place

A. **ancestor** (page 120)
B. **landmark** (page 138)
C. **legend** (page 128)
D. **immigrant** (page 118)
E. **tradition** (page 126)

Test Practice

13. What do the words **national holiday** mean?

    A. a special day for people of a religion

    B. a day when events or people important to a state are honored

    C. a day when events or people important to a nation are honored

    D. a building that honors a famous person

Critical Thinking

Classify

14. Name a state holiday and tell why people celebrate it.

Review and Test Prep

Skillbuilders   Read a Timeline

15. How old is Dan today?

16. What did Dan do when he was six?

Make a Decision

17. What can Nora do? Name two or three choices.

18. Make a chart for each choice to show what is good or bad about it.

Good	Bad

19. What should Nora choose? Tell reasons for your decision.

Unit Activity

Culture Banner

Use pictures to make an American culture banner that shows the many people and symbols that make up our country's culture.

1. Draw or bring in pictures to put on the banner.
2. Write a title and your name on the banner.
3. Arrange the pictures on your banner.

WEEKLY READER — CURRENT EVENTS

Current Events Project

What celebrations are taking place in your community? Make an exhibit about **Celebrations in the News.**

Technology

Read articles about current events at www.eduplace.com/kids/hmss/

In Your Classroom

Look for these Social Studies Independent Books in your classroom.

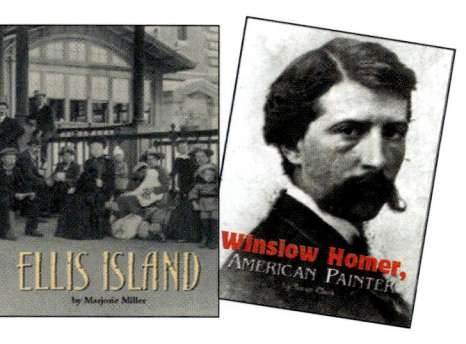

At the Library

You may find these books at your school or public library.

Grandma Maxine Remembers
by Ann Morris

Everybody Brings Noodles
by Norah Dooley

155

UNIT 4

People at Work

"At Dudley Market now I tell
Most kinds of articles they sell:
Hats, caps and bonnets blue
And trousers wide enough for two"
—Ben Boucher, Poet

The Big Idea

What are ways people earn, spend, and save money?

Unit 4 People at Work

Vocabulary Preview

Technology
- e • glossary
- e • word games
www.eduplace.com/kids/hmss05/

producer

A **producer** is someone who provides a service or makes goods. Julie has a dogwalking service, so she is a producer. page 166

consumer

A **consumer** is someone who buys goods or services. You are a consumer when you buy crayons. page 166

158 • Unit 4

Reading Strategy

Use the **question** reading strategy in Lessons 1, 2, and 3 and the **summarize** strategy in Lessons 4, 5, and 6.

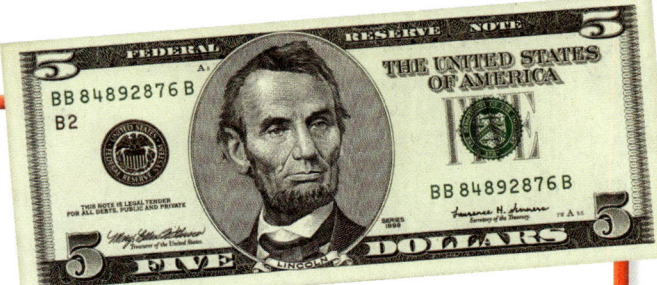

income

The money people earn when they work is their **income.** Sam's income is the $5.00 he earns each week on his paper route.

page 168

price

Price is the amount of money you pay to buy something. If you look in two or three stores, you may find the same toy at different prices. page 180

159

Core Lesson 1

Needs, Wants, and Choices

Vocabulary

needs
shelter
wants

Reading Skill
Predict Outcomes

Build on What You Know

Have you bought anything at a store? What choices did you make?

Needs and Wants

Needs are things that people must have to live. Everyone has to have food, water, clothing, and **shelter.** Shelter is something that protects or covers. Houses, trailer homes, and apartments are kinds of shelter.

Wants are things that people would like to have. People do not have to have those things to live. Everyone has wants and needs.

160 • Unit 4

Making Choices

People cannot have everything they want. People have to make choices about what to buy. If they use all their money to buy one thing, they cannot buy something else.

I have $30 saved. I can buy a computer game and play with it today. Or I can buy a scooter and ride it in the spring.

Sally's Choices

Choices	What I Give Up	What I Get
Buy computer game	Ride scooter in spring	Enjoy computer game today
Buy scooter	Enjoy computer game today	Ride scooter in spring

Review If Sally buys the computer game, what does she give up?

Lesson Review

1. **Vocabulary** Name some **needs** and some **wants**.
2. **Main Idea** Which would you choose, the game or the scooter? Why?

▶ **Activity** List as many kinds of shelter as you can.

161

Extend Lesson 1
Literature

THE MILKMAID

"The Milkmaid" is a tale told in Mexico and many other countries.

❖ ❖ ❖

Maria was a milkmaid who worked for a rich family. Sometimes the family gave Maria their leftover milk. Maria made extra money by selling the milk. One day the family gave Maria enough milk to fill a big jug.

On her way to market to sell the milk she thought, "I will have money to buy a hen that will lay many eggs. I will sell the eggs and use the money to buy a pig."

"When the pig has grown large, I will sell it and buy a cow. My cow will always give me milk to sell."

Maria thought of all the money she would make, and skipped with joy. Then, oops! Down she fell! Crash went the milk jug! Out spilled the milk, and with it Maria's dreams.

Maria cried and cried. Finally she said, "I may not get all I wanted, but I still have what I need."

Activities

1. **Write About It** Make a list of all of Maria's wants.

2. **Think About It** When Maria says, "I still have what I need," what are some needs she may be thinking of?

163

Skillbuilder

Compare Fact and Fiction

Vocabulary

fiction
nonfiction
fact

Fiction books are about made-up things. **Nonfiction** books tell facts. A **fact** is something that is true.

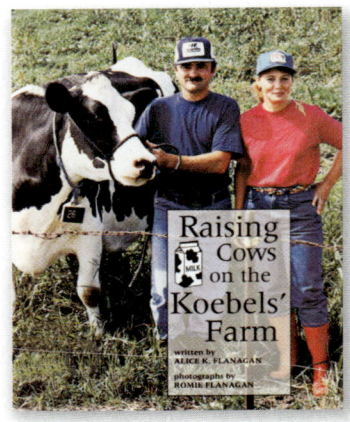

Learn the Skill

Step 1 Read the title. This title shows that the book is a true story about a real family farm.

Step 2 Look at the words and the pictures. The words in this book tell facts. The photographs show real things and people.

Step 3 Decide if the book is fiction, or nonfiction. Tell why you think so.

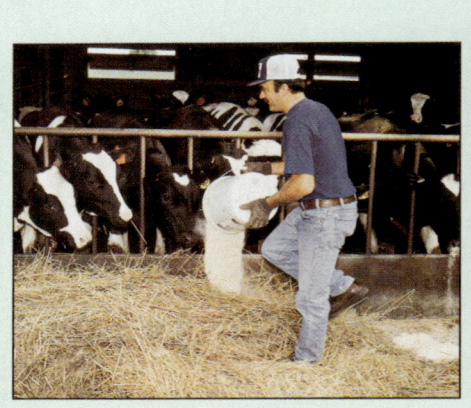

Mr. Koebel is in charge of the cows, or the herd. He is called the herdsman.

10

Apply Critical Thinking

Practice the Skill

Follow the directions.

❶ Look at the book titles below. Which book is fiction?

❷ Look at the book pages. How can you tell that the fiction book is fiction?

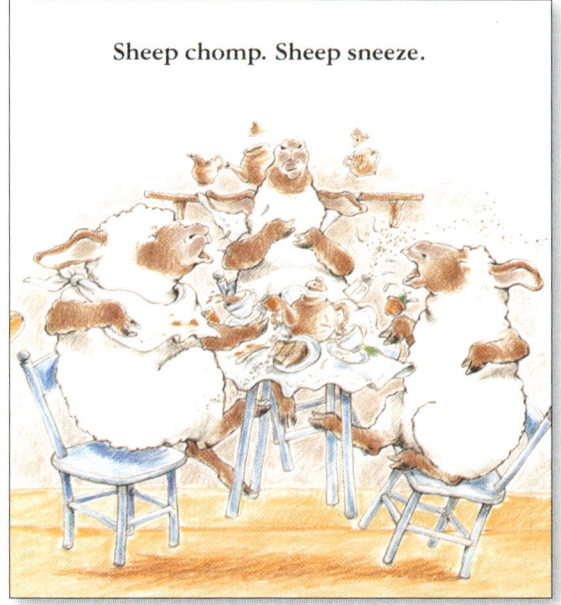

165

Core Lesson 2

Work

Vocabulary
producer
consumer
income

Reading Skill
Draw Conclusions

Build on What You Know
Do you make the things you need and want? Do you buy them?

Getting Things We Need

Hungry? Want an apple to eat? If you are the farmer who grows the apple, you are a **producer.** A producer is a person who makes or grows something. If you are the person who buys the apple and eats it, you are a **consumer.** A consumer is someone who buys or uses things.

goods

What if you grow the apple and eat the apple? Then you are a producer and a consumer.

Review In what ways are you a consumer?

"I am a producer. I make lemonade and sell it."

"I am a consumer. I buy the lemonade and drink it. Yummy!"

Ways to Earn Money

When people work, they usually earn money. This money is their **income.**

One person's income may be earned from selling a painting he made. Another person may earn money by selling a crop she grew. Sometimes people sell their skills or their time. They are paid for teaching in a school or working in a shop. People do different kinds of work.

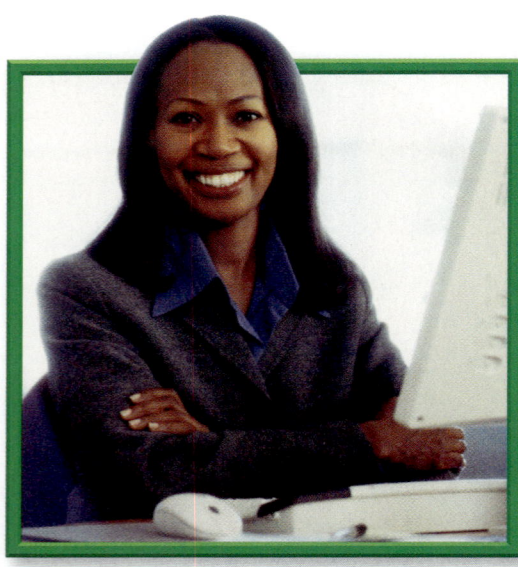

I own a small business. I like to help people with computer problems. I also like being my own boss!

I run this machine. I am really good at making cars.

168 • Unit 4

I work all day. At night, I go to school. I want to be a chef and make really tasty meals for people!

I like to make people's homes look beautiful.

Review What work do people do to earn money?

Lesson Review

1 Vocabulary Name two ways to earn **income.**

2 Main Idea What is a way that someone can be both a producer and a consumer?

Activity Draw a picture that shows a job you might like to do someday.

169

Extend Lesson 2

History

First Farmers

Were people always producers of their food? Look back more than ten thousand years. People did not have cities, towns, or farms. Instead, they moved from place to place. They gathered wild plants to eat.

Then some people took seeds from the strongest wild grains. They planted the seeds. The plants grew well. People picked the grain. They used some of it and saved the rest for planting.

Some of the first farmers lived in Mesopotamia.

1. Making tools
First farmers needed tools to plant seeds and cut grain.

2. Planting seeds
Having plants to care for, farmers began to live near their fields. Small towns grew up nearby.

170 • Unit 4

4. Grinding grain Farmers ground grain into flour.

5. Baking bread Flour was made into bread.

3. Harvesting grain Farmers cut the grain. Some was stored away.

Activities

1. **Chart It** Make a flow chart showing the steps described in the words and pictures on these pages.

2. **Think About It** For thousands of years, people gathered wild grain. Why do you think people decided to grow it instead?

171

Core Lesson 3

Goods and Services

Vocabulary
goods
factory
services

Reading Skill
Classify

Build on What You Know Have you ever wondered how your clothing was made or who made your toys?

Goods

The things people make or grow are called goods. **Goods** are things that you can touch, such as cars, apples, and baseballs. Many goods are made in a **factory.** A factory is a building where people work to make goods.

These people are working in a shoe factory.

172 • Unit 4

Services

Some people are doctors, teachers, or dogwalkers. Those people do not make things. They provide **services.** Services are activities that people do to help other people.

Review What are some services that you use?

Lesson Review

1. **Vocabulary** What are some **goods** that you use?

2. **Main Idea** What is one way goods are different from services?

 Activity Make a picture chart showing goods and services.

173

Extend Lesson 3

Biography

Scientists Serving Others

Some scientists discover things that help many people.

Marie Curie had a good memory that helped her as a student in Poland. When she grew up, she became a scientist. She lived and worked in France with her husband Pierre. Together, they made some big discoveries. Other scientists built on their work to find ways of curing sick people and making energy.

174 • Unit 4

CHARACTER TRAIT: Caring

Louis Pasteur (LOO ee pas TUR) When Louis Pasteur was a boy, his teacher saw that Louis was patient and hardworking. Later, those qualities helped Pasteur become one of France's most famous scientists. He found that heating milk killed germs. That made the milk safer to drink. Pasteur's discoveries have helped millions of people stay healthy. Milk is still heated today. The process is called pasteurization. (pas chuhr ih ZAY shuhn)

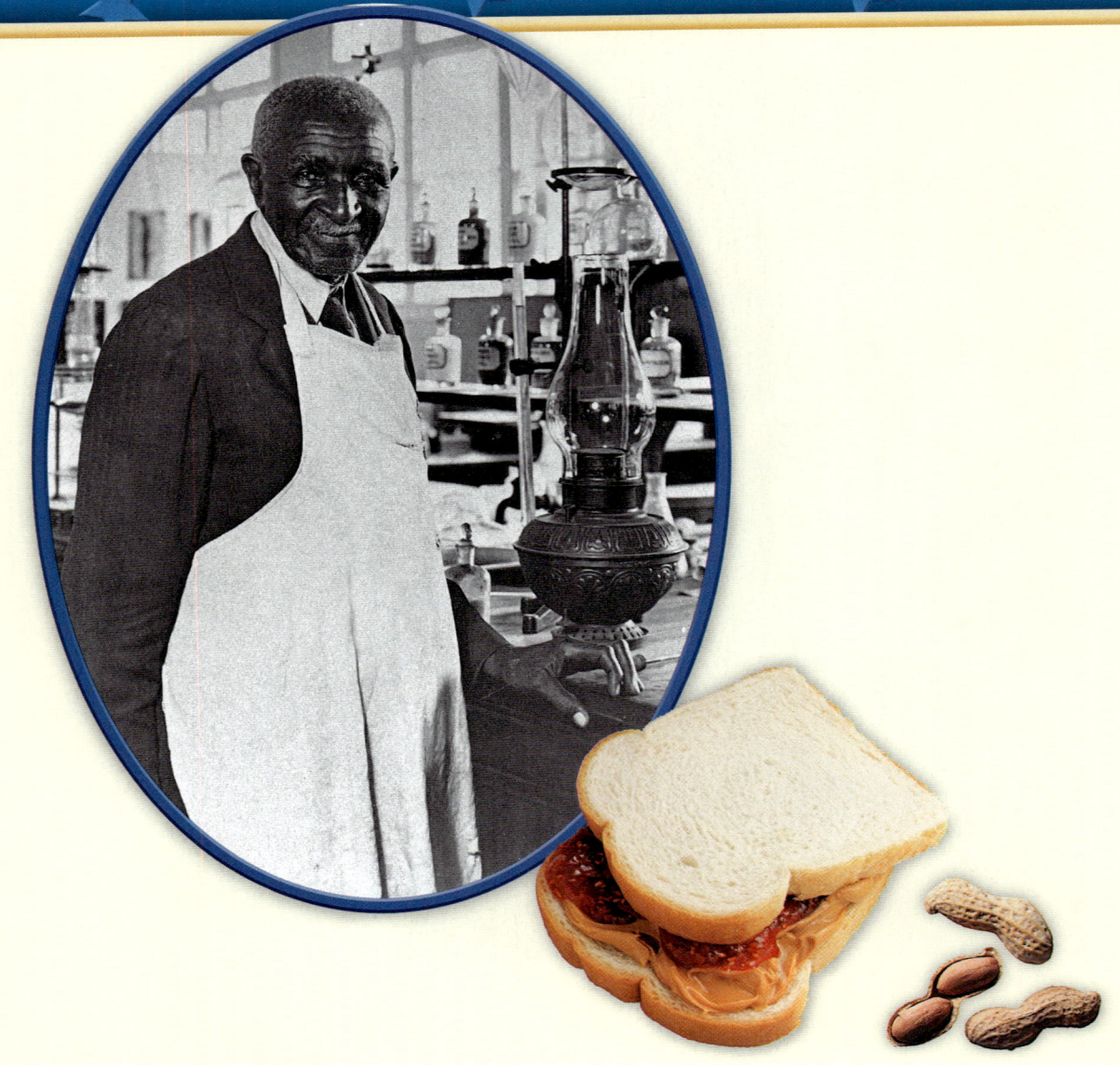

George Washington Carver The plant scientist George Washington Carver wanted to help African American farmers make more money from the crops they grew. After many experiments and much hard work, Carver found hundreds of ways to use peanuts, soybeans, and sweet potatoes. Then, he thought, farmers could earn income by growing these plants too.

CHARACTER TRAIT: Caring

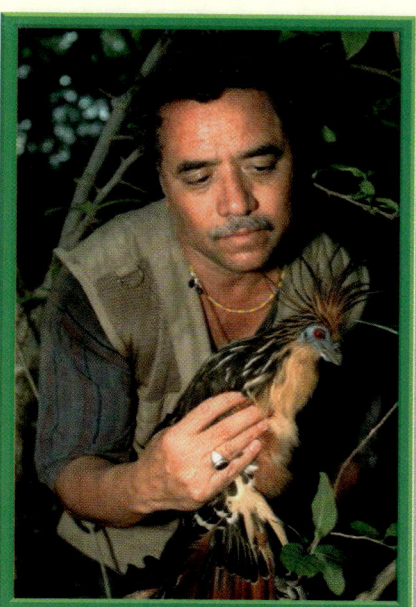

Eloy Rodriguez (ee LOY rahd REE gehs) Think on your feet. Use common sense. Eloy Rodriguez often heard that advice in Spanish from his family. Now he is a scientist who studies how animals use plants to heal themselves. From this he has learned ways that plants can heal people. Also Eloy Rodriguez gets students excited about science. He shares advice that helped him.

Activities

1. **Think About It** What are some ways these scientists show caring for others?

2. **Write About It** Write or tell how people's lives are better because of the work of the scientists you have read about.

177

Skillbuilder
Read a Bar Graph

Many foods are produced in the United States. This bar graph shows how much milk cows produce each year.

> **Vocabulary**
> bar graph

Learn the Skill

Using a **bar graph** is a way to compare things. The bars show how much there is of something.

Step 1 The numbers and words at the side of the graph tell how much. On this graph, the number 30 stands for 30 billion pounds of milk.

Step 2 Along the bottom of the graph are the names of some states in which milk is produced.

Step 3 Look at the bar above California. It goes up to 30. That means that in California, cows produce 30 billion pounds of milk each year. How much milk do cows in Wisconsin produce?

178 • Unit 4

Practice the Skill

Look at the graph below. Then answer the questions.

❶ How much milk is produced in New York each year?

❷ In which state on the graph is the smallest amount of milk produced?

❸ In which state do cows produce more milk each year, Wisconsin or New York?

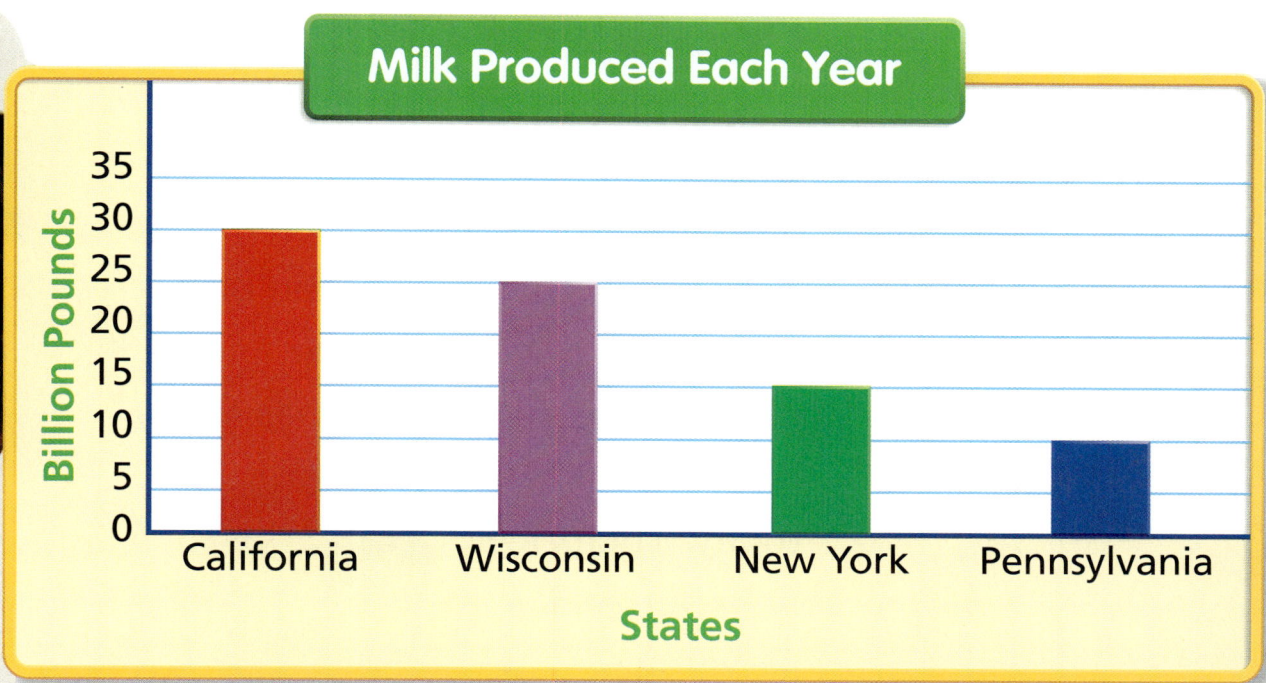

Core Lesson 4

People Save Money

Vocabulary
price
bank
savings account

Reading Skill
Predict Outcomes

Build on What You Know

Suppose you are given $2.00 for helping a neighbor. What will you do with it? Will you buy something now, or keep it for later?

Prices and Choices

The amount of money you pay to buy something is the **price.** In stores, often the prices are printed on or near things that people can buy. Looking at prices helps people decide what to buy. Ken has thirty cents to buy fruit today. The prices help him make his choice.

What do you think Ken's choice will be? Why?

180 • Unit 4

I'm saving for my children to go to college.

We're saving for a trip to Brazil.

I'm saving up to buy roller skates.

These people tell why they are saving money.

Saving Money

Many people are careful not to spend all their income. Some save money so they can pay for what they want. They might save money in a piggy bank. A **bank** is a safe place where people keep their money.

Review Why do people save money?

181

A Savings Account

Most people use a bank that has many services. One service is called a **savings account.** Instead of keeping their money at home, people put it in a savings account. They let the bank use the money. In return, the bank adds a bit more money each month. That money is called interest. Interest helps the amount of money in the account grow.

Review How are banks that are businesses and banks in people's homes alike and different?

What services are in a bank?

Gina Saves

Gina has a savings account at a bank in her town. Last year she put in money every month to save for baseball camp in July. Look at the graph of Gina's account.

Skill **Reading Graphs** What do you think Gina did with her money in July?

Lesson Review

1. **Vocabulary** Describe a **savings account** in a bank.
2. **Main Idea** What is one reason for saving money in banks that are businesses?

Activity Write or tell about a buying choice you have made.

Extend Lesson 4

Economics

Spend Your Dollar

Welcome to Write On store. Take a look at what is for sale. Compare **prices.** Then see what your dollar will buy.

184 • Unit 4

1. Look at the items. Choose the items you like.

2. You have only $1.00 to spend. Check the prices. See what you can buy with your $1.00.

3. Record on a class chart the items you choose. Add the prices and record the total.

Name	30¢	15¢	10¢	Total Spent
Frank	3	0	1	$1.00
Mimi	1	4	1	$1.00
George	2	2	1	$1.00
Amina	0	4	2	$0.80

ECONOMICS

Skillbuilder

Use Reference Books

You can find out more about a topic by using reference books.

▶ **Vocabulary**

dictionary
encyclopedia

Learn the Skill

A **dictionary** is a book that tells what words mean. An **encyclopedia** is a set of books that has articles on different topics. The articles tell facts.

Step 1 The information in reference books is often in ABC order. To find the word **bank** in a dictionary, look in the section that begins with B. To find an article about **banks** in an encyclopedia, look in the book labeled with the letter B.

Step 2 After you find the B section, you need to find the right page. The **guidewords** can help you. They show the first and last word on each page.

Step 3 Use ABC order to find the word **bank.**

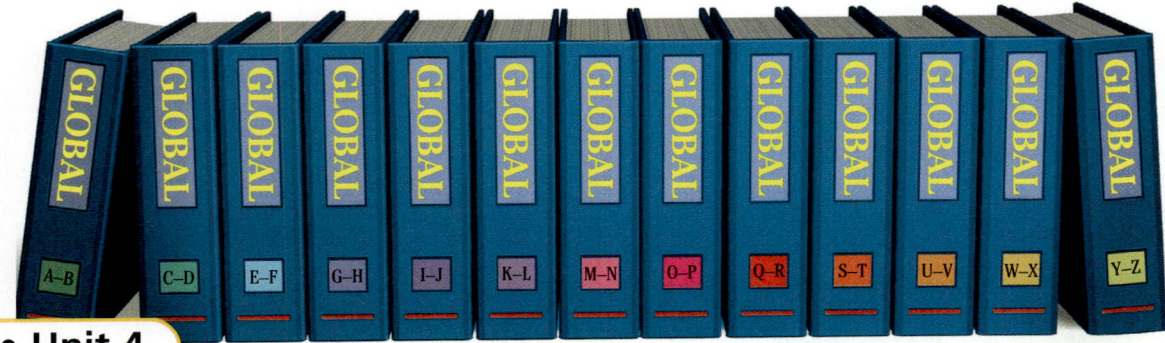

186 • Unit 4

Practice the Skill

Follow the directions.

1 Suppose your teacher asks you to find information about the first factories. Tell which kind of reference book you will use.

2 Use a dictionary to find the definition of these words: **product, income, business**

Guidewords

B b

balloon ◇ bank

balloon
A **balloon** is a kind of bag filled with gas. Some **balloons** are huge and can carry people high into the sky.

banana
A **banana** is a kind of fruit. It has a long curved shape and a yellow skin.

balloon

band

band
A **band** is a group of people who play music together. Everyone in the parade marched to the music of the **band**.

bank
A **bank** is a safe place to keep money. A **bank** can be a small box or jar that you keep at home. A **bank** is also a big building. People can leave money or borrow it at the **bank**.

The first word on this page is **balloon**. It is the first guideword.

The last word is **bank**. It is the second guideword.

Core Lesson 5

From Field to Market

Vocabulary
human resource
capital resource
scarcity

Reading Skill
Sequence

Build on What You Know Do you know how a bunch of grapes becomes the box of raisins in your lunch?

From the Vine to You!

Imagine large farms with row after row of grapevines. In spring, workers start watering the vines. A few months later, the grapes are ripe. Workers pick the grape bunches by hand and place them on clean paper trays. The grapes dry in the sun for two to three weeks. Slowly they become raisins.

Picking grapes

Drying grapes

188 • Unit 4

Workers drive the raisins to the food processing plant. There the raisins are checked and cleaned. Machines take off the stems and package the raisins. Ships, trains, and trucks carry the packages across the country and around the world. Stores sell the raisins to you! It takes many steps to get a box of raisins from a bunch of grapes.

Review When do grapes become raisins?

Cleaning raisins

Sorting raisins

Boxing raisins

Three Kinds of Resources

Raisin producers use natural resources. They need soil, water, and sunshine. Raisin producers also need **human resources.** Human resources are people. They are the farm workers who care for the vines. They are the people who operate machines, sell raisins, and run the business.

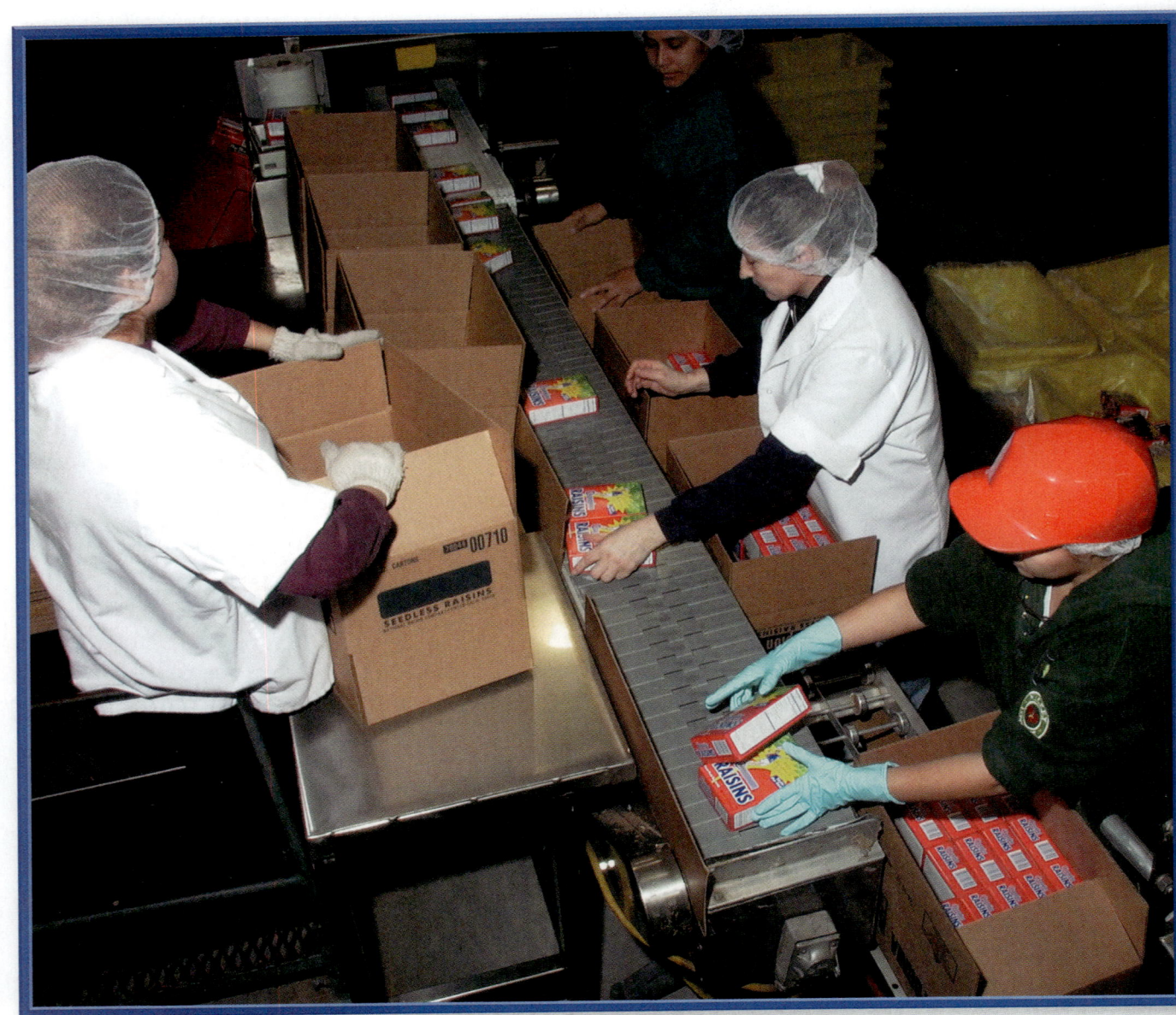

Raisin producers need a third kind of resource. They need capital resources. **Capital resources** are things such as tools, machinery, buildings, and trucks. The buildings where raisins are sorted and cleaned are capital resources. So are the machines that take the stems off the raisins. Producers of raisins and other goods use all three kinds of resources.

Resources

Human Resources	Natural Resources	Capital Resources
farm workers sales people machine operators	soil water	machines trucks tools

191

Scarcity

The three kinds of resources are all limited. The earth has only so many human, natural, and capital resources. However, people have unlimited wants for goods and services. That is why there is scarcity.

Some farmers choose to use their land to grow grapes.

Some farmers choose to use their land for growing vegetables.

Scarcity means we don't have enough resources to produce all the goods and services we want. Because we can't have all we want, we have to make choices in what to make or grow.

Review Why do people have to make choices about what to make or grow?

Lesson Review

1. **Vocabulary** Explain what **scarcity** is.

2. **Main Idea** What are the three kinds of resources people use to produce goods and services?

Activity List one example of each kind of resource in your school.

Extend Lesson 5

History

Keeping Food Cold

A Cool Timeline

For hundreds of years, people have found ways to keep food from spoiling by keeping it cold. There were many ways to keep food cold before people used refrigerators. Look at how the ways have changed.

1750   1800

250 years ago
Settlers dug root cellars inside or outside their homes.

| 1850 | 1900 | 1950 | 2000 |

170 years ago
A big block of ice kept food inside the ice box cold. The iceman delivered a new block of ice every other day or so.

80 to 90 years ago
People began using electric refrigerators with freezers.

Activities

1. **Talk About It** Tell a story about a time when the electricity was out and your family could not keep food cold in the refrigerator.

2. **Think About It** Why do you think a refrigerator is better than an ice box?

Core Lesson 6

People and Nations Trade

Vocabulary
barter
trade
specialize

Reading Skill
Cause and Effect

Build on What You Know

Swapping toys or baseball cards with a friend is one way to get the things you want. What are other ways?

Barter

What you do when you swap toys or cards is called barter. **Barter** takes place when people exchange goods or services without using money. Long ago barter was the main way people got the things they wanted.

I'll give you this pig for two pounds of beets.

I'll trade one pound of beets for your pig.

196 • Unit 4

Skill **Visual Learning** What do people use to help them trade goods?

Trade

Many times, barter does not work very well. That is why most people today pay for goods and services in other ways, often with money. Whether people barter or use money, they are taking part in trade. Trade is the buying and selling of goods and services. You take part in trade when you buy an apple.

Review What is one way you take part in trade?

197

Trading Bananas and Wheat

bananas

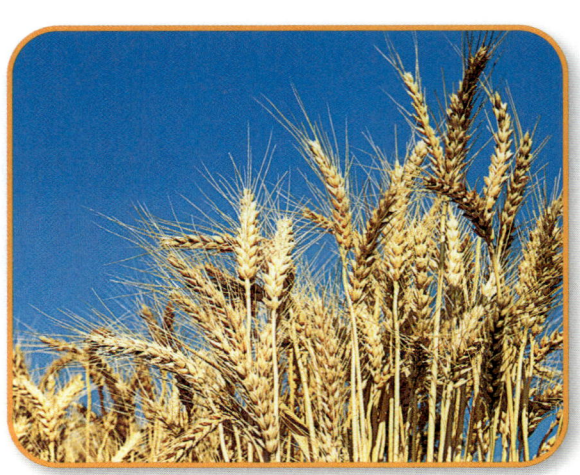
wheat

198 • Unit 4

Depending on One Another

Farmers in the United States specialize in growing wheat, not bananas. Farmers in Costa Rica specialize in growing bananas, not wheat. When farmers **specialize,** that means they choose to grow mainly one crop. Farmers in the United States sell their wheat to consumers in Costa Rica. Farmers in Costa Rica sell their bananas to consumers in the United States. People in countries around the world depend on trade to get the goods and services they want.

Review What does it mean to specialize?

Lesson Review

1. **Vocabulary** The buying and selling of goods and services is called _____.

2. **Main Idea** What is one reason that countries trade with one another?

Activity Draw a picture of something you want. Tell what you would be willing to barter to get it.

199

Extend Lesson 6

  Geography

Money Around the World

There is an old saying that money cannot buy happiness. That's true, but money does buy a lot of other things. People everywhere use metal coins and paper bills to buy goods and services.

Countries around the world have their own money. The United States has the dollar. Jordan has the dinar. Find other money names.

The European Union

euro

2-euro coin

Brazil

real

50-centavo coin

Kenya

shilling

5-shilling coin

GEOGRAPHY

India

rupee

1-paisa coin

Australia

dollar

5-cent coin

Activities

1. **Name It** Which country besides the United States uses a dollar?

2. **Research It** Look up "Money" in an encyclopedia. Find out who is shown on the U.S. penny, nickel, dime, and quarter.

Skillbuilder

Use a Map Scale

Goods need to be moved from place to place. A map scale can tell you how far they go.

Vocabulary

distance
scale

Learn the Skill

Distance is how far one point is from another. You can use a map and a map **scale** to figure out distance.

Step 1 Look at the map scale and the ruler. The blue scale bar measures one inch.

Step 2 Look at the numbers on the scale. They show that one inch on the map stands for 100 miles. How many miles do two inches stand for?

Step 3 It is about five inches on the map from Pittsburgh to Plymouth. So the distance from the real city of Pittsburgh to Plymouth must be about 500 miles.

202 • Unit 4

Practice the Skill

Look at the map. Follow the directions to find distances. Use a ruler.

1. About how many inches is it on the map from Plymouth to Washington, D.C.?

2. How many miles is it from Plymouth to Washington, D.C.? Use the scale to find out.

3. A truck carries clams from Plymouth to Ithaca. How many miles does the truck travel?

Unit 4 Review and Test Prep

Big Ideas

Choose the missing words from the organizer.

1. A _____ makes goods.   2. A consumer buys _____ and services.   3. A consumer may _____ money in a bank.

Facts and Main Ideas

4. What is the difference between needs and wants? (page 160)

5. What is income? (page 168)

6. What is one job that is a service? (page 173)

7. What does **scarcity** mean? (page 193)

204 • Unit 4

Vocabulary

Use words from the box to complete the sentences.

Consumers earn **8.** _____
to pay for needs and **9.** _____ .
One need is **10.** _____ .
Consumers look at the
11. _____ of goods and
12. _____ . Consumers may
save money in a **13.** _____
to pay later for things they want.

A. **prices** (page 180)

B. **income** (page 168)

C. **savings account** (page 182)

D. **services** (page 173)

E. **specialize** (page 199)

F. **wants** (page 160)

G. **shelter** (page 160)

Test Practice

14. What does the word **barter** mean?

　A. earning a small income

　B. saving money in a bank

　C. trading without money

　D. producing many goods

Critical Thinking

Main Idea and Details

15. What are two examples of human resources?

16. What are two examples of trade?

205

Review and Test Prep

Skillbuilders Use a Map Scale

17. On this map, one inch equals _____ .

18. How far is it from Maria's house to the airport?

Read a Bar Graph

19. Which place at school has the fewest workers?

20. How many workers are in the office and the cafeteria altogether?

Unit Activity

Make a Mobile

If you earned $10, how much of your money would you spend and save?

1. Write and draw your choices.
2. Make sure that they add up to $10.
3. Cut out your choices and hang them up to make a mobile. Explain your choices.

CURRENT EVENTS WEEKLY WR READER

Current Events Project

Find articles about jobs around the world. Publish a **Class Newspaper** about people at work around the world.

Rug weaving   Fishing

Technology

Read articles about current events at www.eduplace.com/kids/hmss/

In Your Classroom

Look for these Social Studies Independent Books in your classroom.

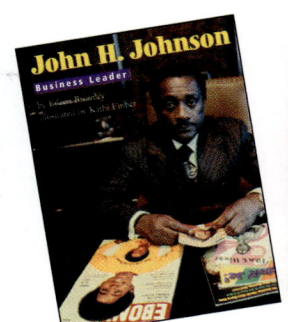

At the Library

You may find these books at your school or public library.

Follow the Money
by Loreen Leedy

The Paperboy
by Dav Pilkey

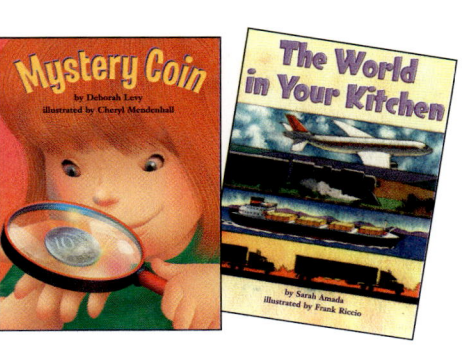

207

UNIT 5

America's Past

"Let Freedom ring."
—Samuel Francis Smith, from "America"

The Big Idea

Why is the past important to you today?

Unit 5 America's Past

Vocabulary Preview

- e • glossary
- e • word games
- www.eduplace.com/kids/hmss05/

colonist

A **colonist** is a person who lives in a colony. Many colonists came to America seeking freedom. page 230

explorer

We remember Christopher Columbus, an **explorer** who traveled to find new things and places. page 222

210 • Unit 5

Reading Strategy

Use the **predict and infer** reading strategy in Lessons 1, 2, 3, and 4 and the **monitor and clarify** strategy in Lessons 5, 6, and 7.

independence

The 13 colonies gained independence from Great Britain. **Independence** is freedom from the rule of another nation. page 242

technology

Technology is the use of science to make new things or to make things work better. page 260

211

Core Lesson 1

Vocabulary
history

Reading Skill
Classify

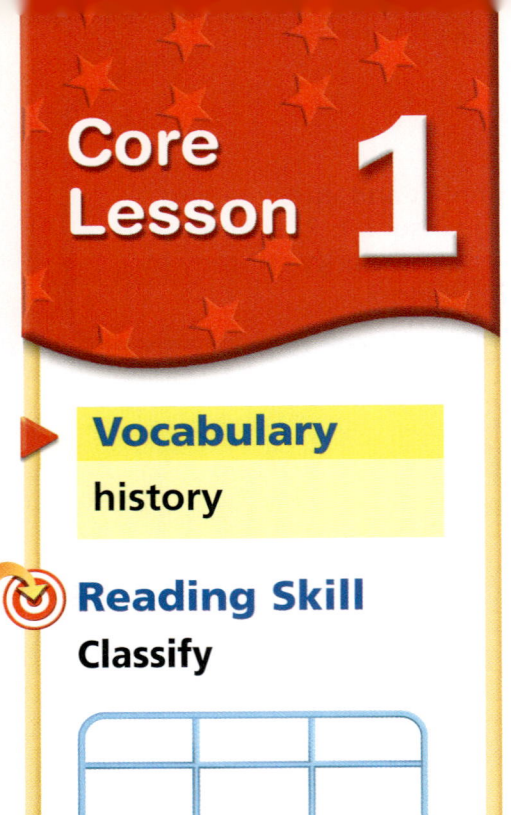

First Americans

Build on What You Know How old are you? Your age now is in the present. You will be a grownup in the future. You were a baby in the past.

History

You remember things that happened in the past. Also you learn about the past from family stories. **History** is everything we can know about the past. History is everything that happened in the lives of people from far back in the past up to the present.

A storyteller in Alaska uses his drum to tell a traditional tale to young people.

The First People in America

Our country's history starts with American Indians. Hundreds of American Indian groups already lived in America more than 500 years ago. They depended on natural resources. American Indians used water, land, and plants in many different ways. Their clothes, tools, and other things from the past help us learn about their lives.

This map locates just four of the many groups of American Indians. They are the four you will learn about on the next pages.

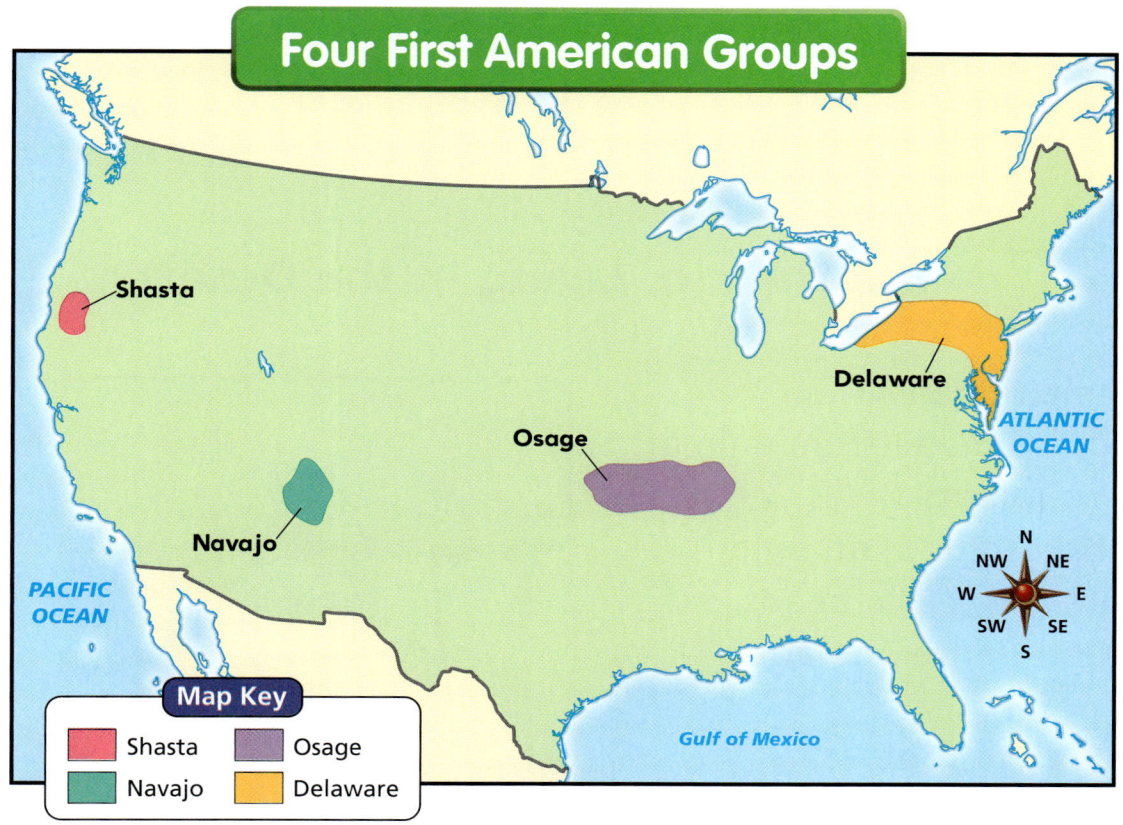

Four First American Groups

Map Key
- Shasta
- Osage
- Navajo
- Delaware

Skill Reading Maps Which group was in the northwest?

213

Compare Groups

The Delaware, Living in Woodlands

Homes winter longhouse for several families; summer wigwam for each family
Clothes made from deerskin
Food nuts, berries, corn, beans, squash, deer meat
Travel by canoe, on foot

The Navajo, Living in the Desert

Home hogan
Clothes made from animal skins, plants
Food cactus fruit, wild potatoes, corn, beans, squash, antelope and deer meat
Travel on foot

The Osage, Living on the Plains

Homes winter longhouses for several families, small summer homes for travelers
Clothes made from deerskin
Food nuts, plums, grapes, potatoes, corn, beans, pumpkins, turkey, buffalo
Travel on foot, by canoe

The Shasta, Living Near the Ocean

Homes winter dwelling house for several families, summer cool brush shelter
Clothes made from animal skins, fur, braided grass
Food bulbs, berries, pine nuts, acorns, turtles, grasshoppers, fish, deer, elk
Travel on foot, with snowshoes in winter, by canoe

Natural Resources and Daily Life

These pictures show some things that American Indians made and used hundreds of years ago. People in the present might see these things in a museum. American Indians used many natural resources to make the things they needed.

Navajo sandals were made from braided leaves of desert plants.

The Osage and other groups who lived on the plains wove baskets from long grasses.

216 • Unit 5

Some American Indian groups in plains and woodlands made dugout canoes from logs of trees.

Review Where might people today see things that people made hundreds of years ago?

Lesson Review

❶ **Vocabulary** Write a sentence that uses the words **history** and **American Indian**.

❷ **Main Idea** Why were natural resources important to American Indians?

Activity Choose two groups and tell a way they were alike and a way they were different.

217

Extend Lesson 1
Literature

The Young Woman and the Thunder Beings

This legend is retold by Joseph Bruchac in his book Between Earth and Sky. In the past, the Seneca told this story. In the present they still tell it. Read it to see why.

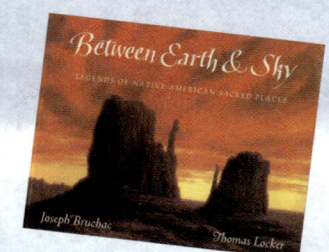

To the North lived the Longhouse People, near the edge of the falls called Ne-ah-ga.

They sometimes spoke of the Thunder Beings who lived in a cave beneath the falls. When a child wanted to give thanks to the Thunderers for the gift of rain, he would place an offering in a canoe and put it in the river to float over the falls.

One day a young woman alone in her canoe was crossing the river far up from the falls when she lost her paddle. The current was swift and she found herself swept away. This brave young woman had always been a friend of the Thunderers, giving them gifts with each new season. So, as she fell, she did not scream or cry. In trust, she asked calmly for help.

The Thunder Beings saved her life, catching her safely in their blanket. Then the chief of the Thunderers asked the young woman to be his wife. She agreed, and to this day, the Seneca say that when the rumbling voices of the Thunder Beings roll across the sky, the brave young woman is keeping watch, reminding us that every gift we give gives us back a blessing.

Activities

1. **Talk About It** Is this a true story? Explain why or why not.

2. **Act It Out** List the characters in the story and act out what they do.

Core Lesson 2

Explorers Travel the World

Vocabulary

explorer
journey

Reading Skill

Compare and Contrast

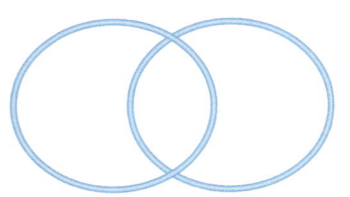

Build on What You Know Have you traveled to a place that was new to you? What did you learn about it?

Explorers from Europe

An **explorer** is a person who travels to find out new things. A **journey** is a trip. Many hundreds of years ago, explorers from Europe made journeys to other lands. They did not have cars, planes, or steam engines then. Their maps did not show much about the places they were going. Their journeys were filled with adventures.

Marco Polo

222 • Unit 5

Marco Polo

More than 700 years ago, a man from Italy named Marco Polo traveled to Asia. He spent many years in China. He told thrilling stories about new things he saw on his journeys. His stories were put into a book. Most people in Europe knew nothing about what Asia was like. Marco Polo's stories made them want to find out more.

Marco Polo in the court of the Chinese emperor

Review Why was Marco Polo important in history?

Christopher Columbus

Christopher Columbus was an explorer from Europe who wanted to find a faster way to reach parts of Asia. Columbus read Marco Polo's stories and studied many maps. He decided to sail west across the Atlantic Ocean. His ships reached land that he thought was Asia. Explorers who came later learned that it was not Asia. It was another continent—now called North America.

Christopher Columbus's First Journey, 1492

Skill Reading Maps What ocean did Christopher Columbus cross?

Christopher Columbus set out from Spain with a crew of ninety sailors in three ships, the **Niña, Pinta,** and **Santa Maria.**

The journeys of Christopher Columbus changed what people knew about the world. North America and South America soon became part of the world map for Europeans. The new knowledge led to other changes for people who lived in the Americas.

Christopher Columbus

Review Why did Christopher Columbus sail west?

Lesson Review

1. **Vocabulary** Write a sentence that uses the words **journey** and **explorer**.

2. **Main Idea** Why was Marco Polo's journey important to Christopher Columbus?

Activity Write or tell a way that Marco Polo and Christopher Columbus were alike and a way they were different.

Extend Lesson 2

History

The Magnetic Compass

How did Christopher Columbus find his way across the Atlantic Ocean? A magnetic compass helped him.

A magnetic compass is like a compass rose. It shows directions: north, south, east and west. But a magnetic compass has something more. It has a needle that is a magnet. Because the needle is a magnet, it always points towards the earth's North Pole. Once you know where north is, you can find east, south, and west too.

People in China were the first to make magnetic compasses.

Read a Magnetic Compass

1 Rest the compass on a table. Find the colored end of the needle. That end points north.

2 Locate the letters N, E, S, and W. Name the direction word that each letter stands for.

3 Gently turn the compass until the needle is in line with the letter N. What does the needle do when you turn the compass?

4 Hold both arms out together ahead of you and face the direction that the compass points. You should be facing and pointing north.

Core Lesson 3

Jamestown and Plymouth

Vocabulary

colony
settlement
colonist
Pilgrim

Reading Skill

Compare and Contrast

Build on What You Know How would you feel about moving to a place far away?

American Land

After Columbus, more explorers from Europe traveled to other parts of North America. They hoped to find gold and other riches. They saw great natural resources in the forests, plains, and rivers. American Indians already lived there. But kings and queens from countries in Europe wanted the land for their countries. They sent people to settle in North America.

228 • Unit 5

English Colonies

A **colony** is a place that is ruled by another country. England was one of the countries that started colonies in North America. People from England traveled in ships to settle there. Their colonies began with small communities called **settlements.** The map shows two of the earliest settlements. See what you can learn about Plymouth and Jamestown from the map.

Skill Reading Maps Why do you think both settlements were built near water?

229

Jamestown

A **colonist** is a person who lives in a colony. The first colonists in Jamestown were men and boys. They worked hard to stay alive. The colonists cut down trees, which they used to build a fort and some houses.

At first they did not have enough food. They ate fish and turtles, even raccoons. Nearby American Indians called the Pamunkey gave them some corn. Also, the colonists had copper that they traded for corn. The Pamunkey wanted the copper to make jewelry.

230 • Unit 5

Later the colonists sent for others in their families. Life was hard for everyone. Children worked along with grownups.

Soon the colonists at Jamestown began to produce goods, such as lumber and window glass. They sent these products to be sold in England.

Skill Visual Learning What are some things in the picture that show what colonists in Jamestown did?

231

Plymouth

Many of the first colonists at Plymouth belonged to the same religious group. They became known as **Pilgrims.** The Pilgrims came to America because they wanted freedom to follow their religious beliefs. Whole families came together. In the first year, they faced sickness, fire, and freezing weather. American Indians called the Wampanoag (wahm puh NOH ag) helped the Pilgrims. The Wampanoag showed the Pilgrims how to plant, hunt, and fish.

232 • Unit 5

Everyone had to help out. Girls and boys helped cook, clean, and look after the younger children. Women kept the gardens. They made and mended the family's clothes. They taught the children to read and write. Men built homes. They hunted and fished and planted corn.

Review In what ways was daily life in Plymouth like daily life in Jamestown?

Lesson Review

1. **Vocabulary** Use the words **Pilgrim** and **colony** to tell something you have learned.

2. **Main Idea** What did colonists from England need to do to live in their new settlements?

Activity Write a description of a way that American Indians helped colonists from England.

Extend Lesson 3

Readers' Theater

The Mayflower Crossing

What was the ocean crossing like for the Pilgrims aboard the Mayflower? Follow them on their journey from England to America.

Characters

Narrator
Mary Brewster: woman
Love Brewster: Mary's son
Constance Hopkins: girl
William Bradford: man
Rose Standish: woman
Elizabeth Tilley: girl
Thomas English: sailor

Scene 1

Narrator: It is September 10, 1620. The **Mayflower** has been at sea for four days.

Love: I am so tired of looking at the ocean, Mother.

Mary: Be patient. There are many days ahead on this little ship.

Thomas: Better go below! A storm is coming! You will find it a little too exciting on deck!

234 • Unit 5

Scene 2

Narrator: Two weeks pass. The sea grows rougher.

Constance: I wish this awful rolling would stop!

Rose: If we only had fresh water.

Love: Or a hot meal. Even beans would do.

Mary: Be glad we have cheese and biscuits.

Elizabeth: Father says the main beam of the ship has cracked.

William: Don't worry. The sailors are fixing it.

Thomas: We'll use these tools to pull the beam together.

READERS' THEATER

Scene 3

Narrator: Halfway through the crossing, during a storm, a cry goes up.

Thomas: Help! John Howland has washed overboard!

Elizabeth: He fell from the main deck!

Love: Wait! He has grabbed hold of a rope.

Elizabeth: They are lifting him out! He is safe, thank goodness.

William: Listen. There is another cry: a new-born baby!

Constance: Mother has had a baby boy. She has named him Oceanus. They are both doing well.

All: Congratulations!

William: This news should give us all hope.

Scene 4

Narrator: In November, more than nine weeks after leaving England, we hear the call we've been waiting for.

Thomas: Land!

Elizabeth: I see it! A long curving beach.

Rose: My husband, Miles, will bring men ashore.

William: We will look for a good place to build our community.

Love: Fresh water!

Rose and Mary: Clean clothes!

William: Friends, it is time to begin our new lives.

Activities

1. **Think About It** What do you think was most difficult for the passengers of the **Mayflower**?

2. **Write About It** Write a letter you might have sent to England if you had sailed on the **Mayflower**.

237

Skillbuilder

Identify Cause and Effect

> **Vocabulary**
> cause
> effect

The Pilgrims wanted to land at the Hudson River. They thought the river was part of Virginia. Why did they land on Cape Cod? Knowing about cause and effect can help you understand what happened.

Learn the Skill

A **cause** makes something happen. Something that happens is an **effect.**

Step 1 Look at this map. The star shows the place the Pilgrims wanted to land. The dots show where the Pilgrims really landed.

Step 2 Use the map to find one thing that caused the **Mayflower** to change its route. The map shows that one cause was a storm.

Step 3 You can explain cause and effect using the word **because.** The **Mayflower** changed its route because it hit a storm.

Apply Critical Thinking

Practice the Skill

Follow the directions to identify cause and effect.

❶ After the **Mayflower** left Cape Cod for the Hudson River, what caused the ship to turn around and go back?

❷ Think about what you have learned. What are two causes for why the Pilgrims landed on Cape Cod?

Hudson River

Plymouth

Storm at sea
B

C

A

Cape Cod   Shallow water

Pilgrims leave England

The Pilgrims wanted to land here.

Route of the Pilgrims, 1620

Map Key
— Route the Pilgrims took
---- Route the Pilgrims planned to take

239

Core Lesson 4

Vocabulary
independence

Reading Skill
Sequence

A New Country

Build on What You Know Have you had to follow rules that didn't seem fair to you?

Many Colonies

After the first settlements in Jamestown and Plymouth, more people came from England to settle in North America. They built homes and churches. They started farms and businesses. Some small communities grew into large towns and cities. People worked and planned together. But they had to follow rules from the king of England, who was the ruler of Great Britain and its colonies.

The map shows thirteen of the colonies in North America in 1763.

Review What were the names of the colonies?

The Thirteen Colonies

Boston

Charleston

Philadelphia

241

Independence

Independence means being free from rule by another nation. More and more colonists in America wanted independence from Great Britain. Some colonists began to act against British rules and taxes. One group of colonists acted against a tax on tea. Their action was called the Boston Tea Party. King George ruled Great Britain then. He sent more and more armies to control the colonists.

Look at events on the timeline.

December 1773
Boston Tea Party

April 1775
British army fights with colonists in Massachusetts

1770 — 1773 — 1775

242 • Unit 5

The Declaration of Independence

People from the thirteen colonies did not all agree about independence from Great Britain. Each colony sent people to Philadelphia to meet and make a decision. People at the meeting chose Thomas Jefferson to write words explaining why the colonies wanted independence. Those words became the Declaration of Independence. <u>By signing the Declaration of Independence, colonists came together for the goal of independence.</u>

Review What did colonists do that showed they wanted independence?

July 1776
Thirteen colonies agree on the Declaration of Independence

1776   1780

This painting shows an artist's idea of how George Washington looked when he crossed the Delaware River during the American Revolution.

The American Revolution

Great Britain would not allow independence. King George sent soldiers to fight a war against the colonists. The war was called the American Revolution. George Washington led the soldiers who fought against Britain. There were terrible battles. The American Revolution lasted eight years. Finally in 1783, the war ended. The colonies had won independence. They became a country called the United States of America.

Leaders for Independence

You have read how George Washington and Thomas Jefferson helped America gain independence. Many others helped too. **Benjamin Franklin** got colonists to think and talk about why they wanted independence. **Abigail Adams** wrote what she saw and thought about the fight for independence. **Samuel Adams** made speeches that got many colonists to fight for independence. **Paul Revere** helped colonists work together against Great Britain.

Benjamin Franklin

Samuel Adams

Review Why did colonists fight in the American Revolution?

Lesson Review

1. **Vocabulary** Use the word **independence** in a sentence about colonists.

2. **Main Idea** Why was the Declaration of Independence important to the colonists?

Activity Draw a picture of a person or an event that helped America become an independent country. Tell why that person or event was important.

245

Extend Lesson 4

Biography

Two Patriots

Abigail Adams and Paul Revere both used their minds and hands to help win independence for their country.

Abigail Adams

Abigail Adams always loved to write long letters. She described events in exciting detail and shared her own ideas.

Abigail married John Adams, who was a leader in the American Revolution. He often traveled far from home. Abigail wrote to him daily. She described life with their children and troubles from the war. Abigail also explained her own ideas about independence.

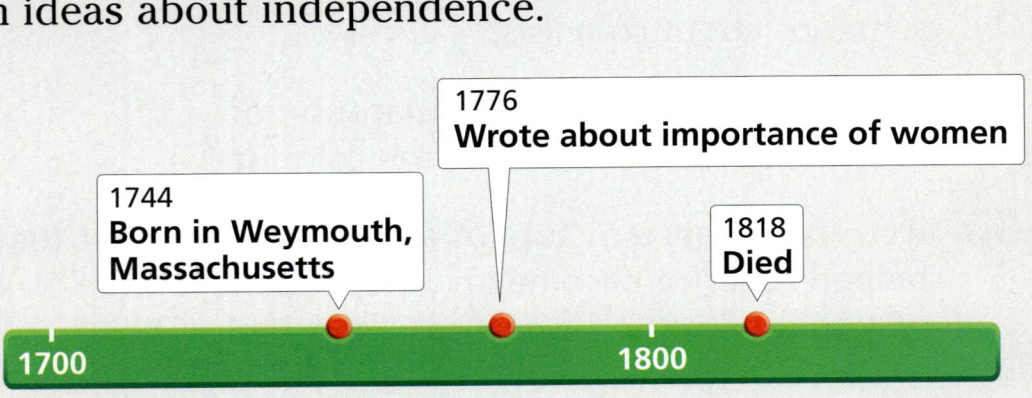

1744
Born in Weymouth, Massachusetts

1776
Wrote about importance of women

1818
Died

1700 — 1800

246 • Unit 5

CHARACTER TRAIT: Patriotism

In this letter, Abigail Adams told John to "remember the ladies…" in the fight for independence.

BIOGRAPHY

Paul Revere

Paul Revere boldly joined other colonists who showed they were against British rule. He kept on doing many things to fight for independence.

At night on April 18, 1775, Paul Revere rode his horse from Boston to warn colonists of a British army plan. This prepared colonists in Lexington to fight a battle that became known as the start of the American Revolution. His brave ride became famous in a poem by Henry Wadsworth Longfellow.

CHARACTER TRAIT: Patriotism

BIOGRAPHY

A picture book of Longfellow's poem

Activities

1. Write About It Write or tell two ways that Paul Revere and Abigail Adams showed **patriotism**.

2. Make It Make a poster that shows something important about the life of Abigail Adams or Paul Revere.

249

Skillbuilder

Compare Fact and Opinion

Vocabulary

fact
opinion

A **fact** is something that is true. An **opinion** is what someone thinks. Two people can have different opinions about the same facts.

Learn the Skill

Step 1 Read the sentences about Independence Day. One sentence tells a fact. The other sentence tells an opinion.

> Independence Day is on July 4 every year.

> I think Independence Day is the best national holiday.

Step 2 A fact is something that is true. You can check to see if a fact is true. A fact is probably true if two or more good nonfiction books agree.

Step 3 Opinions use words such as "I think."

Apply Critical Thinking

Practice the Skill

Read the sentences. Then follow the directions.

❶ In what way is a fact different from an opinion?

❷ Which sentences below tell facts?

❸ Which sentence below tells an opinion? Tell how you know that it is an opinion.

George Washington was the first President of our country.

John Hancock's signature is the largest on the Declaration of Independence.

I think Benjamin Franklin was the greatest inventor of all time.

251

Core Lesson 5

Vocabulary
hero
invention

Reading Skill
Classify

Past Heroes

Build on What You Know Think of a person who is special.

Heroes

A **hero** is someone who does something brave for the good of others or works hard to help others. Some heroes are strong leaders of a group. Some heroes are inventors. An inventor is someone who finds new ways to do things. Look at some heroes from the past. They were important to people in the past, and they are still important today.

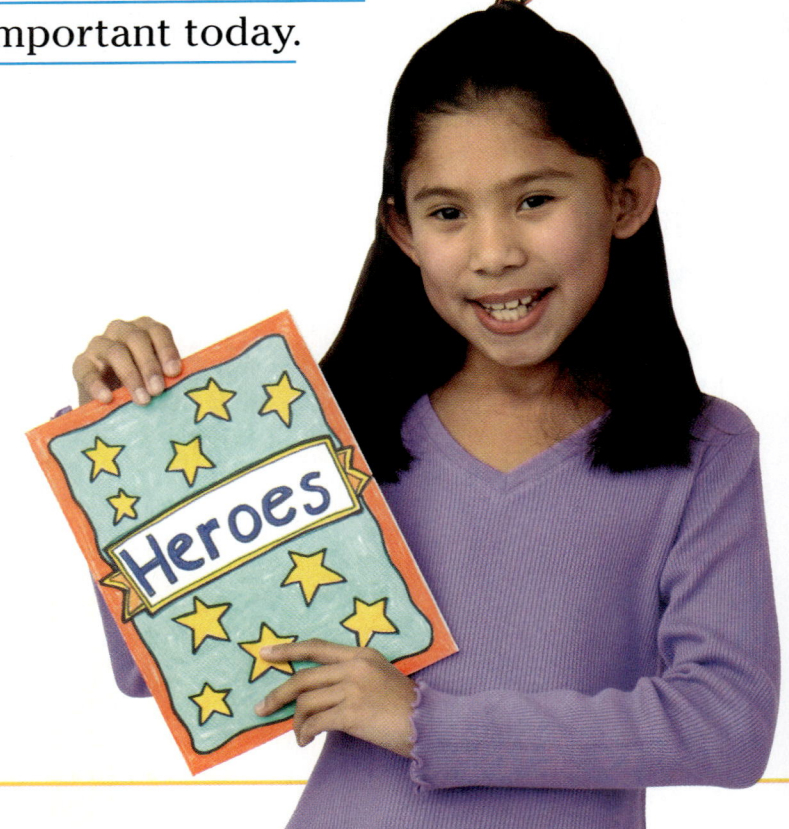

252 • Unit 5

★ Sitting Bull ★

Sitting Bull was a leader of the Lakota nation. He was known for being powerful, brave, and wise. He believed strongly in Lakota traditions.

Sitting Bull was against the United States control of Lakota land. He helped the Lakota nation to fight the United States Army. He always stood firmly for a way of life he felt was right.

Sitting Bull

Review Why is Sitting Bull still a hero?

253

★ Golda Meir ★

Golda Meir was a Jewish immigrant from Russia to the United States. As a young woman, she joined others who worked to start a Jewish nation called Israel. Golda Meir gave strong speeches. She worked hard to start the new nation. Golda Meir was a leader of Israel. She was one of the first women to lead a country.

Golda Meir

254 • Unit 5

★ Jackie Robinson ★

Jackie Robinson was excellent in many sports. In 1947, he became the first African American baseball player in the National League. At that time, many people did not want African American players to be with white players. They did hurtful things to make him quit. But Jackie Robinson did not quit. He kept playing baseball. He set a great example. Other African American players began to join teams with white players.

Jackie Robinson

Review What are some ways that Jackie Robinson, Golda Meir, and Sitting Bull are alike?

★ Thomas Edison ★

Thomas Edison was a great inventor. Even as a boy, he loved to try out new ideas. He learned science on his own. In his life, he produced more than a thousand inventions. An **invention** is something new that someone makes or thinks of. Two of Thomas Edison's inventions were the electric light bulb and sound recordings. These inventions changed people's daily lives.

Thomas Edison

★ Albert Einstein ★

Albert Einstein grew up in Germany. As a young child, he was excited by science questions. As an adult, Albert Einstein kept thinking about science. He explained how light works. He changed ideas in science about time and space. His work helped people understand the world.

Review What is a way that Albert Einstein and Thomas Edison are alike?

Albert Einstein

Lesson Review

1 Vocabulary Write a sentence that tells why one of the people you have read about is a **hero.**

2 Main Idea Why are heroes from the past still important to people today?

Activity Choose a hero in the lesson. Write or tell two things the hero could feel proud about.

257

Primary Sources

LEARN FROM A LETTER

Do you like to save letters or cards from people you know? Branch Rickey saved a thank-you letter from Jackie Robinson. Now, more than fifty years later, we can learn from it.

Branch Rickey was the manager of the Brooklyn Dodgers baseball team. When he hired Jackie Robinson for the Dodgers, some people said that the team was headed for big trouble. Jackie Robinson wrote this letter after three years of great playing for the Dodgers. He wrote because Branch Rickey was leaving the team.

... It has been the finest experience I have had being associated [a friend] with you and I want to thank you very much for all you have meant not only to me and my family but to the entire country and particularly [mostly to] members of our race. . . .

My wife joins me in saying thanks very much Mr. Rickey. . .

Activities

1. **Talk About It** What did Branch Rickey do to show respect for Jackie Robinson?

2. **Write About It** Name someone you would like to thank. Write a letter to the person with your reasons for thanking him or her.

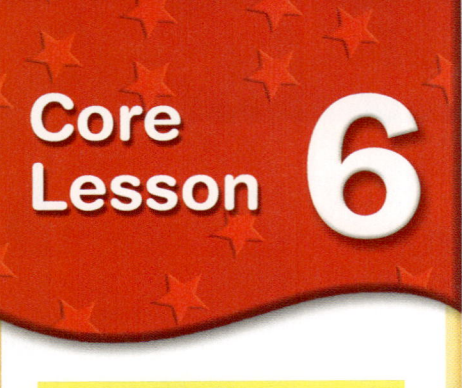

Core Lesson 6

Communities Change

Vocabulary

transportation
technology

Reading Skill

Sequence

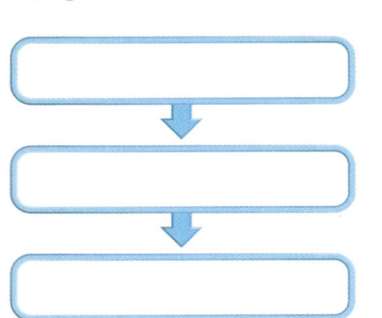

Build on What You Know What are some ways that you have traveled? Do you think those ways were possible for people two hundred years ago?

Transportation

Transportation is any way of moving things or people from one place to another. When people travel or move goods, they use transportation.

Technology is using science to make things work better. Inventors have used technology to make transportation faster, stronger, and safer. Technology has helped them make new kinds of transportation. New kinds of transportation have changed how people live in a community.

260 • Unit 5

The two maps show changes in one community: Plainfield, Illinois. Compare the roads on both maps.

Plainfield, Illinois, more than 100 years ago

Plainfield today

Review What is a way that technology has changed communities?

261

Transportation Changes Plainfield

Look at some changes in transportation that brought more people and business to this community.

1850 — **1900**

1834

People came by stagecoach to settle in the new town. Stagecoaches also brought travelers who stopped for food and rest.

1904

People rode streetcars on railways between towns. Many came to Plainfield for vacations in a place called Electric Park.

1920

The first paved highway to cross the country went through Plainfield. Cars and buses brought more people. Trucks brought goods quickly. More businesses opened.

Review What were three kinds of transportation that went through Plainfield?

2000

2004

Now many highways go around and through Plainfield. It is a suburb of Chicago. People have built more homes and schools. Families keep moving to Plainfield.

Lesson Review

❶ **Vocabulary** Tell a way that technology has changed transportation.

❷ **Main Idea** Give an example of how transportation changed Plainfield.

Activity Name a kind of transportation that people use today. Explain how it helps people.

263

Extend Lesson 6

Biography

Two Inventors

Both inventors found new ways to do things in transportation.

Granville T. Woods

Train crashes were a big problem when Granville T. Woods was a young man. He invented a Railway Telegraph that located moving trains. It kept trains from crashing. Granville T. Woods invented much more. He invented a grooved wheel that allowed a street car, or trolley, to receive electricity to move it along tracks. Granville T. Woods started a company to make and sell his inventions.

Taylor G. Wang

Taylor Wang is a scientist, an inventor, and a college teacher. He wanted to find new ways for scientists to work in space. To do this he became an astronaut. He set up a science lab on the space shuttle. During the flight he was always solving problems in the lab. Taylor Wang and other scientists still use what he learned in space.

Activities

1. **Act It Out** Act out or describe something Granville T. Woods or Taylor Wang did as an inventor.

2. **List It** Make a list of facts about Granville T. Woods and another list of facts about Taylor G. Wang. Use the lists to compare the two inventors.

265

Skillbuilder

Understand Point of View

Vocabulary
point of view

A **point of view** is what someone thinks about something. When people give reasons for what they think, they help others understand their point of view.

Learn the Skill

Step 1 Read this question. **What do you think was the best invention in transportation? Tell why.**

Step 2 Read two different points of view.

- **Jeff:** I think the railroad train was best, because more people could travel across land after that.
- **Sheera:** I think the airplane was the best invention. Flying helped people get places much faster.

Step 3 Both Jeff and Sheera gave reasons for their points of view. Tell two ways their points of view are different.

Apply Critical Thinking

Practice the Skill

1. Look at the pictures of inventions in transportation below. Which do you think was the best invention?

2. Give your answer. Make sure to tell a reason for your point of view.

3. Tell a way that your point of view is different from Jeff's or Sheera's or the point of view of someone in your class.

267

Core Lesson 7

Communication Changes

Vocabulary
communication

Reading Skill
Main Idea and Details

Build on What You Know What are some ways that you can leave a message for someone? Which of those ways were possible 200 years ago?

Communication in History

Communication is any way of sharing information. Communication has changed over the years.

Mail by Stagecoach

In 1776, Benjamin Franklin headed the American postal system. He got stagecoaches to carry mail between post offices. This helped letters reach people faster.

268 • Unit 5

Telegraph

In 1844, an American, Samuel Morse, invented a telegraph system. People could then send messages along a wire. They used a code of clicks to stand for letters of the alphabet. They could send news quickly along hundreds of miles of wire.

Telephone

In 1876, Alexander Graham Bell showed how people could send voice messages along a wire. These were the first telephones. Once telephone wires were strung across the country, people could talk even if they lived far apart.

Review In what way were the telegraph system and postal system alike?

Radio

By 1900, inventors had used technology to send messages by airwaves. This led to the radio. Over time, people began to have radios at home. Families around the country could listen to the same music, news, or speeches. People heard plays, comedies, and stories too.

Television

In the 1920's and 1930's, inventors showed how people could see events live on television. Then some inventors found ways to make it work well in homes. By the 1950's many families had television.

Internet

By 1975, inventors had ways to connect computers. They called these networks. People could send messages between computers in a network. Soon computers around the world could join one huge network called the Internet. What can you do on the Internet?

Review In what ways were radio and television alike?

Lesson Review

1. **Vocabulary** Use the word **communication** in a sentence about something you use now.

2. **Main Idea** Give two examples of something that changed communication after 1775.

Activity Choose one of the ways of communicating shown in this lesson. Make a chart comparing it with something you use now.

271

Extend Lesson 7
History

Runners with a Message

Long ago in South America people called the Incas got messages from runners. The runners were young men who trained to run very fast. They had to learn to remember every word of the message. They had to speak it very clearly. One runner started with a message. He ran for miles along a road to a spot where another runner waited. Each runner had to listen closely and then run on with the message. What could happen if one runner did not listen well?

Inca pots had paintings of Inca runners.

272 • Unit 5

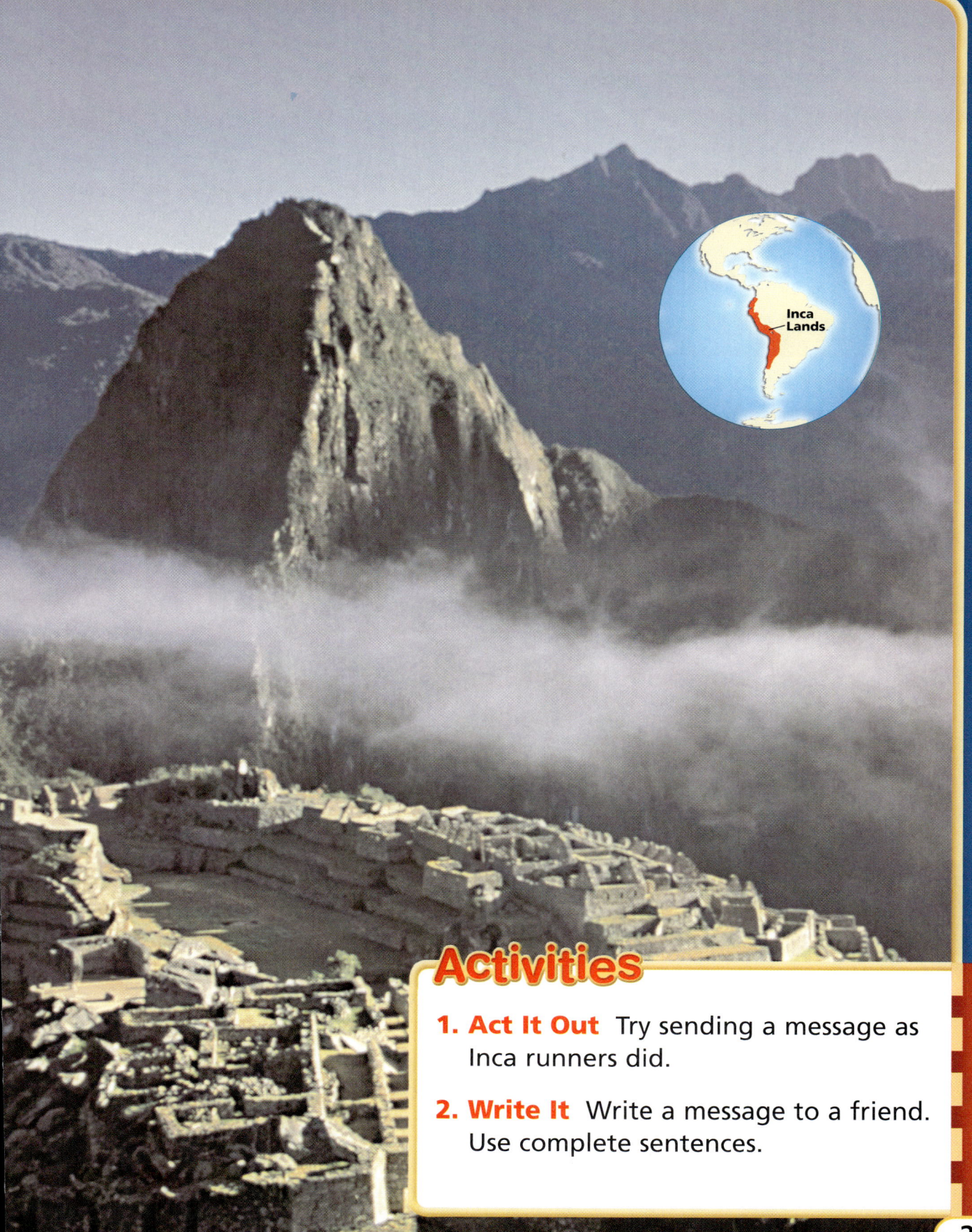

Activities

1. **Act It Out** Try sending a message as Inca runners did.

2. **Write It** Write a message to a friend. Use complete sentences.

273

Unit 5 Review and Test Prep

Big Ideas

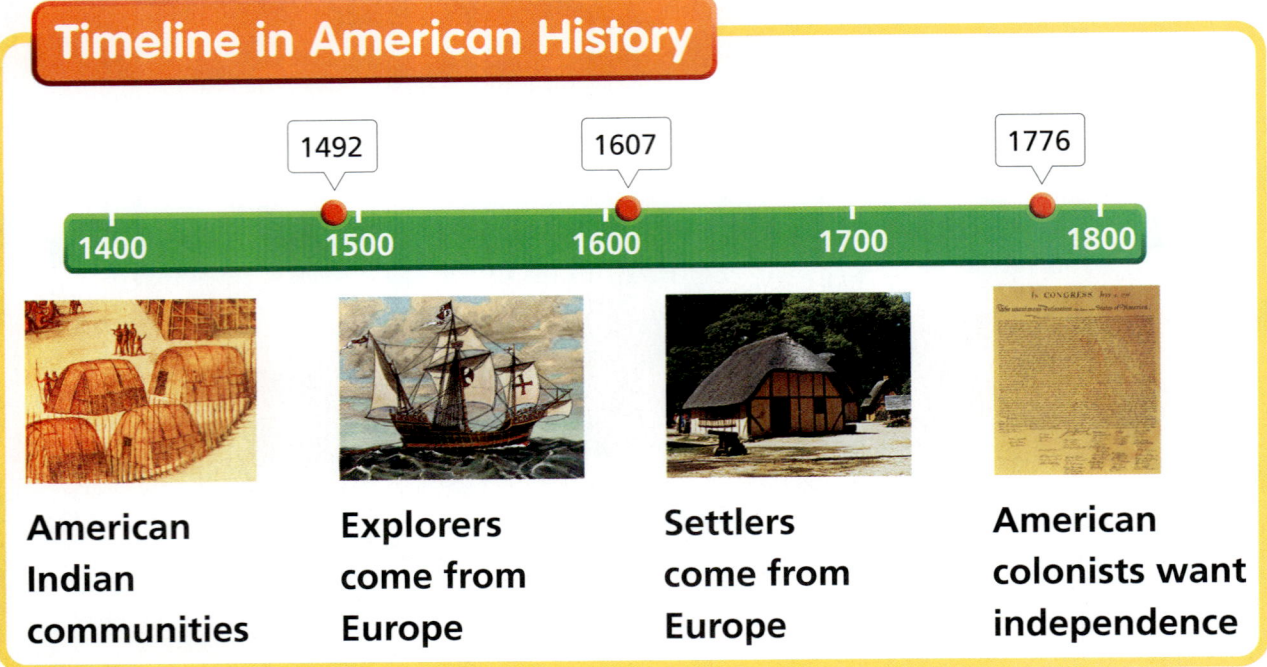

Find the missing words on the timeline.

1. _____ lived in America before explorers came.
2. _____ came after explorers from Europe.
3. In 1776, _____ said they wanted independence.

Facts and Main Ideas

4. What was a food that American Indians ate? (pages 214, 215)

5. Name two kinds of work the Plymouth colonists did. (pages 232, 233)

6. Name two leaders who wanted independence from Great Britain. (pages 243, 244, 245)

7. Who were two American inventors? (pages 256, 257, 264, 265)

274 • Unit 5

Vocabulary

Choose the letter of the word that best matches the picture.

8.
9.
10.
11.
12.

A. **explorer** (page 222)
B. **colonist** (page 230)
C. **settlement** (page 229)
D. **communication** (page 268)
E. **transportation** (page 260)

Test Practice

13. What does the word **history** mean?

    A. a long trip
    B. a Plymouth colonist
    C. everything you can know about the past
    D. new things people make or think of

Critical Thinking

Sequence

14. Who came first? Who came next? List these people in time order.

    a. Christopher Columbus   b. Marco Polo   c. Thomas Jefferson

275

Review and Test Prep

Skillbuilders **Identify Cause and Effect**

Read the paragraph and answer the questions.

When colonists in America wanted independence, the king of England sent the British army to control them. More colonists became angry at the actions of the king. They decided to fight for independence.

The Beginning of the American Revolution

15. Why did the king of England send armies to America?

16. Why did the colonists fight the British army?

Compare Fact and Opinion

A fact is something that is true. An opinion is what someone thinks.

17. Which sentence tells a fact?

18. Which sentence is an opinion? Tell if you agree or disagree.

A. I think it would be fun to sail on the **Mayflower.**

B. The **Mayflower** landed in America in 1620.

276 • Unit 5

Unit Activity

Make a History Puppet

Choose a person from American history and make a puppet of that person.

1. Make the puppet's head and costume.
2. Write three questions that you would like people to ask your puppet.
3. Use your hand and voice so that your puppet answers the questions.

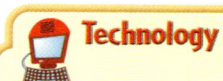

CURRENT EVENTS WEEKLY WR READER

Current Events Project

What events are taking place in your area? Make an **Events in the News Timeline.**

Technology

Read articles about current events at www.eduplace.com/kids/hmss/

In Your Classroom

Look for these Social Studies Independent Books in your classroom.

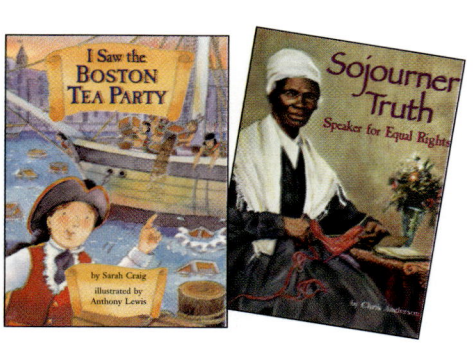

At the Library

You may find these books at your school or public library.

Life in a Colonial Town
by Sally Senzell Isaacs

Thomas Edison
by Lola Schaefer

277

UNIT 6

America's Government

"My country 'tis of thee,
Sweet land of liberty,
Of thee I sing."
—Samuel Francis Smith
from "America"

The Big Idea

What does government mean to you and your family?

Unit 6 America's Government

Vocabulary Preview

Technology
e • glossary
e • word games
www.eduplace.com/kids/hmss05/

government

Government is a group of people who make and carry out laws. page 283

citizen

A **citizen** is a member of a community, state, or country. You are a citizen of your class too. page 292

280 • Unit 6

Reading Strategy

Use the **summarize** reading strategy in Lessons 1, 2, and 3 and the **question** strategy in Lessons 4, 5, and 6.

election

An **election** is a time when people vote. You can hold a class election to make a choice. page 308

Constitution

The **Constitution** is a plan for making rules for the United States government. page 316

281

Core Lesson 1

Government and People

Vocabulary

government
capital
tax

Reading Skill

Draw Conclusions

Build on What You Know

Who are the people who help run your school? What are some ways they work together?

Communities are like schools. A community needs a group of people working together to help it run well.

A school principal raises the flag with the help of students.

282 • Unit 6

Most communities have a city or town hall building where people work to run local government.

Local Government

A **government** is a group of people who work together to run a community, state, or country. The government of a community is called a local government. People in your local government decide how to use money for schools, police, and other community needs. They try to solve community problems too.

Review What do people in government do?

Three Governments

Your state also has a government. Each state has a **capital**, which is a city where the people in government work. The United States has a government, too. That is the national government. It is in Washington, D.C., the nation's capital. Everyone has three governments: local, state, and national.

Look at Robin, for example.

I live in Duluth, Minnesota. Leaders of my **local** government meet in Duluth.

Leaders of my **state** government meet in St. Paul, the capital of Minnesota.

Leaders of my **national** government meet in Washington, D.C.

284 • Unit 6

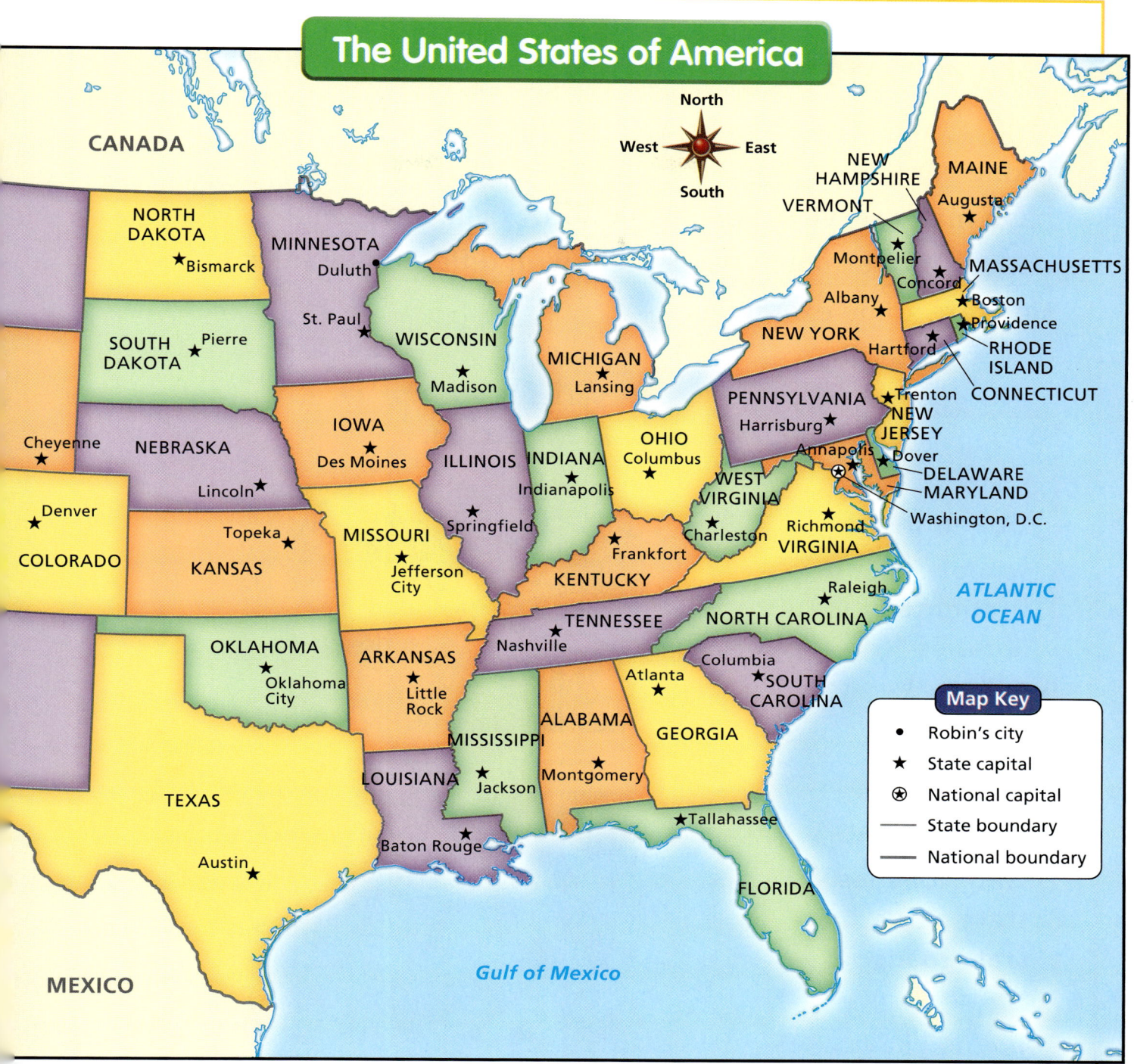

Skill Reading Maps Find Duluth, Minnesota. Is Duluth north, or south, of the state capital of Minnesota?

285

Government Services

Remember the services you read about in Unit 4. Fixing cars and cutting hair are services. Governments have many services for people too. Local, state, and national governments each help with different services. Here are some examples.

Services

Local Government

schools
firefighters
libraries
police

State Government

state colleges
state parks
state roads

National Government

National Park Service
U.S. Post Office
Coast Guard

Taxes

How do governments pay for services? Governments collect money called **taxes.** Workers pay income taxes from the money they earn. Businesses also pay income taxes. In most states, people pay sales taxes when they buy goods such as bikes or baseballs. Governments use money from taxes to pay for services such as parks, police, and roads.

Review Why do governments need taxes?

Baseball Bat	35.00
Baseball	8.00
Baseball glove	40.00
SUBTOTAL	83.00
Georgia Tax 4.00%	3.32
TOTAL	$86.32
Cash	90.00
Cash Change	3.68

Lesson Review

❶ **Vocabulary** Write a sentence that explains what **taxes** are.

❷ **Main Idea** What are the three governments that people have?

Activity Write or tell about a local government service you use. Explain how it helps you and other people.

287

Extend Lesson 1
Literature

Fire Fighters

From **The Fire Station** by Stuart A. Kallen

When a fire alarm rings, fire fighters race into action. Fire fighters are men and women who risk their lives every day. Their most important job is to put out fires that threaten lives and property. They must learn how to do this at fire fighters' school.

Fire fighters drive long red fire trucks to help pump the water onto fires. Huge hoses shoot water onto fires. Fire fighters use ladders to climb into the windows of burning buildings. They use axes to break through burning doors and walls.

LITERATURE

289

Fighting fires is hard, dangerous work. Sometimes fire fighters lose their lives in fires. Almost every city and town has a monument to fire fighters. Some are honored with medals and decorations.

Fire fighters don't just rescue people. They rescue dogs, cats and other pets.

You can be sure that if there is an emergency a firefighter will be there as soon as possible.

A fire fighter uses an extension ladder to get water to fires in skyscrapers.

LITERATURE

A fire fighters' memorial

Activities

1. **Talk About It** Draw a fire fighter at work. Tell about your drawing.

2. **Write About It** Write about how a fire fighter shows courage.

291

Core Lesson 2

Citizens Make a Difference

Vocabulary

citizen
right
responsibility

Reading Skill
Classify

Build on What You Know

Think of ways students have made your school a good place to learn. You will read about how you are a citizen in your school, community, and nation.

You Are a Citizen

A <mark>citizen</mark> is a person who belongs to a place. You are a citizen of the community where you live and the nation where you were born. You can also become a citizen of the United States even if you were not born here.

292 • Unit 6

Citizens Have Rights

As a citizen, you have rights that the government protects. A **right** is something you may do. As a citizen of the United States, you have a right to speak freely and to practice your religion. You also have the right to privacy. That means you may decide what to show or tell someone and what not to tell.

Review What rights do you have as a citizen?

Citizens Have Responsibilities

Along with rights, citizens have responsibilities. A **responsibility** is something that you should do. A responsibility may be following rules or doing a chore. It may be treating others fairly. Name some responsibilities you have. What would happen if you did not do them?

Skill **Reading Visuals** What are the citizens doing for their community?

294 • Unit 6

Being a Good Citizen

Good citizens care about people's rights. They try to make things fair and safe for everyone. Good citizens work together to solve problems. Children can be good citizens by solving problems together in their school or community. Look at the four steps.

How to Solve a Problem
1. Name the problem.
2. List ways to solve it.
3. Choose the best way.
4. Find out if it solves the problem.

Review How can you be a good citizen?

Lesson Review

1. **Vocabulary** Name two **rights** of **citizens** in the United States.

2. **Main Idea** Copy this sentence. Fill in the blanks. Citizens of the United States have _____ and _____.

Activity Draw a poster that shows how to be a good citizen. Write sentences to explain your ideas.

Extend Lesson 2

Readers' Theater

Solving Problems

Read about some students who take **responsibility** to try to solve a problem at their school.

Cast

Narrator

Lisa: student

Greg: student

Mimi: student

Don: student

Mr. Vacca: teacher

Ms. Leroy: principal

Scene 1

Narrator: We are in Mr. Vacca's classroom. It's a Friday in May. Our class is almost ready to go home. Then the principal, Ms. Leroy, speaks on the intercom.

Ms. Leroy: Next week the builders will start the new addition to our school. They will have to take out all the bike racks. After that, no one can ride a bike to school.

296 • Unit 6

Lisa: So we can't ride our bikes to school all spring!

Mr. Vacca: Everyone listen, please!

Ms. Leroy: Please make sure to take my letter home to your families. It tells why students cannot ride bikes to school.

Mr. Vacca: Now everyone may go, quietly! Have a good weekend.

Don: How can we have a good weekend with bad news like that?

Mimi: Maybe it will be good if we can solve the bike problem!

Lisa: Let's meet at the bike racks to talk about it.

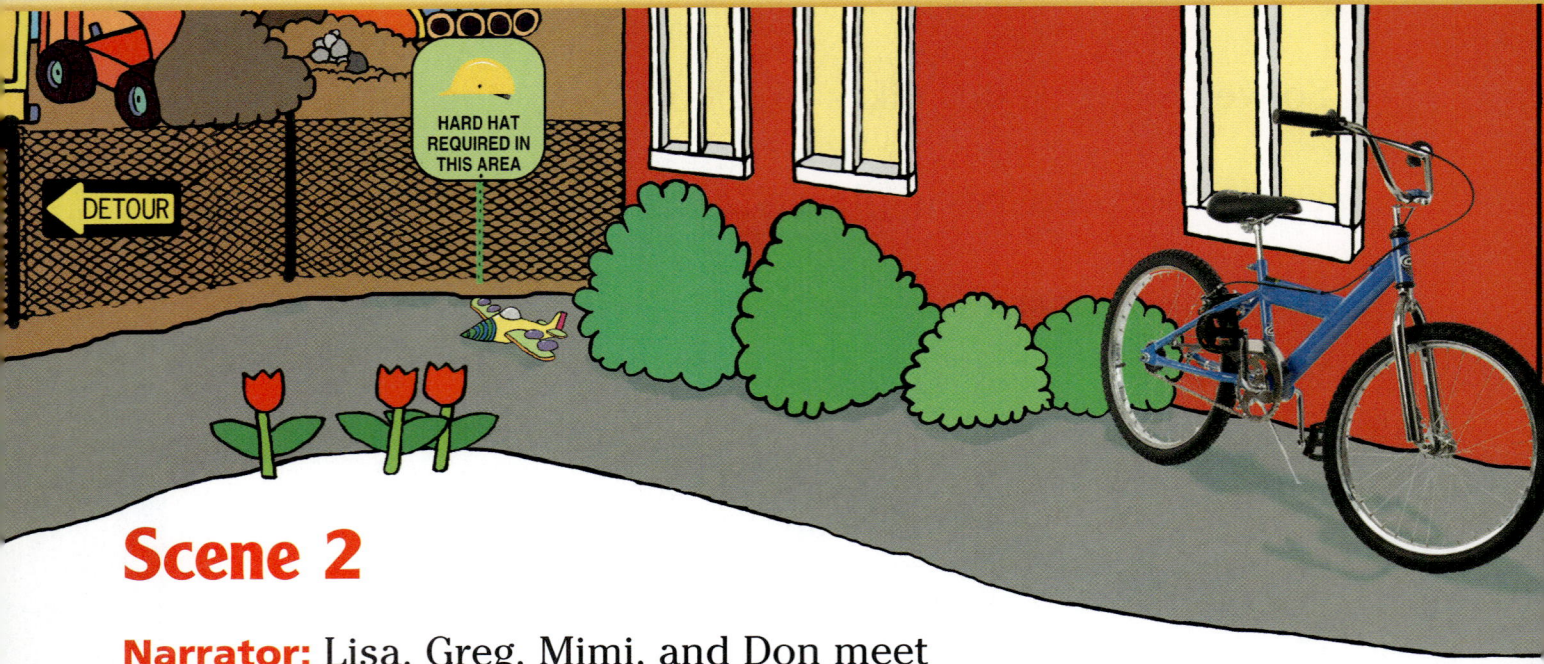

Scene 2

Narrator: Lisa, Greg, Mimi, and Don meet at the bike racks.

Lisa: First we have to name the problem.

Greg: The problem is we want to ride our bikes to school, but now we can't.

Lisa: Next we should name the reasons why we can't ride our bikes.

Greg: Because they're building where the bike racks are.

Mimi: Then let's tell them not to build!

Don: But we want them to build. They are building a theater and a new gym.

Mimi: What if we hid Ms. Leroy's letter from our families and rode our bikes anyway?

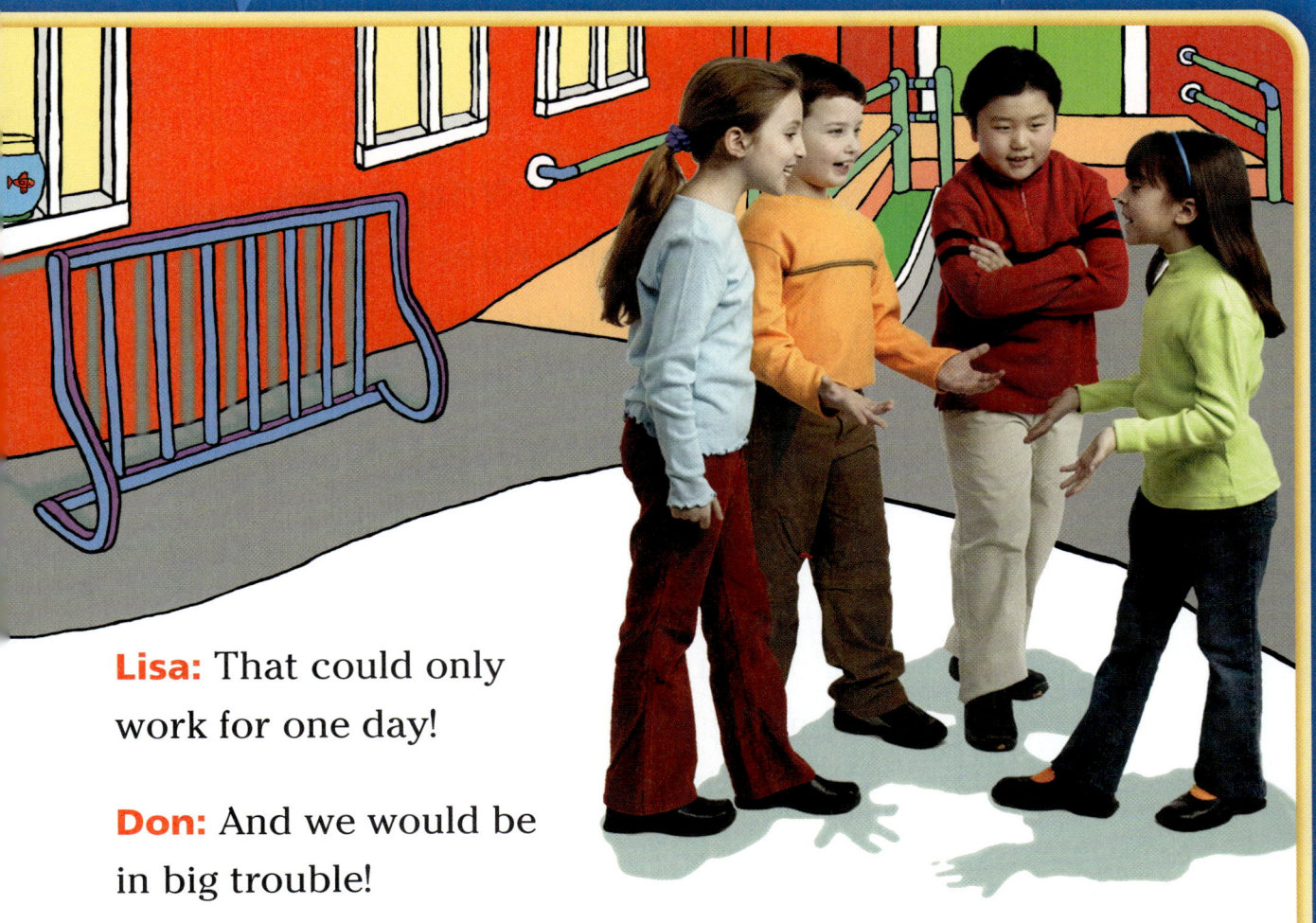

Lisa: That could only work for one day!

Don: And we would be in big trouble!

Greg: Here's another idea. Maybe they can move the bike racks to the other side of the school.

Lisa: That should work! Let's go talk to Ms. Leroy.

Don: I'll bet she'll listen. She likes kids to show responsibility. Maybe she can help us think of another way to solve the problem if our idea doesn't work.

Activities

1. **Think About It** Do you like the way the students tried to solve the problem? Why?

2. **Write About It** Write or tell what Ms. Leroy might say when the students talk to her.

Core Lesson 3

Laws

Build on What You Know
What are some rules in your school or classroom? Learn how they are like rules in a community, state, or country.

Vocabulary
law
judge

Reading Skill
Main Idea and Details

Laws Are Important
A **law** is a rule that everyone in a community, state, or country must follow. Laws keep people safe and help them get along with one another. What do you think would happen if there were no traffic laws?

Review Why are laws important?

The signs on this page tell people about laws.

300 • Unit 6

Police stop drivers who speed.

Police Help with Laws

Local, state, and national governments have laws. Police help with government laws. They tell people how to obey (oh BAY) laws. They stop people who break laws. Look at the picture on this page. What do you think is happening? Think of another way that police help with laws.

In Court Judges work in courts, where people come when they have problems with laws. Here two lawyers talk to a judge.

Judges Help with Laws

A **judge** is someone who helps decide when people don't agree about laws. Governments have many, many laws. Judges know the laws well. They help decide if someone has broken a law. Judges say what people must do to make up for breaking laws.

Citizens Help with Laws

Citizens protect each other when they know and follow laws. When people obey a traffic law, they help keep others safe. When you follow laws in a park, you help others enjoy the park. Citizens help by choosing good people to make laws. Also citizens can work together to make better laws.

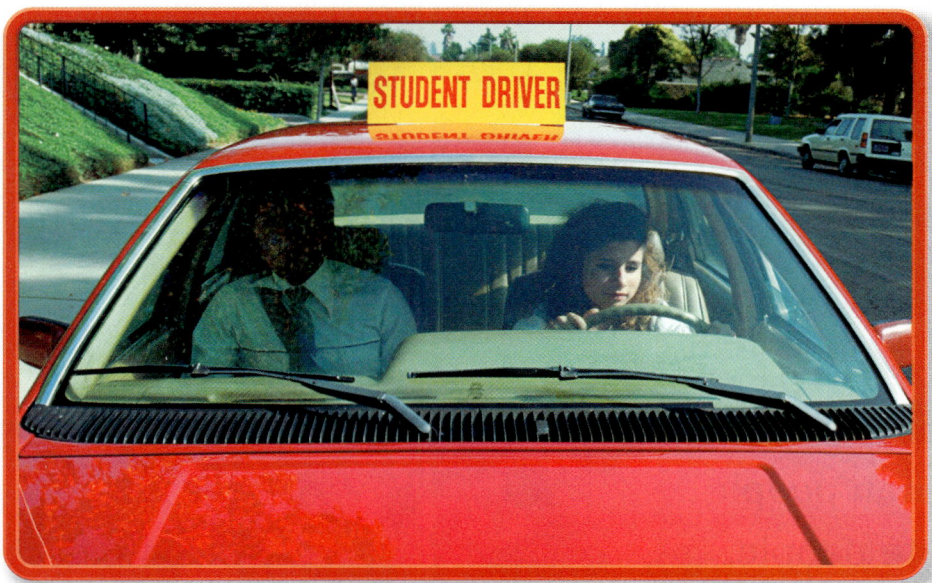

States have laws about driving. In many states, you must be sixteen before you can get a permit to learn to drive.

Review What can citizens do to help with laws?

Lesson Review

1. **Vocabulary** Tell two things that **judges** do.
2. **Main Idea** What would happen if drivers did not pay attention to traffic lights?
▶ **Activity** Name a law that you think is important. Write or tell why you think it is important.

303

Extend Lesson 3

Biography

Rosa Parks

Rosa Parks in 1999

Not everyone is brave enough to risk jail for what they believe is right. In 1955, Rosa Parks showed courage when she stood up for her beliefs.

At that time Rosa Parks was living in Montgomery, Alabama. The state's **laws** and rules did not give African American people the same rights as white people. This seemed very wrong to Rosa Parks. She began to work with others who wanted fair laws and rights for everyone.

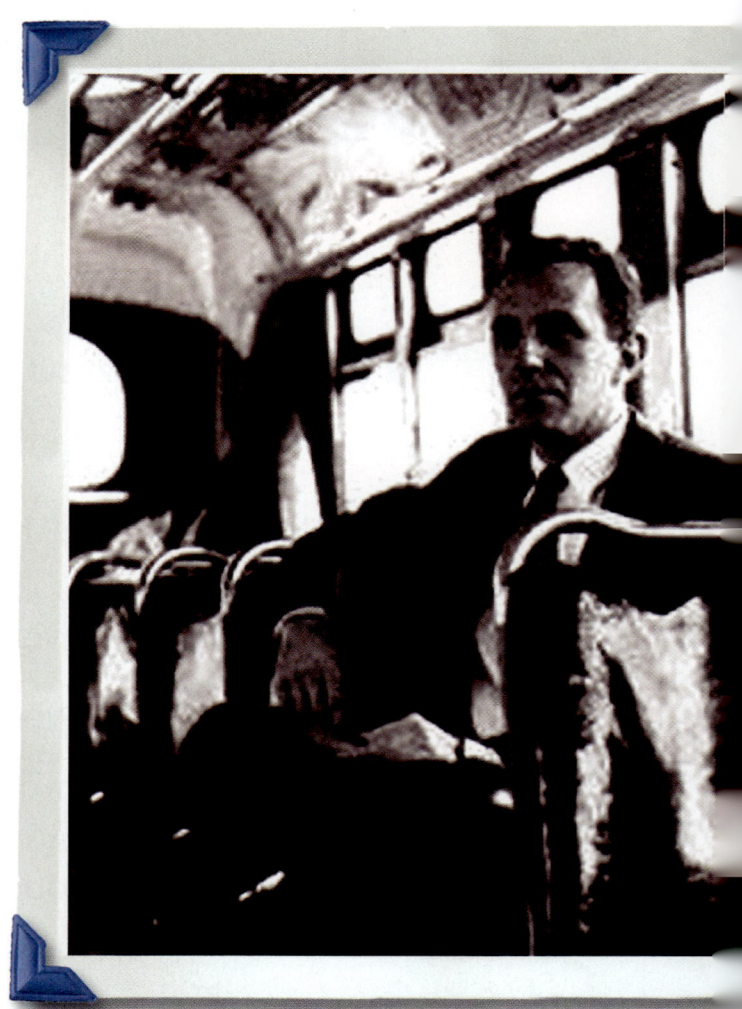

Rosa Parks helped change a law that was unfair to African American people on buses.

CHARACTER TRAIT: Courage

Taking Action

On December 1, 1955, Rosa Parks acted against an unfair law. The law made African Americans give up their bus seats to white people.

Rosa Parks stayed firmly in her seat when the bus driver tried to make her give it up. For this she had to go to jail. Her action led many others to work together to change the unfair law.

Activities

1. **Talk About It** How did Rosa Parks show courage?

2. **Build It** Make a mobile that shows pictures of citizens who did something brave.

Skillbuilder

Read a Pictograph

Vocabulary
pictograph

A school started a project to recycle cans. The children used a pictograph to keep track of the cans they collected.

Learn the Skill

A **pictograph** is a way to compare things. A pictograph uses pictures to show numbers of things.

Step 1 Look at the title. It tells what the pictograph is about.

Step 2 Look at the key. It shows what each picture of a can stands for.

Step 3 Count the cans for Class A. There are seven cans. So Class A collected seven 10s, or seventy, cans.

Practice the Skill

Look at the graph below. Then follow the directions.

1. What is the title of this pictograph?

2. How many cans did Class C collect?

3. How many cans did Class E collect?

4. How many cans did Classes B and D collect together?

Core Lesson 4

Leaders

Build on What You Know

Sports teams and school bands have leaders. What are some other kinds of leaders? Governments have leaders too.

Choosing Leaders

Did you ever choose a leader for a team? When you show or write a choice, you **vote.** Your school might have an **election,** which is a time when people vote. When you turn eighteen, you will have the right to vote in government elections. You may vote for many different leaders in one election. The chart shows three examples.

Vocabulary
vote
election
ballot

Reading Skill
Sequence

308 • Unit 6

Government Leaders

Local Government
Citizens may vote for mayor of their city or town.

State Government
Citizens may vote for governor of the state where they live.

National Government
Citizens may vote for President of the United States.

Government leaders have important jobs. Some make laws. Others make sure the laws work well. In elections, citizens get to choose leaders who they think can do these jobs the best.

Review Why should citizens vote in government elections?

309

Before You Vote

What can citizens do to choose the best leaders? They can read newspapers and watch television. They can ask questions of leaders. They can ask themselves questions.

Will you add more bus stops?

What can you do to fix our playgrounds?

My Questions

★ Is this person honest and smart?

★ Will this person work hard for all citizens?

★ Can this person run the government best?

Leaders and Citizens

A **ballot** is a form on which people mark their choices. In elections, citizens vote on ballots.

Leaders who win elections need to keep listening to citizens. Citizens need to keep telling leaders what they want for their community, state, and country. Citizens and leaders together help governments work well.

People who run for election explain how they will work for citizens.

Review Why should leaders talk with citizens?

Lesson Review

1. **Vocabulary** Use the words **vote** and **election** to tell some things you know about leaders.

2. **Main Idea** Tell something that government leaders do.

   Activity Write or tell two things a voter can do before an election.

311

Extend Lesson 4

Citizenship

Voting with Ballots

The eagle is a symbol for our national government. You can choose an animal to be a symbol for your class. Think of animals that stand for something you feel proud about, such as being kind or smart.

Choose between the two animals you see on the box, or decide on two different animals to choose from. Have an election in your classroom. Use a ballot to mark your choice. Then count the votes to know the winning symbol for your class.

❶ Look at the two animals. Think about their special features. Decide which is the best symbol for your class. Make speeches and signs.

❷ Mark your ballot with your choice. Do not write your name on your ballot! It's a secret vote. Add your ballot to a big box.

❸ Help count the votes for each animal. Write down the totals. Check your counts and totals. Which symbol won? Plan together how to show your new class symbol.

313

Skillbuilder

Resolve a Conflict

People in classrooms and communities don't always agree. When people disagree, it is called a **conflict.** Together, people can resolve conflicts.

Vocabulary
conflict

Learn the Skill

Follow the steps to help resolve a conflict.

Step 1 Look at the picture. Describe the conflict. Two children want to use the computer at the same time.

Step 2 Think about what each child wants to do.

| Write | Play Games |

Step 3 Think of ways to resolve the conflict.

- Take turns.
- Writer uses pencil.
- Game player plays board game.

Step 4 Ask yourself about each idea: Can both children do some of what they want? Choose the best way to resolve the conflict.

314 • Unit 6

Apply Critical Thinking

Practice the Skill

Work with a small group. Look at the picture below. Then follow the directions.

1 Tell in your own words what the conflict is. What does each group want?

2 List some ways to resolve the conflict.

3 Choose the best solution. Tell why your solution is the best one.

315

Core Lesson 5

National Government

Build on What You Know

When you start a class project, you may write a plan for how it will work. In a way, that is like the plan that early leaders wrote for our nation's government.

Vocabulary

Constitution
democracy
liberty
justice

Reading Skill
Classify

A Plan for Government

In Unit 5 you read about the Revolutionary War. When that war ended, American leaders did not want a king to rule the new nation. The leaders met and wrote a new plan for the government. That plan is called the **Constitution**.

Review What is the Constitution?

316 • Unit 6

Skill **Visual Learning** Leaders worked on the Constitution in Philadelphia in 1787. What do you notice about their clothes and hair?

Important Words

The writers of the Constitution planned a **democracy,** which is government by the people. They used words that they believed were important in a democracy. One word was **liberty,** which means "freedom." Another was **justice,** which means "fairness." Why are they still important words today?

317

Government in Three Parts

The Constitution is more than 200 years old. It is still the plan for our government today. The Constitution describes a government in three parts, or branches. Each branch has its own building in Washington, D.C. On these pages you can read about the people who work in those buildings.

Review How many branches does the government have?

White House

The President of the United States is the leader of the nation. The President lives and works in the White House.

318 • Unit 6

Capitol

The members of Congress make laws. Men and women in Congress come from all fifty states. They work in the Capitol Building.

Supreme Court

The Supreme Court has nine judges who look carefully at laws. They decide if the laws are fair and protect citizens' rights. They meet in the Supreme Court Building.

Lesson Review

1 **Vocabulary** When do you say, "with **liberty** and **justice** for all"? Tell what it means.

2 **Main Idea** What are the three branches of the national government?

 Activity Make a chart that shows who works in the three branches of government.

319

Extend Lesson 5

Citizenship

Democracy

Democracy is government that comes from the people. In a democracy, people make choices about their leaders and their laws. They may do this by voting in an election.

In the United States, citizens may vote for a leader of their community or state. They may also vote for a few people from their state to go to Washington, D.C. Those people are members of Congress. In Congress, they vote to make laws for all citizens in the country. Look at examples of democracy in the United States.

School
Students vote on where to have their class picnic.

Community
This city council votes on how much money to spend on city services.

320 • Unit 6

Nation

People vote for a new President of the United States.

State

People hear a speech before they vote for governor.

Activities

1. **Talk About It** Tell how democracy is part of what happens in your class or school.

2. **Write About It** Write about why voting is important in a democracy.

CITIZENSHIP

321

Core Lesson 6

Our Nation and the World

Vocabulary
aid

Reading Skill
Problem and Solution

Build on What You Know

Have you ever worked with a friend to solve a problem? Sometimes nations work together to try to solve problems.

Nations Help Each Other

The United States is one of more than two hundred nations in the world. Nations work out ways to help each other. If storms destroy crops in one nation, other nations may send aid. **Aid** is help. It can be money, goods, or services. What goods or services might people need after a big storm?

U.S. troops give bags of food to people in Honduras after a hurricane.

322 • Unit 6

United States President Jimmy Carter sits between President Anwar el-Sadat of Egypt (left) and Prime Minister Menachem Begin of Israel after the signing of a peace treaty between Israel and Egypt.

Leaders Work Together

Every nation has a government. Government leaders from different nations work together. They talk about how to make the earth cleaner and safer. Leaders have meetings about trade, health, and peace. Government leaders travel to visit each other. They stay in touch by phone, mail, and the Internet.

Review Why do leaders from different countries work together?

323

Meetings Around the World

Here are a few places where world leaders have met to discuss problems.

President George W. Bush met in Washington, D.C. with President Vladimir Putin from Russia.

324 • Unit 6

China

Jiang Zemin, the president of China (left) met with Prime Minister Tony Blair of Great Britain in Beijing.

South Africa

Review Why are meetings with leaders from different countries important?

Palestinian leader Yasir Arafat met with President Nelson Mandela of South Africa in Johannesburg.

Lesson Review

1. **Vocabulary** Give an example of government **aid.**

2. **Main Idea** What are two ways that government leaders from different countries stay in touch?

 Activity Choose a leader whose country is not shown on the map on page 324. Find his or her country on a world map.

325

Extend Lesson 6
Geography

Flags of Different Nations

Did you know that there are more than 200 nations in the world? Every one of them has a different flag.

I live in **Mexico**. The eagle holding a snake is important in a legend of our country. Red, white, and green stand for our independence.

326 • Unit 6

I live in **Japan**. The word Japan means "land of the rising sun." The red circle is the rising sun. It has been a symbol of my country for a very long time.

I live in **Ghana** in Africa. The black star on our flag is a symbol of freedom. The stripes have colors that are important in the flags of many African nations.

Activities

1. **Talk About It** What is one way that the three flags are alike?

2. **Write About It** Write something you learned about one of the three flags.

327

Unit 6 Review and Test Prep

Big Ideas

Fill in three missing words that help describe the chart.

Each citizen has 1. _____ , 2. _____ , and 3. _____ governments. (page 284)

Facts and Main Ideas

4. Why do governments collect taxes? (page 287)

5. What is one responsibility that citizens have? (page 294)

6. What are two things citizens can do to choose good leaders? (page 310)

7. What is the Constitution? (page 316)

Vocabulary

Write the letter of the correct answer.

8. The money that people pay to a government

9. A person who belongs to a place

10. A freedom that government must protect

11. A time when people vote

A. **right** (page 293)

B. **election** (page 308)

C. **taxes** (page 287)

D. **citizen** (page 292)

E. **judge** (page 302)

Test Practice

12. What does the word **government** mean?

    A. A person who belongs to a place, such as a state

    B. A group of people who make and carry out laws

    C. A leader of a community, state, or country

    D. Something that people should do for others

Critical Thinking

Compare and Contrast

13. What are some ways that your local government is like your national government?

14. What are some ways that your local government is different from your national government?

329

Review and Test Prep

Skillbuilders

Read a Pictograph

Mrs. Tan's class is choosing a place for a field trip. The pictograph shows the class's votes.

Votes for Our Field Trip	
Aquarium	✔✔✔✔✔✔
Fire Station	✔✔✔
Bakery	✔✔✔✔
Dairy Farm	✔✔✔✔✔✔

15. Which choice has the most votes?

16. Which has the fewest?

17. How many children voted?

Resolve a Conflict

Jack, Lena, Darryl, and Kay all want another slice of pizza. There are only 2 slices of pizza left.

18. Choose the best way to resolve the conflict.

A　　　　B　　　　C

330 • Unit 6

Unit Activity
The Big Idea

Make Up a Riddle

Think of a person, place, or thing you learned about in this unit. You might choose a government leader or service worker. Keep your choice secret.

1. Fold a sheet of paper in half and write two riddle clues on the outside. Write your secret answer inside.
2. Show your clues to others. Can they guess?

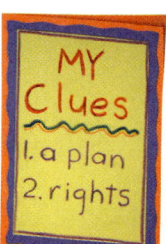

CURRENT EVENTS WEEKLY WR READER

Current Events Project

Find out what your local government is doing. Make a **Government in the News Big Book**.

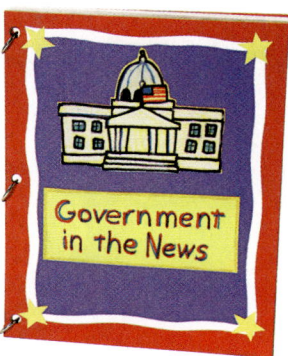

Technology

Read articles about current events at www.eduplace.com/kids/hmss/

In Your Classroom

Look for these Social Studies Independent Books in your classroom.

 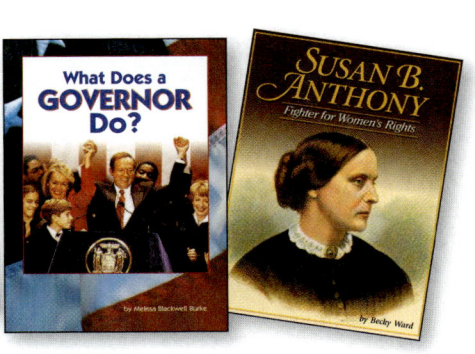

At the Library

You may find these books at your school or public library.

We the Kids
by David Catrow

City Green
by DyAnne DiSalvo-Ryan

331

• November •

Veterans Day

Veterans Day honors people who were in the army and other armed forces. Soldiers, sailors, and pilots who served the United States are veterans.

Many veterans march in Veterans Day parades. People thank our veterans for helping our country when it is at war and at peace.

A Purple Heart medal

Activity

Thank You Letter

1. Write a thank you letter to a veteran.
2. You may display your letter or mail it to a group of veterans.

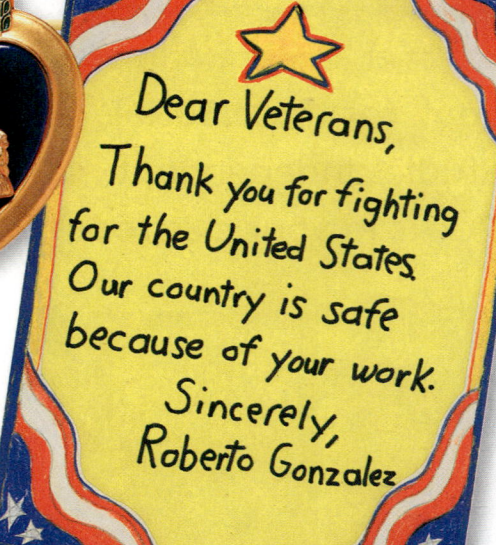

Dear Veterans,
Thank you for fighting for the United States. Our country is safe because of your work.
Sincerely,
Roberto Gonzalez

332 • Holidays

Thanksgiving

On Thanksgiving Day people give thanks for what they have. This is a tradition that began long ago when Pilgrims shared their first harvest with the Wampanoag.

In 1863, President Abraham Lincoln thought the United States should have a day of thanks. He started the national holiday we celebrate today.

American families of many backgrounds celebrate Thanksgiving Day. People may eat foods from their own culture and also turkey and cranberry sauce. Many families talk about why they feel thankful. Some go to church.

Activity

Thanksgiving Stick Puppets

1. Make stick puppets of the Pilgrims and the Wampanoag.

2. What do you think the Pilgrims and the Wampanoag felt thankful for? Use the puppets to act out your ideas.

Martin Luther King, Jr. Day

Dr. Martin Luther King, Jr., worked to make laws that would be fair to all people. Each year, Americans honor his work.

Like many people, Dr. King knew that some laws were not fair to African Americans. He gave speeches and marched to show the need to change the unfair laws. He shared his dream of good lives for all. He received the Nobel Peace Prize for his work.

Activity

Dream Doves

1. Think of a dream that you believe is good for everyone.
2. Write your dream on the shape of a dove.

334 • Holidays

Presidents' Day

On Presidents' Day, people honor two important Presidents of the United States.

George Washington helped make the United States a free country. He led the army for the new country in the American Revolution. He was the first President of the United States.

Abraham Lincoln was another great President. He helped to make all people in the United States equal and free. Lincoln helped keep the states together in one country.

Activity

"If I Am President" Poster

1. Think about what you would do if you were the President of the United States.

2. Make a poster to show your ideas.

Memorial Day

Vietnam Veterans Memorial

On Memorial Day, citizens of the United States remember the people who fought and died in wars.

A memorial is something that helps people remember a person, a group, or an event from the past. A memorial can be a statue, a sign, or a building. On Memorial Day, people gather at memorials and cemeteries.

People put flowers and flags on memorials and graves. Towns and cities have parades or speeches. Citizens honor the people who fought for the United States.

Activity

Make a Memorial Circle

1. Think of a person or an event you want to remember.
2. Write the words on a circle of colored paper. You may add a picture.

Flag Day

The United States flag stands for our country. On Flag Day, many communities have parades and sing the national anthem.

Our country's first flag had only 13 stripes and 13 stars. They stood for the 13 colonies that formed our country. Later the colonies became states.

Now there are 50 states in the United States. The United States flag has 50 stars that stand for our 50 states. It still has 13 stripes.

Activity

State Stars

1. Cut out the shape of a white star.
2. Write the name of a state in red. Write the capital of the state in blue.

Independence Day

On the Fourth of July, we celebrate our country's birthday.

The United States was born on July 4, 1776. On that day, our leaders signed an important paper. It said that our land and our people were now free from Great Britain.

Independence is another word for **freedom**. Every Fourth of July, we celebrate our country's freedom. Towns and cities have parades and picnics. Many communities have fireworks at night.

Activity

Freedom Poem

1. Think of some things that United States citizens are free to do.
2. Write a poem about your freedoms. You may start with the words "I am free. . . ."

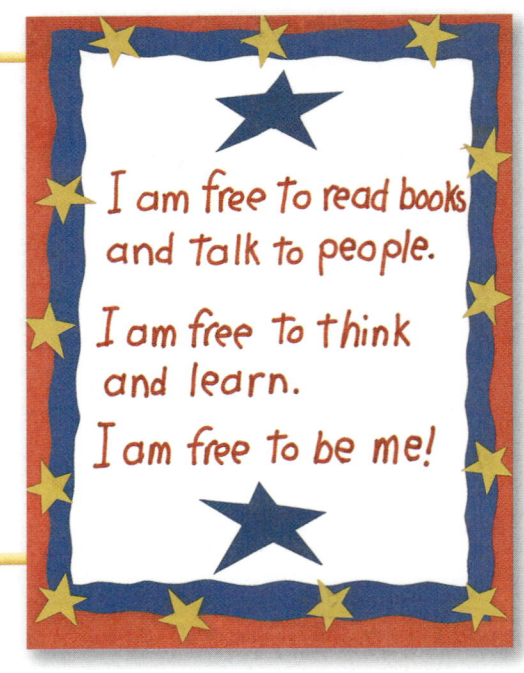

I am free to read books and talk to people.

I am free to think and learn.

I am free to be me!

338 • Holidays

References

Citizenship Handbook

Our Flag	R2
Songs of Our Nation	R4
Character Traits	R8

Resources

Geographic Terms	R10
Atlas	R12
Picture Glossary	R20
Index	R36
Acknowledgments	R43

R1

Our Flag

Pledge of Allegiance

I **pledge allegiance** to the flag
of the United States of America
and to the **Republic** for which it stands,
one Nation under God, **indivisible**,
with **liberty** and **justice** for all.

What does the Pledge of Allegiance mean? Use the vocabulary to explain.

pledge: promise
allegiance: loyalty
republic: nation
indivisible: cannot be divided
liberty: freedom
justice: fairness

R2 • Citizenship Handbook

Rules about the Flag

Look at some rules about our national flag. They come from a law called the United States Flag Code.

- **The flag should have thirteen stripes, red and white. It should have white stars on a blue background. It should have a star for each state.**

- **To salute the flag, stand straight and face the flag. Put your right hand on your heart.**

- **Say the pledge while you salute.**

- **Do not let the flag touch the ground.**

- **Fly the United States flag above any state flag.**

- **At night, take down the flag or light it up.**

R3

Songs of Our Nation

On page 143, you can read the words to "The Star-Spangled Banner," our national anthem. Many other songs also show our pride in our country. How did they come to be?

In 1893, a teacher from the East named Katharine Lee Bates took a trip to the West. The beauty of mountains, plains, and open skies inspired her to write a poem. Bates's poem became the words for the song "America the Beautiful."

"America the Beautiful"

by Katharine Lee Bates

O beautiful for spacious skies,
    For amber waves of grain,
For purple mountain majesties
    Above the fruited plain.
America! America!
    God shed His grace on thee
And crown thy good with brotherhood
    From sea to shining sea.

Vocabulary

spacious: spread over a large area
amber: golden brown
majesties: powers
fruited: successfully planted
shed: give out
grace: blessing
thee: you
brotherhood: friendship

What does the song mean to you?
The words above help explain the song.

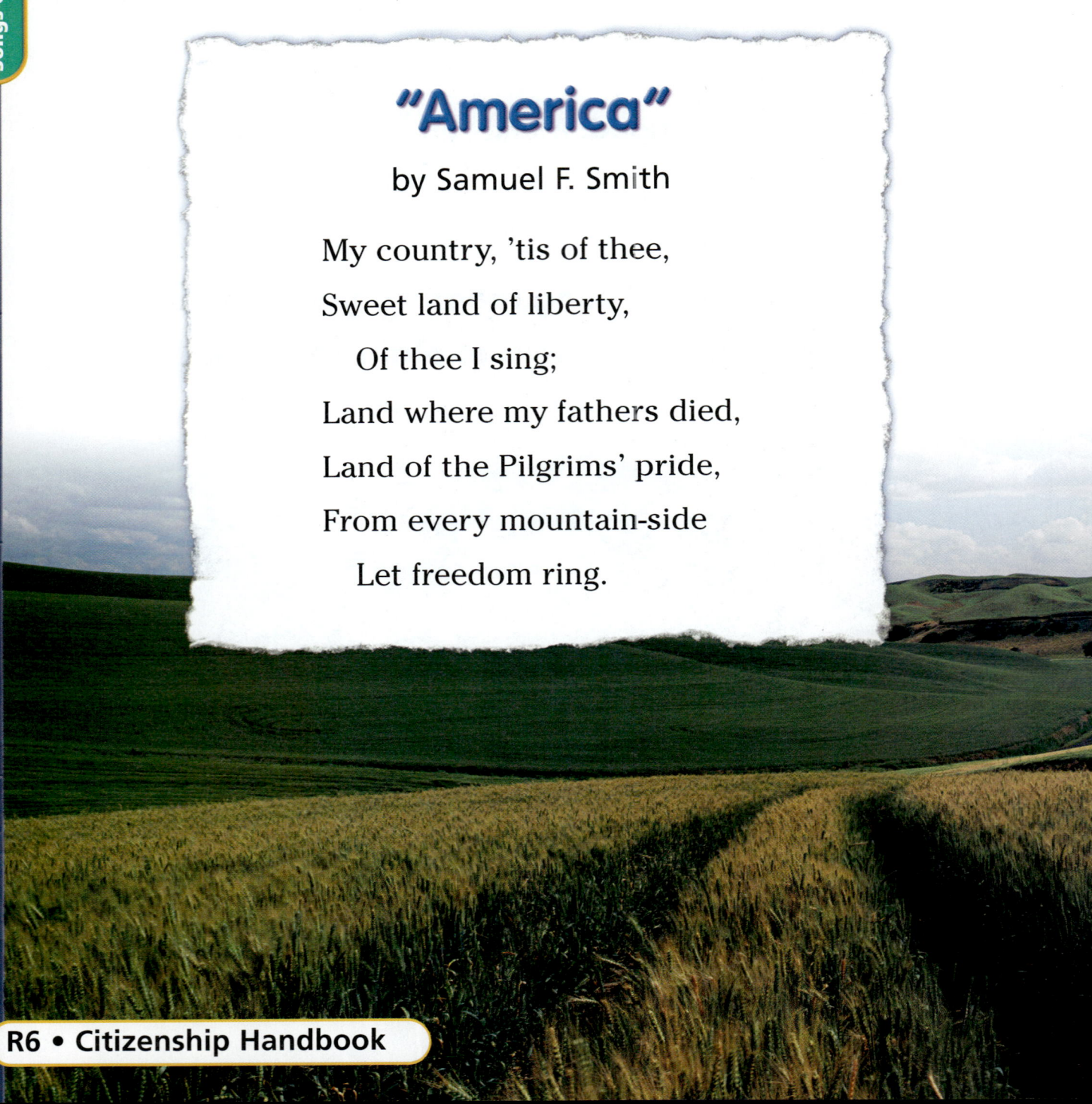

Samuel F. Smith heard the British national anthem in 1832 and liked the music. He wrote words so that Americans could sing it. "America," or "My Country, 'Tis of Thee," quickly became a favorite of many people in the United States. People still love to sing it today.

"America"

by Samuel F. Smith

My country, 'tis of thee,
Sweet land of liberty,
  Of thee I sing;
Land where my fathers died,
Land of the Pilgrims' pride,
From every mountain-side
  Let freedom ring.

Irving Berlin first wrote "God Bless America" for a show in 1918 but did not use it then. Twenty years later, when it seemed that war would break out at any minute, he decided to revise the song. Kate Smith, a famous singer, sang it on a radio program. People loved the song, and it has been an American favorite ever since.

"God Bless America"

by Irving Berlin

God bless America,

Land that I love,

Stand beside her and guide her

Through the night with a light from above.

From the mountains, to the prairies,

To the oceans white with foam,

God bless America,

My home sweet home.

Character Traits

A character trait is something people show by the way they act. A person who acts bravely shows courage, and courage is a character trait.

Character traits are also called "life skills." Life skills can help you do your best, and doing your best leads to reaching your goals.

Paul Revere
Patriotism
Paul Revere showed patriotism by riding to warn the colonists about the plans of the British army.

Coretta Scott King
Courage
Coretta Scott King showed courage by speaking out for the rights of African Americans.

R8 • Citizenship Handbook

Courage means acting bravely. It takes courage to be honest and tell the truth.

Patriotism is being proud of your country and working for your country's goals.

Responsibility means doing all your work. You can count on people who show responsibility. They will do all the things they are asked to do.

Respect means paying attention to what other people want and believe. Treating others with respect helps everyone get along.

Fairness means acting to make things fair for everyone.

Civic virtue is good citizenship. It means doing things to help communities live and work well together.

Caring is helping others. Listening to how other people feel is also caring.

Character Traits

R9

Geographic Terms

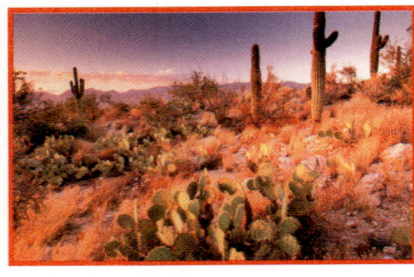

▲ **desert**
a dry area where few plants grow

forest
a large area of land where many trees grow

hill
a raised mass of land, smaller than a mountain

▲ **island**
land with water all around it

lake
a body of water with land all around it

R10 • Resources

mountain
a steep mass of land, much higher than the surrounding country

▲ **ocean**
a salty body of water covering a large area of the earth

peninsula
land that sticks out into water

plain
a broad, flat area of land

plateau
an area of flat land that is higher than the land around it

river
a large stream of water that runs into a lake, ocean, or another river

valley
low land between mountains or hills

Geographic Terms

valley

peninsula

plain

R11

Atlas

The World: Political

R12 • Resources

The World: Physical

The United States

Atlas

ALASKA
0 500 kilometers
0 500 miles

WASHINGTON
OREGON
IDAHO
MONTANA
WYOMING
NEVADA
UTAH
COLORADO
CALIFORNIA
ARIZONA
NEW MEXICO

North / West / East / South

Map Key
- ★ National Capital
- ▬ National Boundary
- — State Boundary

HAWAII
0 200 kilometers
0 200 miles

R18 • Resources

Picture Glossary

aid
Help to others is a kind of **aid**. (p. 322) The United States often sends **aid** to countries where an earthquake has struck.

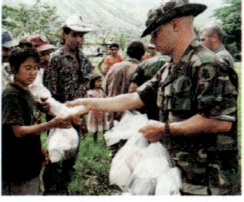

ancestor
A family member who lived before you is an **ancestor.** (p. 120) An **ancestor** of mine lived in China in the 1600s.

ballot
A **ballot** is a form on which people mark their choices in an election. (p. 311) Many communities have switched from paper **ballots** to voting machines.

bank
A **bank** is a safe place to keep money. (p. 181) Dad went to the **bank** to get money for gas.

bar graph
A **bar graph** is a chart that uses bars to show amounts. (p. 178) The **bar graph** shows the number of different workers in a school.

barter
The exchange of goods or services without the use of money is called **barter.** (p. 196) **Barter** takes place when you swap goods or services with someone.

R20 • Resources

calendar

A **calendar** is a chart that shows the months, weeks, and days of the year. (p. 50) I marked my birthday on the **calendar**.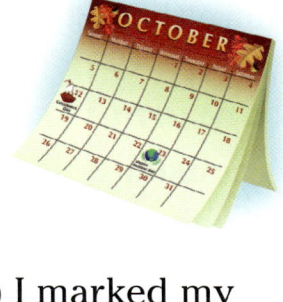

capital

A **capital** is a city where the people in a government work. (p. 284) The **capital** of New Jersey is Trenton.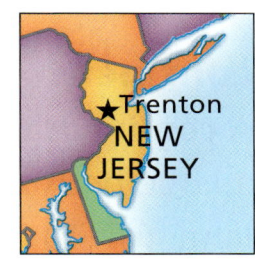

capital resource

Something other than natural or human resources, that people need in order to produce goods is a **capital resource**. (p. 191) **Capital resources** include tools, machinery, buildings, and trucks.

cause

A **cause** is something that makes something else happen. (p. 238) The **cause** of the fire was a lightning strike.

citizen

A **citizen** is a person who belongs to a place. (p. 292) You are a **citizen** of the community where you live.

climate

The usual weather of a place over a long time is called **climate**. (p. 85) Southern Michigan has a **climate** with cold winters and warm summers.

colonist

A **colonist** is a person who lives in a colony. (p. 230) The **colonists** at Jamestown came from England.

colony

A **colony** is a place that is ruled by another country. (p. 229) England's first **colony** in North America was Jamestown.

Picture Glossary

R21

communication

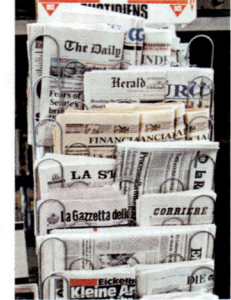

Any way of sharing information is **communication**. (p. 268) Newspapers and magazines are kinds of **communication**.

community

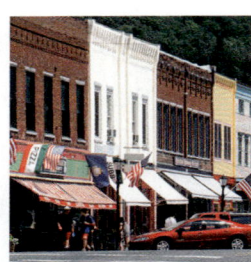

A **community** is a place where people live. (p. 38) Cities and towns are **communities**.

compass rose

A **compass rose** is a drawing that shows directions on a map. (p. 34) Use the **compass rose** to find north.

conflict

A **conflict** is a disagreement. (p. 314) Good citizens try to resolve **conflicts** peacefully.

Constitution

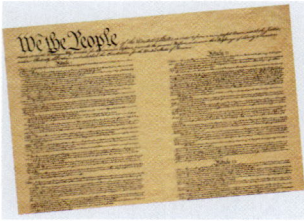

The **Constitution** is a plan for the government of the United States. (p. 316) The United States **Constitution** is more than 200 years old.

consumer

A **consumer** is someone who buys or uses goods or services. (p. 166) I am a **consumer** when I buy food at a store.

continent

A **continent** is a large body of land. (p. 68) The earth has seven **continents**.

country

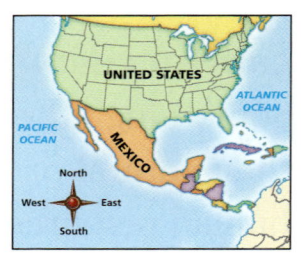

A **country** is a land where people have the same laws and leaders. (p. 67) Mexico is the **country** south of the United States.

culture

The way of life of a group of people is called **culture**. (p. 117) Religious beliefs are part of people's **culture**.

R22 • Resources

custom

A **custom** is something that people usually do at a certain time. (p. 116) It is our **custom** to wear party hats at birthday parties.

decision

A **decision** is the act of deciding or of making a choice. (p. 150) I had to make a **decision** about doing my homework before or after supper.

democracy

A **democracy** is government by the people. (p. 317) People in a **democracy** choose their leaders.

detail

A **detail** is a small piece of information. (p. 98) Make sure you support your idea with **details**.

Main Idea
Details
1.
2.
3.
4.
5.

dictionary

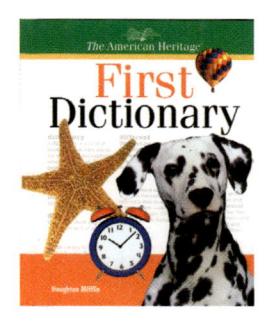

A **dictionary** is a book that gives the meanings of words. (p. 186) Look up new words in a **dictionary**.

distance

The word **distance** means how far one point is from another. (p. 202) The **distance** across the table is 30 inches.

effect

An **effect** is something that happens as a result of a cause. (p. 238) An **effect** of playing in puddles is wet clothing.

election

An **election** is a time when people vote. (p. 308) We have an **election** to choose a new President every four years.

R23

encyclopedia

An **encyclopedia** is a book or set of books that gives information about many topics. (p. 186) Look up a topic in an **encyclopedia** to find out more about it.

environment

The **environment** is the natural world around you. (p. 103) Land, water, plants, animals, and people are all part of the **environment.**

equator
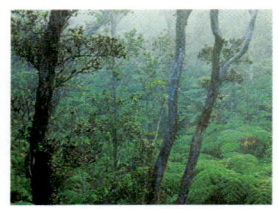
The **equator** is an imaginary line that divides the earth into its northern and southern halves. (p. 72) You can only see the **equator** on maps.

explorer
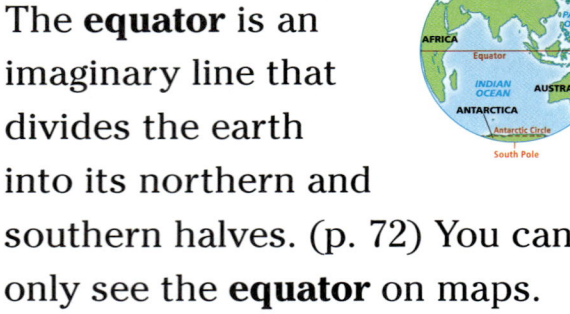
An **explorer** is a person who travels to find new things and places. (p. 222) Columbus was an **explorer** who traveled to the Americas.

fact
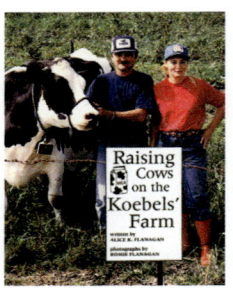
A **fact** is something that is true. (pp. 164, 250) A book about seashells has many **facts** in it.

factory
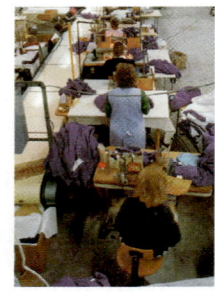
A **factory** is a place where goods are made. (p. 172) It would be fun to go to a sneaker **factory.**

fiction
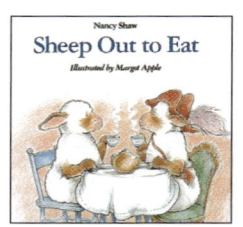
Written works that tell about made-up events and characters are called **fiction.** (p. 164) The stories "Cinderella" and **Sheep Out to Eat** are **fiction.**

globe

A **globe** is a ball-shaped model of the earth. (p. 32) A **globe** shows the true shape of the earth.

R24 • Resources

goods

Things people make or grow are called **goods.** (p. 172) Goods are things such as trucks and apples.

government
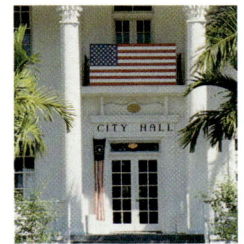
A group of people who work together to run a community, state, or country make up a **government.** (p. 283) Some people in our **government** work at city hall.

grid

A **grid** is a pattern of lines that form boxes. (p. 42) A **grid** helps you find places on a map.

group

A **group** is a number of people who live together, work together, or spend time together. (p. 26) A soccer team is a **group.**

hemisphere

A **hemisphere** is half the earth. (p. 72) North America is in the Western **Hemisphere.**

hero

A **hero** is someone who is admired for great courage or for doing something important. (p. 252) **Heroes** can be found in medicine, sports, science, or other areas.

history
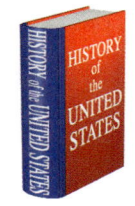
Everything people can know about the past is called **history.** (p. 212) The invention of the computer was an important event in **history.**

human resource
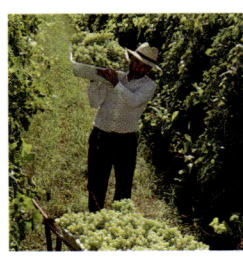
A **human resource** is a person who helps make a product. (p. 190) A worker in a factory or other places is a **human resource.**

R25

immigrant
An **immigrant** is a person who moves from one country to another. (p. 118) In the 1970s, many **immigrants** came to the United States from Asia.

income
The money people earn when they work is called **income.** (p. 168) My mother uses her **income** to pay for our food.

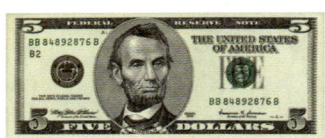

independence
Independence means freedom from the rule of another nation. (p. 242) The 13 colonies wanted **independence** from Britain.

interview
An **interview** is a meeting in which one person asks another person questions. (p. 134) In our **interview** with the mayor, we asked five questions.

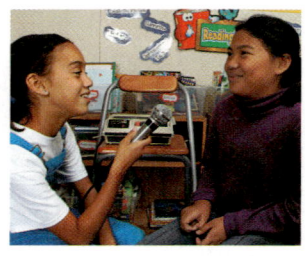

invention
An **invention** is something new that someone makes or thinks of. (p. 256) Thomas Edison thought of many important **inventions.**

island
An **island** is a piece of land with water all around it. (p. 76) Greenland is a very large **island.**

journey
A **journey** is a long trip. (p. 222) Colonists from England made a **journey** from Europe to North America.

R26 • Resources

judge

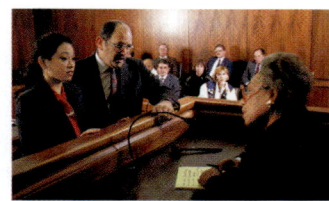

A **judge** is someone who studies the laws and decides the best way to follow them. (p. 302) A **judge** may decide what a person must do to make up for breaking a law.

justice

Justice means fairness. (p. 317) A good judge treats everyone with **justice**.

lake

A body of water with land all around it is called a **lake**. (p. 78) Most **lakes** have fresh water.

landform

A **landform** is one of the shapes of land found on the earth. (p. 74) A mountain is a **landform**.

landmark

A **landmark** is something that helps people know a place. (p. 138) The Gateway Arch is a **landmark** of St. Louis, Missouri.

law

A rule that everyone in a community, state, or nation must follow is called a **law**. (p. 300) A driver who doesn't stop at a stop sign is breaking a **law**.

leader

A **leader** is someone who leads others. (p. 28) A community **leader** guides the work of others.

legend

A **legend** is a story that people have passed along for many years. (p. 128) Most cultures have a **legend** that explains weather.

liberty

The word **liberty** means freedom. (p. 317) The **Liberty** Bell is a symbol of our nation's freedom.

location

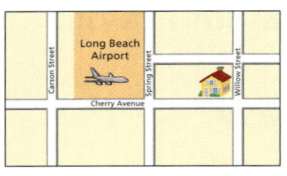

A **location** is a place. (p. 42) An airplane symbol may mark the **location** of an airport on a map.

M

main idea

The most important thought on a page is called a **main idea.** (p. 98) The **main idea** on that page is that people have many kinds of pets.

market

A **market** is any place where people buy and sell things. (p. 55) A small store is one kind of **market.**

memorial

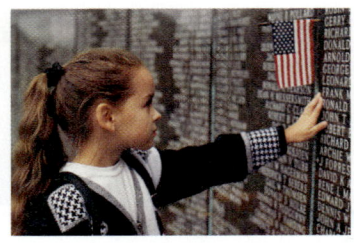

A **memorial** is something, such as a building or statue, that honors a hero or an event. (p. 140) The Vietnam Veterans **Memorial** honors Americans who were killed in the Vietnam War.

monument

A **monument** is something, such as a building or statue, that honors a hero or an event. (p. 140) Many towns have a **monument** to people who served in a war.

N

nation

Nation is another word for country. (p. 69) Canada is a **nation** to the north of the United States.

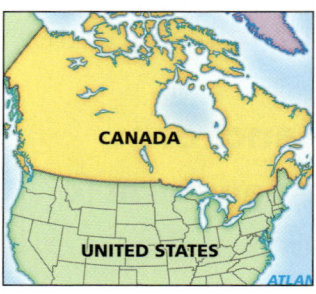

national holiday

A **national holiday** is a holiday that honors someone or something that is important to a country. (p. 144) Independence Day is a **national holiday** that honors the beginning of the United States.

natural resource

Something in nature that people use is a **natural resource**. (p. 100) Water is an important **natural resource**.

needs

Things that people must have to live are called **needs**. (p. 160) Our **needs** are food, water, clothing, and shelter.

neighborhood

A neighborhood is a part of a city or town. (p. 36) Each year, people in my **neighborhood** get together for a picnic on Labor Day.

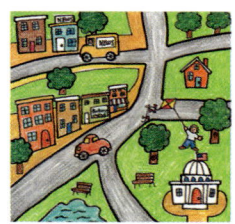

nonfiction

Written materials that are about true things are **nonfiction**. (p. 164) **Sheep on the Farm** is a **nonfiction** book.

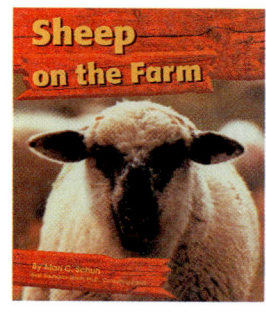

northeast

The direction between north and east is called **northeast**. (p. 82) New York City is **northeast** of Trenton, New Jersey.

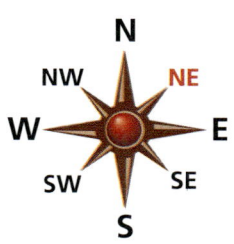

northwest

The direction between north and west is called **northwest**. (p. 82) Montgomery, Alabama is **northwest** of Tallahassee, Florida.

opinion

An **opinion** is a belief based on what you think or feel, rather than on facts. (p. 250) In my **opinion** soccer is better than baseball.

R29

peninsula
Land that sticks out into water is called a **peninsula.** (p. 76) A **peninsula** has water on three sides.

pictograph
A **pictograph** is a chart that shows information by using small pictures to stand for amounts. (p. 306) Each picture of a tomato can on the **pictograph** stood for ten tomatoes.

Pilgrim
A **Pilgrim** was one kind of colonist at Plymouth. (p. 232) The **Pilgrims** came to America to find religious freedom.

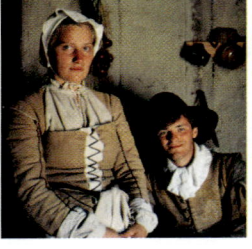

point of view
A way of looking at things is called a **point of view.** (p. 266) We each had a different **point of view** about which play to put on.

pole
The place on the earth that is farthest north or south is a kind of **pole.** (p. 72) The North **Pole** and the South **Pole** are very cold.

president
A **president** is the leader of a country or nation. (p. 138) John Adams was the second **President** of the United States.

price
The amount of money you pay to buy something is called **price.** (p. 180) The **price** of a box of cereal is $2.79.

R30 • Resources

producer

A **producer** is a person who makes or grows something. (p. 166) A baker is a **producer** of bread and rolls.

R

region

A **region** is an area that has some shared natural or human feature that sets it apart from other areas. (p. 92) The state of Iowa is in a plains **region.**

religious holiday

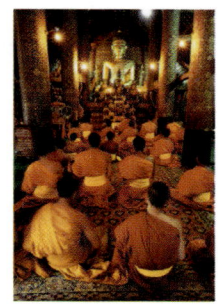

A special day that is important to people in a religion is called a **religious holiday.** (p. 146) In April, Buddhists celebrate the birthday of their founder on a **religious holiday** called Wesak.

responsibility

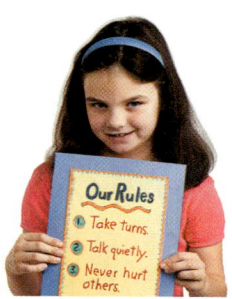

A **responsibility** is something that you should do. (p. 294) Everyone has the **responsibility** to obey the law.

right

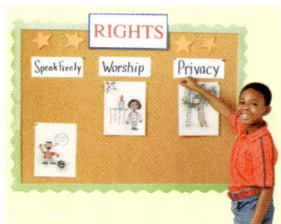

A **right** is something you are free to do. (p. 293) You have the **right** to speak freely.

rule

A statement or an idea that tells people what they should or should not do is called a **rule.** (p. 29) One school **rule** says that you may not run in the hallway.

rural area

A **rural** area is a place that has fewer stores, schools, and homes than a city or suburb has. (p. 53) Farms and forests are found in **rural areas.**

Picture Glossary

R31

savings account

A **savings account** is a service from a bank that allows people to earn interest on their money. (p. 182) Aki's **savings account** earned 11 cents in interest last month.

scale

A line with a series of marks used to find distance on a map is a **scale.** (p. 202) Use a map **scale** to find how far apart two places are.

scarcity

Not having enough resources to meet people's unlimited wants is called **scarcity.** Because of scarcity, people must make choices in what to make or grow. (p. 193)

service

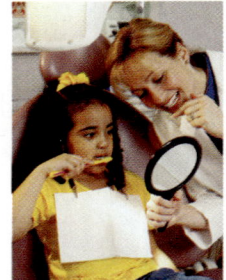

An activity that people do to help other people is called a **service.** (p. 173) A dentist provides a **service.**

settlement

A **settlement** is a small community started by people from another land. (p. 229) St. Augustine in Florida is the oldest lasting European **settlement** in America.

shelter

Something that protects or covers is called a **shelter.** (p. 160) Houses are kinds of **shelter.**

southeast

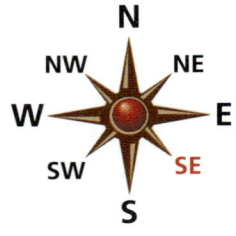

The direction between south and east is called **southeast.** (p. 82) Springfield, Illinois, is **southeast** of Des Moines, Iowa.

southwest

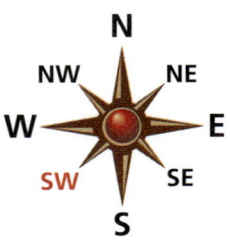

The direction between south and west is called **southwest.** (p. 82) Frankfurt, Kentucky is **southwest** of Columbus, Ohio.

specialize
Choosing to grow mainly one crop or to make only one main kind of product is to **specialize**. (p. 199) Farmers in Costa Rica **specialize** in growing bananas.

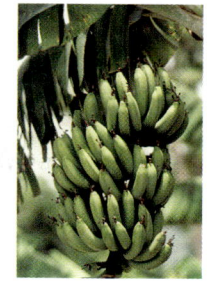

state
Part of a country is called a **state**. (p. 67) Ohio is one **state** of the 50 in the United States.

suburb
A **suburb** is a community near a city. (p. 46) Many people who live in a **suburb** work in the city.

symbol
A **symbol** is a picture, place, or thing that stands for something else. (pp. 34, 137) An eagle is a **symbol** of freedom.

tax
A **tax** is money that a government collects from citizens and businesses. (p. 287) A local government uses the **tax** money it collects to pay for services such as police.

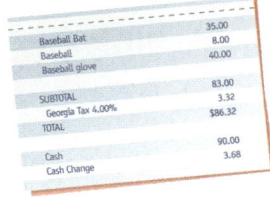

technology
The use of science to make new things or to make things work better is called **technology**. (p. 260) People used **technology** to make faster and safer cars.

timeline
A **timeline** is an ordered group of words and dates that show when events happened. (p. 124) A **timeline** must be divided into equal parts.

R33

trade

The buying and selling of goods and services is called **trade**. (p. 197) People in this country take part in **trade** in many ways.

tradition

A **tradition** is something that people do the same way year after year. (p. 126) One **tradition** in my family is that you choose what is served for dinner on your birthday.

transportation

Any way of moving things or people from one place to another is called **transportation**. (p. 260) Cars are one kind of **transportation**.

urban area

Urban area is another name for city. (p. 44) An **urban area** has many buildings and people.

valley

The low land between mountains or hills is called a **valley**. (p. 75) A **valley** often has a river running through it.

vote

To **vote** means to show or make a choice for a leader or a law. (p. 308) You may **vote** for class president or team captain.

wants

Things that people would like to have, but do not have to have to stay alive are called **wants**. (p. 160) A new bike and roller skates are on my list of **wants**.

weather

What the air is like outside at any given time is called **weather**.
(p. 84) Today the **weather** is warm and rainy.

world map

A **world map** is a flat drawing of the earth. (p. 32) You can see the whole earth at once on a **world map**.

Index

Page numbers with *m* after them refer to maps. Page numbers in italics refer to pictures.

A

Adame-Moliner, Alicia, 130
Adams, Abigail, 245, 246–247
Adams, Samuel, 245
Address, in geography, 66
African Americans, 254, 258–259, 304–305, 334
Aid, 322
American Indians, 118–*119*
  canoes, 217
  Cherokee, 80–81
  Delaware, *213m*–214
  "Great Smokies, The," 80–81
  history of, 213–215
  legends, 218–221
  natural resources, 216
  Navajo, 214
  Osage, 215
  Pamunkey, 230
  powwows, 119
  Shasta, 215
  Sitting Bull, 253
  totem poles, *129*
  Wampanoag, 232
American Revolution
  causes, 242
  events, 243, 244
  people, 242–249
Ancestors, 120–121
Arafat, Yasir, 325
Art and artists, 129–131
Artifacts, 139, 209, 216, 217, 226, 243, 247, 258, 269–272, 281, 316, 332, 334
Australia, 201, R13, R15

B

Ballots, 311
Banks, 181
  savings accounts, 182–183
Bar graphs, 178–179
Barter, 196
Begin, Menachem, *323*
Bell, Alexander Graham, *269*
Blair, Tony, *325*
Boston, Massachusetts, *241*
Boston Tea Party, 242
Branches of government, 318–319
Brazil
  money of, 200
Bush, George W., 309, *324*

C

Calendars, 50–51
California,
  Palm Springs, 86
  San Diego, 47
  Spring Valley, 46
Canada, 69
Capital resources, 191. *See also* Resources.
Capitals, 284
Capitol, 319
Caring, 174–177, R9
Carter, Jimmy, *323*
Carver, George Washington, 176
Cause and effect, 238
Cent, 201
Centavo, 200
Cervantes, Maggie, 40–41

Character traits, R8–R9
  caring, 174–177, R9
  civic virtue, 40–41, R9
  courage, 304–305, R8, R9
  fairness, 148–149, R9
  patriotism, 246–249, R8, R9
  respect, 258–259, R9
  responsibility, 270–271, R9
Charleston, South Carolina, *241*
Chavez, Cesar, 148–149
Cherokee
  folklore, 80–81
Chicago, Illinois, *45*
Chinese New Year, 118
Choices, economic, 161
Cincinnati, Ohio, 79
Cities, 44–45
  characteristics of, 44–45
  as "communities," 38
  neighborhoods, 36
Citizens, 292
  definition of, 280, 292, 329
  elections, 309–311
  good citizens, 295
  government, 293, 309–311
  laws and, 303
  responsibilities of, 294, 296–299
  rights of, 20–21, 293
  voting and, 311
Citizenship
  civic understanding, 40–41, 294, 295, R9
  civic virtue, 294, 295
  Constitution, 316–318
  democracy, 317, 320–321
  elections, 308–311
  government defined, 283
  judges, 302
  laws, 300–305

R36 • Resources

Einstein

leaders, 308–311
police, 301
responsibilities, 294
rights, 293
Citizenship Handbook, R2–R9
Citizenship skills, 150–151, 266–267, 314–315
Climate, 85–87. *See also* Weather.
Coleman, Michael B. (Columbus, Ohio, mayor), 309
Colonies, 229, 240, *241m*
American Revolution, 244
Declaration of Independence, 243
Jamestown, *229m*, *230–231*
Plymouth, *229m*, *232–233*
Colonists, 230
Colorado, 75
Columbus, Christopher, 224–225
Columbus, Ohio, 83
mayor of, 309
Communication, 268
Inca messengers, 272–273
Internet, *271*
radio, *270*
telegraph, *269*
telephone, *269*
television, *270*
Communities, 38
Community activities, 39
Compass rose, 34
Compasses, 226–227
Conflict resolution, 314–315
Congress, 319
Constitution Day and Citizenship Day, 20–21
Constitution of the United States, 316–317
branches of government, 318–319

Consumers, 166–167
Continents, 68–69
Country, definition of, 67
Courage, 304–305, R8, R9
Critical thinking,
cause and effect, 238–239
classify, 153
compare and contrast, 59, 109
conflict resolution, 296–299, 314–315
decision making, 150–151
main idea and details, 205
sequence, 275
Cultural holidays, 147
Culture
ancestors and, 120–121
art, 129
customs, 116–117
dance and, 131
families and, 117
holidays and, 144–148
immigrants, 118–119, 122–123
landmarks, 138–139
language, 117
literature and, 128
monuments, 140, 141
music and, 130–131
sharing, 126–131
stories, 128
symbols, 118–119, 136
traditions from, 126–127
Curie, Marie, 174
Customs, 116–117

Decision making, 150–151
Declaration of Independence, 243
Delaware Indians, *213m*–214
Delaware River, *79*

George Washington crossing, *244*
Delmarva Peninsula, 76
Democracy, 320–321
Dictionaries, 186–187
Directions, geography, 82
Distance on a map, 202
Dollar, 201
Drums, *130*
Duluth, Minnesota, 284, *285m*

Earning money, 168
Easter, 146. *See also* Holidays.
Economics
banks, 182
barter, 196
capital resources, 191
choices, 161, 180, 184–185, 193
consumers, 166–167
free enterprise, 192–193
goods, 172
human resources, 190
income, 168
interest, 182
needs, 160, 162–163
opportunity cost, 161
price, 180
producers, 166–167, 170–171, 204
saving, 181–183
savings account, 182–183
scarcity, 192–193
services, 173, 174–177
specialization, 199
trade, 197–198
wants, 160
Edison, Thomas, 256
Einstein, Albert, 257

R37

Elections

Elections, 308–313
Electric light bulb, 256
Ellis Island, 122–123
Encyclopedias, 186
English colonies, 229, 240, *241m*
  American Revolution, 244
  Declaration of Independence, 243
  Jamestown, *229m*, 230–231
  Plymouth, *229m*, 232–233
Environment, 103
  harm to, 104–105
  protection of, 104–105
Equator, 72
European Union
  money of, 200
Explorers, 222, 228
  Christopher Columbus, 224–225
  Marco Polo, 222, 223

Fact and fiction, comparing, 164
Fact and opinion, comparing, 250
Factories, 172
Fairness, 148–149, 317, R9
Families
  ancestors, 120–121
  cultures and, 117
  customs, 116
  groups, 26, 27
  sharing traditions, 126–127
Fargo, North Dakota, *86*
Farms and Farming
  first farmers, 170–171
  in Mesopotamia, 170–171
  raisin production, 188–191
  specializing in, 199
Fire fighters, 288–291

Fish markets, *57*
Flag Day, 337
Flags
  Ghana, *327*
  Japan, *327*
  Mexico, *326*
  United States, *136–137*
Florida
  cities, 38–39
Folktales
  "Fox and the Crab, The," *128*
  "Great Smokies, The," 80–81
  "Milkmaid, The," *162–163*
  "Young Woman and the Thunder Beings, The," 218–221
Food, keeping cold, 194–195
Forest regions, 94
Forests, 54, 95
Fort McHenry, *142*
Fourth of July, 338
Franklin, Benjamin, 245, *268*
Freedom, 20–21, 317, 338

Geography, 66–107
  climate, 85–87
  continent, 68–69
  country, 66–67
  environment, 103–105
  human regions, 92, 96–97
  landforms, 74–77
  location, 66–69
  nation, 69
  natural resources, 100
  nonrenewable resources, 102
  physical regions, 92–95
  regions, 92–97

  renewable resources, 102
  resources, 100–107
  states, 67
  synthetic resources, 101
  water, bodies of, 78–79
  weather, 84–85, 88–91
Globes, 32–33
  parts of, 72–73
Goods, 172
Government
  branches of, 318–319
  Constitution and, 20–21, 317
  institutions, 284, 286, 301–302
  leaders, 308–310
  local, 283
  national, 284
  services, 286
  state, 284
  taxes, 287
  working together, 323
  world leaders, 323–325
Governors, 309
Granholm, Jennifer (Michigan governor), *309*
Grassland regions, 94
Graph and chart skills, 124–125, 150–151, 178–179, 306–307
Great Lakes, 78
"Great Smokies, The," 80–81
Grids, 42
Groups, 26–27
  leaders, 28
  rules, 29

Hawaii forest, *95*
Hemispheres, 72

R38 • Resources

Heroes, 252
Hezekiah, Alan, 130
Highways, 263
History
American Indians, 212–217
American Revolution, 242–249
changes over time, 260–263
colonists, 230–233, 240–243
communication changes, 268–271
Declaration of Independence, 243
explorers, 222–225
inventions, 227, 262–263, 264–265, 268–271
Jamestown, 230–231
Plymouth, 232–233
timelines, 124–125, 154, 194–195, 242–243, 246, 248, 262–263, 274
transportation changes, 264–265
Holidays
Cesar Chavez Day of Service and Learning, 145, 148
Constitution Day and Citizenship Day, 20–21
cultural holidays, 147
Flag Day, 337
Independence Day, 338
Martin Luther King, Jr. Day, 334
Memorial Day, 336
national holidays, 144
Patriots' Day, 145
Presidents' Day, *144*, 335
religious holidays, 146
state holidays, 145
Thanksgiving, 333
Veterans Day, 332
Human regions, 92

Human resources, 190, *191*
Hurricane Katrina, 96–97
Hurricane Rita, 96–97

Immigrants, 118
at Ellis Island, 122–123
Inca messengers, 272–273
Income, 168
Independence, 242
American Revolution, 244
Declaration of Independence, 243
leaders of, 245
Independence Day, 338
India, money of, 201
Internet, 56, *271*
Internet marketplace, *56*
Inventions, 256
in communications, 268–271
in transportation, 260–263
Islands, 76

Jamestown, *229m*, 230–231
Japan, *326m*
flag, *327*
market, 57
Jefferson, Thomas, 141, 243
Jefferson Memorial, 141
Judges, 302
Supreme Court, 319
Justice, 317

Katrina, Hurricane, 96–97
Kenya, *201m*
money of, 200

Key, Francis Scott, 142
King, Coretta Scott, R8
King, Martin Luther, Jr., 334

Lakes, 78
Landform regions, 93
Landforms, 74
islands, 76
peninsulas, 76
plains, 77
valleys, 75
Landmarks, 138–139
Liberty Bell, 139
Mount Rushmore, 138
Statue of Liberty, 139
See also Memorials; Monuments.
Laws
citizens' obedience to, 303
environment and, 105
importance of, 300
judges and, 302
police and, 301
Leaders, 28
government, 20, 308–311, 323–325
of independence, 245
Legends, 128, 218–221
Liberty, 317
Liberty Bell, 139
Lincoln, Abraham
Lincoln Memorial, *140*
Presidents' Day, *335*
Literature
Fire Station, The, 288–291
"Great Smokies, The," 80–81
"Maple Talk," 106–107
"Milkmaid, The," 162–163

Literature

Index

R39

Local government
"Recess Rules," 30–31
"Star-Spangled Banner, The," 142–143
"Young Woman and the Thunder Beings, The," 218–221
Local government, 283
mayors, 309
services, *286*
Location, on grid, 42
Logs, *54*
Longhouses, 214, 215

Magnetic compasses, 226–227
Mail, by stagecoach, *268*
Mandela, Nelson, *325*
"Maple Talk," 106–107
Map and globe skills, 32–35, 42–43, 72–73, 82–83, 202–203
Map scale, 202
Maps of the world, 32–33
Markets, 55–57
Marrakesh market, 56
Martin Luther King, Jr. Day, 334
"Mayflower Crossing, The," 234–237
Mayors, 309
Meir, Golda, 254
Memorial Day, 336
Memorials, 140, 141
Lincoln Memorial, 140
Thomas Jefferson Memorial, 141
Mesopotamia, 170
Message runners, 272–273
Mexico, 69
flag, *326*
music and dancing, *131*

Michigan
governor of, 309
"Milkmaid, The," 162–163. See also Folktales.
Minneapolis, Minnesota, 44
Minnesota, 44
Money
Australian, 201
Brazilian, 200
earning money, 168
European Union, 200
Indian, 201
Kenyan, 200
saving money, 181
Monuments, 140
Morse, Samuel, *269*
Mount Rushmore, 138
Musical traditions, 130, 133

National anthem, 142–143
National government, 284
branches of government, 318–319
Constitution of the United States, 316, *317*
President of the United States, 138, 309, 318
services, *286*
National holidays, 144
Constitution Day and Citizenship Day, 20–21
Flag Day, 337
Independence Day, 338
Martin Luther King, Jr. Day, 334
Memorial Day, 336
Presidents' Day, 335
Thanksgiving, 333
Veterans Day, 332

Nations, 69
flags of, *326–327*
working together, 322–325
Native Americans, 118, *119*
Delaware, 214
"Great Smokies, The," 80–81
history of, 213–215
natural resources, use of, 216
Navajo, 214
Osage, 215
Pamunkey, 230
powwows, *119*
Shasta, 215
Sitting Bull, 253
totem poles, *129*
Wampanoag, 232
Natural resources, 100, *191*
American Indians' use of, 216
raisin producers, 190
replacement of, 102
Navajo, 213*m*, 214, 216
Needs, 160
Neighborhood activities, 37
Neighborhoods, 36. See also Communities.
Nevada, 83 (map), 311 (candidate in photo)
New England forest, *95*
New Orleans, Louisiana, 96–97
New York City, 48–49
immigrants, *119*
Nonfiction, 164
North America, 69
North Pole, 72
Northeast, 82
Northwest, 82

R40 • Resources

Ocean water, 78
Ohio, 79, 83, 309
Ohio River, 79
Oil, replacement of, 102
Opinion and fact, 250
Origami, 127
Osage, 213*m*, 215–216

Palm Springs, California, 86
Pamunkey, 230
Parks, Rosa, 304–305
Passover, 146
Pasteur, Louis, 175. *See also* Scientists.
Pasteurization, 175
Patriotism, 246–249, R8, R9
Patriots' Day, 145
Peninsulas, 76
Philadelphia, 241
  Liberty Bell, 139
Pictographs, 306–307
Pilgrims, 232
  "Mayflower Crossing, The," 234–237
  in Plymouth Colony, 232–233
Plainfield, Illinois, 261–263
Plains, 77
Plant regions, 94–95
Plymouth Colony, 229*m*, 232–233
Police, 301
Polo, Marco, *222,* 223
Powwows, *119*
Presidents' Day, 335

Presidents of the United States, 138, 309, 318
  Bush, George W., 309, 324
  Carter, Jimmy, 323
  Jefferson, Thomas, 141, 243
  Lincoln, Abraham, 140, 335
  Seal of the President, 136
  Washington, George, 140, 335
Prices, 180
  comparing, 184–185
Primary sources, 22, 41, 62, 71, 80, 112, *116*–119, *120*–121, *122*–127, 130–131, 134, 143, 148, 156, 208, 218–221, 233, 243, 247, 258–259, 278, 316, R2, R4, R6–R7
Producers, 166–167
  raisin production, 188–191
Putin, Vladimir, *324*

Radios, *270*
Railways, 262
Rainfall, in the United States, 99
Raisin production, 188–191
Ramadan, 146
Readers' Theater, 88–91, 234–237, 296–299
Reading skills
  cause and effect, 44, 196, 338–339(s)
  classify, 66, 136, 144, 172, 212, 252, 292, 316
  compare and contrast, 26, 52, 74, 222, 228
  draw conclusions, 116, 166, 282
  fact and opinion, 250–251(s)

  main idea and details, 36, 84, 92, 98, 126, 268, 300
  predict outcomes, 160, 180
  problem and solution, 314–315(s), 322
  sequence, 100, 188, 240, 260, 308
Reading strategies
  monitor and clarify, 65, 211
  predict and infer, 25, 115, 211
  question, 65, 159, 281
  summarize, 25, 115, 159, 281
"Recess Rules," 30–31
Recycling, 105
Regions, 92
  human regions, 92
  landform regions, 93
  plant regions, 94–95
Religious holidays, 146
Reno, Nevada, 83
Resources, 100
  capital resources, 191
  human resources, 190, *191*
  natural resources, 100, 102, 190, *191*, 216
  scarcity of, 192–193
  synthetic resources, 101
Respect, 258–259, R9
Responsibilities, 270, 271, 294, R9
Revere, Paul, 245, 248, *249*
Revolutionary War. *See* American Revolution.
Ride, Sally, 70–71
Rights, 293
  of African Americans, 255, 258–259, 293, 304–305, 334, R8
  of American Indians, 253, 293

Rita
    of Mexican Americans, 148–149
    of women, 40–41, 70, 254, 293
Rita, Hurricane, 96
Rivers, 79
Robinson, Jackie, 255, 258–259
Rodriguez, Eloy, 177
Rules, 29
    "Recess Rules," 30–31
Rural areas, 53

S

Sadat, Anwar el, *323*
Saint Patrick's Day parade, *147*
St. Paul, Minnesota, 83
San Diego, California, 47
    Spring Valley suburb, 46
San Juan Mountains, Colorado, 75
Saving money, 181
Savings accounts, 182–183
Scarcity of resources, 192–193
School class, 26, 27
Scientists, 174–177
Seneca
    legends, 218–221
Services, 173
    government services, 286
Settlements, 229
    Jamestown, *229m*, 230–231
    Plymouth, *229m*, 232–233
Shasta, 215
Shelter, 160
Sitting Bull, 253
Skills,
    citizenship,
        conflict resolution, 314–315

decision making, 150–151
        point of view, 266–267
    graph and chart,
        bar graph, 178–179
        calendar, 50–51
        pictograph, 306–307
        timeline, 124–125
    map and globe,
        compass rose, 34–35
        globe, 32, 72–73
        grid, 42–43
        intermediate directions, 82–83
        map scale, 202–203
        symbols, 34–35
    reading and thinking,
        cause and effect, 238–239
        fact and fiction, 164–165
        facts and opinions, 250–251
        main idea and details, 98–99
    Study,
        interviewing, 134–135
        reference books, 86–87
Skyscrapers, 49
Small towns, 52
Soil loss, 104
South Pole, 72
Southeast, 82
Southwest, 82
Space shuttle science lab, 265
Specialization, 199
Spring Valley, California, 46, *47m*
Stagecoaches, 262
    mail by, *268*
"Star-Spangled Banner, The," 142–143
State
    capitals, 284
    definition of, 67
    government, 284

governors, 309
    holidays, 145, 148
    laws, 300–301, 303–304
    services, 286
    United States, 66–67, 203*m*, 284–285*m*, R18–R19*m*
Statue of Liberty, 139
Story sharing, 128
Streetcars, 262
Study skills, 186–187, 238–239
Suburbs, 46–47
Supreme Court, 319
Symbols, 34, 137
    American symbols, 136–137
Synthetic resources, 101

T

Taxes, 287
Teams as "groups," 26
Technology, 260
Telegraph, *269*
    Railway Telegraph, 264
Telephone, *269*
Television, *270*
Thanksgiving, 333
Thomas Jefferson Memorial, *141*
Timelines, 124–125, 154, 194–195, 242–243, 246, 248, 262–263, 274
Totem poles, *129*
Towns
    as "communities," 38
    neighborhoods, 36
    small towns, 52
Trade, 197, *198*
Traditions, 126–127
Transportation, 260
    Plainfield, Illinois, 262–263

R42 • Resources

Trees
honey mesquite, 98
"Maple Talk," 106–107
replacement of, 102

Uncle Sam, *137*
United States Constitution, 20–21, 316–317
branches of government and, 318–319
United States of America, *67,* 244
Urban areas, 44, 47, 49, 55

Valleys, 75
Veterans Day, 332

Vietnam Veterans Memorial, 336
Voting, 308–313

Wampanoag, 232
Wang, Taylor G., 265
Wants, definition of, 160
War for Independence. *See* American Revolution.
Washington, D.C., 284
Washington, George
crossing the Delaware River, *244*
Presidents' Day, *144,* 335
Washington Monument, *140*
Water, bodies of, 78–79

Weather, 84
Weather reports, 84
Wheat, *198*
White House, 318
Woods, Granville T., 264
Work, 166–169
World leaders, 323–325
World maps, 32–33

"Young Woman and the Thunder Beings, The," 218–221
Yo-Yo Ma, 132–133

Zemin, Jiang, 325

Acknowledgments

Permissioned Material

Excerpts from "*The Fire Fighter's Job*" and "*Brave Fire Fighters,*" from *The Fire Station,* by Stuart A. Kallen. Copyright © 1997 by Abdo Consulting Group, Inc. Reprinted by permission of Abdo Publishing Company.

"God Bless America," by Irving Berlin. © Copyright 1938, 1939, © copyright renewed 1965, 1966 by Irving Berlin. © Copyright assigned to the Trustees of the God Bless America Fund. International Copyright Secured. All Rights Reserved. Reprinted by permission of the Irving Berlin Music Company.

Lyrics from "I Live in a City," words and music by Malvina Reynolds. Copyright © 1961 by Schroder Music Co. (ASCAP) Renewed 1989. Used by permission. All rights reserved.

Excerpt from "Jackie Robinson's letter to Branch Rickey," [1950], by Jackie Robinson, Copyright © Jackie Robinson. Reprinted by permission of The Jackie Robinson Foundation.

Excerpt from *Journey to Ellis Island: How My Father Came to America,* by Carol Bierman with Barbara Hehner. Text copyright © 1998 by Carol Bierman. Jacket copyright © 1998 by The Madison Press Limited. Reprinted by permission of Madison Press Books.

"Maple Talk," from *Poems Have Roots,* by Lilian Moore. Text copyright © 1997 by Lilian Moore. Reprinted with the permission of Atheneum Books for Young Readers, an imprint of Simon & Schuster Children's Publishing Division and Marian Reiner for the author.

Excerpt from "North" ("The Young Woman and the Thunder Beings"), from *Between Earth & Sky: Legends of Native American Sacred Places,* by Joseph Bruchac. Text copyright © 1996 by Joseph Bruchac. Reprinted by permission of Harcourt, Inc. and Barbara S. Kouts Agency.

Excerpt from "Our Family Comes From 'Round the World," from *Fathers, Mothers, Sisters, Brothers,* by Mary Ann Hoberman. Copyright © 1991 by Mary Ann Hoberman. Reprinted by permission of Little, Brown and Company, (Inc.) and Gina Maccoby Literary Agency.

Excerpt from *Raising Cows on the Koebels' Farm,* by Alice K. Flanagan. Copyright © 1999 by Alice K. Flanagan and Romie Flanagan. All rights reserved. Reprinted by permission of Children's Press, an imprint of Scholastic Library Publishing, Inc.

"Recess Rules," from *Lunch Money,* by Carol Diggory Shields, illustrated by Paul Meisel. Text copyright © 1995 by Carol Diggory Shields. Illustrations copyright © 1995 by Paul Meisel. Used by permission of Dutton Children's Books, a division of Penguin Young Readers Group, a member of Penguin Group (USA) Inc., 345 Hudson Street, New York, NY 10014. All rights reserved.

Excerpt from *Sheep on the Farm,* by Mari C. Schuh. Copyright © 2002 by Capstone Press. All rights reserved. Reprinted by permission of Capstone Press.

Excerpt from *Sheep Out to Eat,* by Nancy Shaw, illustrated by Margot Apple. Text copyright © 1992 by Nancy Shaw. Illustrations copyright © 1992 by Margot Apple. Reprinted by permission of Houghton Mifflin Company.

Excerpt from "South" ("The Great Smokies"), from *Between Earth & Sky: Legends of Native American Sacred Places,* by Joseph Bruchac. Copyright © 1996 by Joseph Bruchac. Reprinted by permission of Harcourt, Inc. and Barbara S. Kouts Agency.

Assignment Photography Credits

27, 29, 37, 66–67, 89–91, 114 (l), 128, 134, 159 (r), 180, 184–185, 227 (b), 235–237, 252, 267, 312–315, R22, R30 © HMCo./Ken Karp. 130–131, 139–131, 247 (bkgd), 284, 287, 292–293, 297–299, 328, © HMCo./Angela Coppola. 187, 227 (tr) © HMCo. 308 © HMCo./Jade Albert. 189, 190, 191, R21 (capital resource) © HMCo./JPMaroot.

Illustration Credits

All cartographic maps done by Ortelious Design. 24 Ron Berg. 36 Alex Burnet. 43 Bob Depew. 46–47 Nathan Jarvis. 51 Christiane Beauregard. 58 Hector Borlasca. 60 Chris Lensch. 75–78 (borders) Sally Vitsky. 84 Mark and Rosemary Jarman. 86 Mark and Rosemary Jarman. 88–91 Steve Costanza. 92–93 Michael Maydak. 98 Jeffrey Mangiat. 103 Bob Depew. 106–107 Lucia Washburn. 151 Nathan Jarvis. 152 Promotion studios. 154 Nathan Jarvis. 162–163 Doris Barrette. 170–171 Len Ebert. 186 Peter Richardson. 194–195 Kathryn Mitter. 196 Lisa Campbell Ernst. 200 (br, cr) Jeffrey Mangiat. 204 Anthony Lewis. 214–215 Robert Van Nutt. 218–222 Richard Cowdrey. 230–233 Martha Aviles. 234–237 Jui Ishida. 239 Frank Riccio. 241 Viviana Diaz. 276 Leah Palmer Preiss. 284–285 Ortelius Cartography 294 Kathi Ember. 300 Ron Berg. 306 Jeff Mangiat. 310 Christiane Beauregard. 330 Nathan Jarvis. R20 (barter) Lisa Campbell Ernst. R21 (calendar) Chris Lensch. R23 (decision) Nathan Jarvis. R24 (encyclopedia) Peter Richardson

Photography Credits

4 © Arthur Tilley/Taxi/Getty Images. **5** © Photodisc/Getty Images. **6** (r) Dave G.Houser/Corbis. **7** © HMCo./Ken Karp Photography. **8** © PhotoEdit. **9** © Doug Armand/Stone/Getty Images. **10** © Corbis. **11** Keren Su/Corbis. **20** © Ariel Skelley/Getty Images. **22–23** Kwane Zikomo/Superstock. **24** Gibson Stock Photography. **25** (l) Wes Thompson/Corbis; (r) Claver Carroll/Botanica/Getty Images. **26** Arthur Tilley/Taxi/Getty Images. **28** (l) SW Productions/Photodisc Red/Getty Images; (r) Rhoda Sidney/Photo Edit, Inc. **39** (c) Digital DataStream Inc/Paint Your Heart Out Tampa; (tr) Richard Steinmetz. **40–41** Courtesy of Maggie Cervantes. **44** © Chris Gregerson/cgstock.com. **45** (tl) Owaki–Kulla/Corbis; (tr) Gibson Stock Photography. **46** (lc) Mark Richards/Photo Edit; (tr) Stephen Schauer/Stone/Getty Images. **48** (inset) Brinsley Ford Collection, London, UK/Bridgeman Art Library. **48–49** (bkgd) Andrew Gordon 2003/Panoramic Images. **50** Mitch Hrdlicka/Photodisc Green/Getty Images. **52** J Sohm/VOA LLC/Panoramic Images. **53** (br) Burwell/Folio Inc.; (c) Larry Lefever/Grant Heilman Photography. **54** (br) Jeff Green Berg/Photo edit; (c) Alan Oddie/Photo Edit; (lc) Alec Pytlowany/Masterfile; (tr) Kitayama Sugi/Photonica. **55** (c) Rachel Epstein/Photo Edit; (inset) Richard Hamilton Smith/Corbis. **56** (b) David South/Image State–Pictor/PictureQuest; (t) Jon Riley Index Stock Imagery. **57** (l) TRBfoto/Photodisc/Getty Images; (r) TSUVOI/Masterfile. **62–63** (bkgd) Jesse Kalisher Gallery/Superstock; (inset) Palmer Kane Studios. **64** Mark Heifner/Pan Stock/Picturequest. **65** (l) Michael Melford/Imagebank/Getty Images;(r) Dan Budnik/Woodfin Camp & Associates. **70–71** (inset) NASA; (bkgd) Image produced by F. Hasler, M. Jentoft–Nilsen, H. Pierce, K. Palaniappan, and M. Manyin. NASA Goddard Lab for Atmospheres—data from National Oceanic and Atmospheric Administration NASA. **74–75** (b) Thomas Winz/Panoramic Images. **75** (t) © John Shaw/Panoramic Images. **76** Tony Arruza/Corbis. **77** Terry Thompson/NGS Images.com/Panoramic Images. **78** Steve Dunwell/Getty Images. **79** © Richard Cummins/SuperStock. **80–81** (bkgd) Donovan Reese/Panoramic Images. **81** (tr) ABPL Image Library/Animals Animals/Earth Scenes. **86** (bl) Lonnie Duka/Index Stock Imagery; (br) Brad Wrobleski/Masterfile. **87** Alan and Sandy Carey/Photodisc Green/Getty Images. **94** C. C. Lockwood Bruce Coleman. **95** (tc) James Schwabel/Panoramic Images; (tl) New Moon/Panoramic Images; (tr) (c) HMCo./Photo Disk. **96** Courtesy of Habitat for Humanity. **96–97** © NOAA/Handout/Reuters/Corbis. **100** International Stock/Imagestate. **101** (br) Dwayne Newton/Photo Edit; (t) R. Ian Lloyd/Masterfile. **102** (l) Grant Heilman Photography; (r) Gibson Stock Photography. **104** Collart HERVE/Corbis. **105** (tl) Gibson Stock Photography; (tr) Gibson Stock Photography. **112–113** Banana Stock. **114** (r) Paul Barton/Corbis. **115** (r) Nik Wheeler/Corbis; (tl) Jerry Wachter/Photo Researchers. **116** Ariel Skelley/Corbis. **117** Tony Freeman/Photo Edit. **118** Lawrence Migdale. **119** (b) Rudi Von Briel/Index Stock Imagery, Inc.; (t) Dave G. Houser/Corbis. **120** Courtesy of Aparna Agrawal; **121** Courtesy of Maria Carter; **122–123** (bkgd) North Wind Picture Archive. **123** (c) Bettmann/Corbis. **124** (b) Burke/Triolo/Retrofile; (t) Myrleen Ferguson Cate/Photo Edit. **125** (c) Claudia Kunin/Corbis; (l) Horace Bristol/Corbis; (r) Don Mason/Corbis. **126** Paul Barton/Corbis; (tr) Creatas. **127** (bl) Creatas; (c) David Young–Wolff/Photo Edit. **129** (b) Mark Gibson/Index Stock; (bl) Superstock. **132–133** (b) Osamu Honda/AP World Wide Photo; **133** (tr) AP World Wide Photos. **136** (b) Superstock. **136–137** (tl) Ken Davies/Masterfile. **137** (br) Thinkstock/Getty Images. **138** (b) ro-ma stock/Index Stock Imagery, Inc. **139** (b) Leif Skoogfors/Woodfin Camp & Associates; (t) Danny Lehman/Corbis. **140** (b) Craig Aurness/Corbis; (t) Photolink/Photodisc Green/Getty Images. **141** James P. Blair/Corbis. **142–143** (b) Richard T. Nowitz/Corbis. **143** (r) Photodisc/Getty Images. **144** (frame) © HMCo./C. Squared Studios/Photodisc/Getty Images; (frame) HMCo./C. Squared Studios/Photodisc/Getty Images; (l) Francis G. Mayer/Corbis; (r) Corbis. **145** Connie Ricca/Corbis. **146** (b) Roger Ressmeyer/Corbis; (c) Bob Krist/Corbis; (t) Michael Newman/Photo Edit. **147** Tim Boyle/Getty News and Sports/Getty Images. **148** (inset) Hulton Archive/Getty Images. **148–149** (bkgd) Walter P. Reuther Library, Wayne State University. **154** (c) Bob Thomas/Stone/Getty Images; (l) Jim Craigmyle/Corbis; (r) ImageState Pictor/PictureQuest. **156–157** David Young-Wolff/Photo Edit. **158** (l) Thinkstock/Getty Images; (r) Robert W. Ginn/Photo Edit. **160** Frank Siteman/Index Stock. **161** Superstock. **166** Photodisc/Getty Images. **167** LWA–Dann Tardif/Corbis. **168** (l) Jose Luis Pelaez, Inc./Corbis; (r) Ed Lallo/Index Stock Imagery. **169** (l) Stone/Getty Images; (r) Comstock Images. **172** Rogério Reis/Tyba Brazil Photos. **173** Corbis. **174** (bc) Scott Barrow/Image State; (r) Photo Researchers. **175** (cr) Photodisc/Getty Images; (tl) Albert Gustaf Aristeded Edelfelt/SuperStock. **176** (c) Photodisc/Getty Images; (cr) Photodisc/Getty Images; (tl) AP WorldWide Photos. **177** (l) Goldberg Diego/Corbis; (r) Goldberg Diego/Corbis. **178** G. K. & Vikki Hart/Getty Images. **181** (bl) Walter Hodges/Corbis; (br) © HMCo./C Squared Studios/Photodisc/Getty Images; (cr) Stone/Getty Images; (tl) John Coletti/Index Stock Imagery; (tr) Steve Cole/Photodisc/Getty Images. **182** Steve Dunwell/Indexstock Imagery. **183** Wonderfile. **188** (bl) Corbis; (br) Alan Pitcairn/Grant Heilman Photography; (c) Ed Young/Corbis. **189** (tr) Corbis. **191** (c) Taxi/Getty Images. (l) Ed Young/Corbis. **192** (l) Taxi/Getty Images; (r) Larry Lefever/Grant Heilman Photography. **193** David Young-Wolff/Photo Edit. **197** (tl) Allan Davey/Masterfile; (tr) Taxi/Getty Images. **198** (l) Dan Gair Photographic/Indexstock/PictureQuest; (r) Gibson Stock Photography. **208–209** John McGrail. **210** The Bridgeman Art Library; (r) Maryann and Bryan Hempill/Index Stock. **211** (l) Bettmann/Corbis; (r) H.P. Merten/Zefa/Masterfile. **212** YVA Momatiuk & John Eastcott/Woodfin Camp & Associates. **216** (bl) Jules Frazier /Photodisc/Getty Images; (br) J. A. Kraulis /Masterfile; (tl) Scott T. Smith/Corbis; (tr) Marilyn "Angel" Wynn/NativeStock. **217** (tl) Marilyn "Angel" Wynn/Nativestock; (tr) Larry Ditto/Bruce Coleman. **222** The Granger Collection, New York. **223** The Bridgeman Art Library. **225** The Bridgeman Art Library. **226** Keren Su/Corbis. **228** John Anderson/Animals Animals. **242** Courtesy Don Troiani, Historical Military Imagebank. **244** Bettmann/Corbis. **245** (b) New York Historical Society/ The Bridgeman Art Library; (t) Tom McHugh/Photo Researchers. **246** Photo Edit. **247** (tl) Massachusetts Historical Society. **248** Freelance Photography Guild/Corbis. **249** Rick Friedman/Photo Edit. **251** (c) Bettmann/Corbis; (frame) HMCo./Image Farm; (l) Museum of the City of New York/Corbis; (r) Bettmann/Corbis. **253** The Bridgeman Art Library. **254** Bettman/Corbis. **255** Hulton Archive/Getty Images. **256** Bettmann/Corbis. **257** Bettmann/Corbis. **258** (br) © HMCo./C Squared Studios/Photodisc/Getty Images; (cr) Bettmann/Corbis. **259** Library of Congress. **260** Hulton–Deutsch Collection/Corbis. **262** (l) Underwood Photo Archives; (r) Minnesota Historical Society/Corbis. **263** (l) Underwood & Underwood/Corbis; (r) Courtesy of the Village of Plainfield. **264** (bl) Underwood & Underwood/Corbis; (tr) The Associated Publishers New York Public Library. **265** (bl) NASA/Science Source/Photo Researchers, Inc.; (tr) NASA. **266** (inset bl) George H.H. Huey/Corbis; (inset br) Bettmann/Corbis. **267** (bl) Bettmann/Corbis; (br) Mark M. Lawrence/Corbis; (cl) Hulton–Deutsch Collection/Corbis; (cr) Sean Sexton Collection/Corbis. **268** Tony Mc Grath/Hulton Archive/Getty Images. **269** (b) Underwood & Underwood Corbis; (t) Hulton Archive/Getty Images. **270** (br) Takaharu Yoshizawa/Photonica; (tl) Hot Idea's Collection/Index Stock. **271** Peter Cross's Collectiion/Index Stock. **272** (br) Museum of Mankind, London, UK/The Bridgeman Art Library. **272–273** (bkgd) Galen Rowell/Corbis. **274** (l) British Museum London/Art Resource, NY; (lc) Bettmann/Corbis; (r) Joseph Sohm/Corbis; (rc) Richard T. Nowitz/Corbis. **275** (bl) Richard T. Nowitz/Corbis; (lc) Archivo Iconografico, S.A./Corbis; (r) Burstein Collection/Corbis; (tl) Colin Garratt; Milepost 92 1/2/Corbis; (tr) Photonica. **276** The Granger Collection. **278–279** (l) Ariel Skelley/Masterfile. **280** (l) Michael Crabtree/Getty Images. **280–281** (b) Getty Images. **281** (lc) Joseph Sohm Visions of America/Corbis; (tr) Photodisc/Getty Images. **282** Richard Hutchings/Photo Edit. **283** Paul Colangelo/CORBIS. **286** (c) Elena Rooraid/Photo Edit; (b) IndexStock Imagery. **288–289** (bkgd) Skip Nall/Photodisc/Getty Images. **289** (inset) Chad Slattery/Stone/Getty Images. **301** Bonnie Kamin/Photo Edit. **302** © John Neubauer/Photo Edit. **303** Jose Carillo/Photo Edit. **304** Reuters NewMedia Inc./Corbis. **304–305** Bettmann/Corbis. **309** (br) Bell/Folio Inc.; (cr) AP World Wide Photos; (tr) Office of the Mayor, Columbus Ohio. **310** (cl) Steven Begleiter/Image State; (cr) Jim and Mary Whitmer. **311** AP Photo/Jae C. Hong. **317** The Granger Collection. **318** Peter Gridley/Getty Images. **319** (bl) Peter Gridley/Taxi/Getty Images; (tr) Doug Armand/Stone/Getty Images. **320** (br) Ghislain & Marie David de ossy/Imagebank/Getty Images; (tr) Index Stock. **321** (bl) Wilfredo Lee/AP Wide World Photo; (tr) Richard Hutchings/Photo Edit. **322** (b) AFP Corbis. **323** Wally McNamee/Corbis. **324** Mark Wilson/ Getty Images News and Sports/Getty Images. **325** (r) AFP/Corbis; (tl) Stephen Shaver, Pool/AP World Wide Photos. **326** (bl) Lawrence Migdale; (cl) Stockbyte/Punchstock. **327** (bc) David Young-Wolff/Photo Edit Inc; (c) Henryk T. Kaiser/Index Stock Imagery/Picturequest; (tc) Jack Star/Photolink/PhotoDisk/Getty Images; (tr) Dorian Weber/Index Stock Imagery. **332** (tl) Mark Gibson Stock Photography. (c) © Davies and Starr/The Image Bank/Getty Images. **333** © Ronnie Kaufman/Corbis. **334** (tl) © Hulton-Deutsch Collection/Corbis; (Inset) © The Nobel Foundation. **335** © The Granger Collection; (cr) © Corbis; (r) © HMCo./Jade Albert. **336** (tl) © Philip James Corwin/Corbis. **337** (tl) © Stone/Getty Images. **338** (tl) © Maroon/Folio, Inc. **R1** © Corbis. **R2** (l) © Pete Turner/The Image Bank/Getty Images; © Elyse Lewin/Photographer's Choice/Getty Images. **R3** (tr) © Bruce Burkhart/Corbis; (b) © Annie Griffiths Belt/Corbis; (bc) © AFP/Corbis; (bl) © Mark Thiessen/Corbis. **R4–R5** © Digital Vision/Getty Images. **R6–R7** © Thomas Wiewandt/Visions of America/Corbis. **R8** (l) © Bettmann/Corbis; (r) © Arnold Michaelis/Pix Inc./Time & Life Pictures/Getty Images. **R10** (tl) © Art Wolfe/Stone/Getty Images; (tr) © Michael T. Sedman/Corbis. **R11** (tl) © Orion Press/Stone/Getty Images; (br inset) © D. Rose/Zefa/Masterfile. **R20** (aid) © AFP/Corbis; (ancestor) Courtesy of Aparna Agrawal; (ballot) © Joe Sohm, Chromosohm/Stock Connection/PictureQuest. (bank) Steve Dunwell/Index Stock Imagery. **R21** (citizen) © Tom & Dee Ann McCarthy/Corbis; (climate) © Photodisc/Getty Images; (colonist) Maryann and Bryan Hemphill/Index Stock Imagery. **R22** (communication) © Jack Star/Photolink/Photodisc/Getty Images; (community) © Owaki–Kulla/Corbis; (culture) © Ariel Skelley/Corbis. **R23** (custom) © Tony Freeman/ Photo Edit; (democracy) Zefa Visual Media/Index Stock Imagery; (election) © HMCo./Jade Albert. **R24** (environment) New Moon/Panoramic Images; (explorer) The Bridgeman Art Library; (factory) Diaphor Agency/Index Stock Imagery. **R25** (goods) © Allan Davey/Masterfile; (government) © Paul Colangelo/Corbis; (group) © Arthur Tilley/Taxi/Getty Images; (hero) © Hulton Archive/Getty Images; (human resource) © Ed Young/Corbis. **R26** (immigrant) Courtesy of Aparna Agrawal; (interview) © Michael Newman/Photo Edit; (invention) Bettman/Corbis **R27** (judge) © John Neubauer/Photo Edit; (justice) © David Young-Wolff/Stone/Getty Images. (lake) © Steve Dunwell/Getty Images. (landform) Thomas Winz/Panoramic Images; (landmark) © Corbis; (leader) © Photodisc/Getty Images. **R28** (liberty) © Leif Skoogfors/Woodfin Camp & Associates; (market) David South/Image State-Pictor/PictureQuest; (memorial) © Philip James Corwin/Corbis; (monument) © Bettmann/Corbis. **R29** (national holiday) © IPS/Photonica/Getty Images; (natural resource) © Arthur Tilley/Taxi/Getty Images; (needs) Robert W. Ginn/Photo Edit. **R30** (peninsula) © Tony Arruza/Corbis; (Pilgrim) © Catherine Karnow/Corbis. (point of view) (inset l) George H. H. Huey/Corbis; (nset r) Bettmann/Corbis; (president) © Bettmann/Corbis. **R31** (producer) © Charles Gupton/Corbis; (region) © Mark Heifner/Pan Stock/PictureQuest; (religious holiday) © MI Sinibaldi/Corbis; (right) © HMCo./Angela Coppola; (rural area) Larry Lefever/Grant Heilman Photography. **R32** (service) © Corbis; (settlement) © Lee Snider/Corbis; (shelter) © Michael Melford/Image Bank/Getty Images. **R33** (specialize) Dan Gair Photographic/Index Stock/PictureQuest; (suburb) © Stephen Schauer/Stone/Getty Images; (technology) © HP Merten/Zefa/Masterfile. (timeline) baby © Jim Craigmyle/Corbis. boy © Bob Thomas/Stone/Getty Images. boy standing © Imagestate-Pictor/PictureQuest **R34** (trade) © LWA Dann Tardif/Corbis; (tradition) © Paul Barton/Corbis; (transportation) © Bettmann/Corbis; (urban area) © Jeffrey Greenberg/Folio, Inc; (valley) © Joseph Sohm;Visions of America/Corbis. **R35** (wants) © Photodisc/Getty Images.